W9-BVY-934

THE
Angels'
Share

A NOVEL

GARFIELD ELLIS

This is a work of fiction. All names, characters, places, and incidents are the product of the author's imagination. Any resemblance to real events or persons, living or dead, is entirely coincidental.

Published by Akashic Books
©2016 Garfield Ellis

ISBN: 978-1-61775-373-2
Library of Congress Control Number: 2015934082

First printing

Akashic Books
Twitter: @AkashicBooks
Facebook: AkashicBooks
E-mail: info@akashicbooks.com
Website: www.akashicbooks.com

FEB / ' 2016

CONELY BRANCH

For Garfield, my son;
it's not just the experiences but the lessons we take from them.

CONELY BRANCH

ONE

I t may be anywhere between four and five a.m. Monday morning. I am wide awake and panting. My girlfriend Audrey is grinding backward up against me ferociously.

This is her favorite position, this is her favorite time: on the still edge of morning, her body twisted slightly on its side, one leg wrapped back almost around my waist, a hand tight on my neck as I thrust deeply into her with long, strong, deliberate strokes.

She has been here since yesterday, using her marketing expertise to help me all day with my presentation, which is to be made to the board of directors later today. Last night I had been too tired to attend to her, and now she is intent on making up for the last three weeks.

And I don't mind, for I can be greedy that way, myself . . . when I am in the mood.

So I am panting, grinding back, aiming along her heaving, moist crevices, so I may synchronize and glide true and deep with the thrusts she craves.

And then the phone rings, shattering the morning like a stone splintering a glass window. I freeze and everything in me grows cold and still. Phones do not ring innocently at five o'clock in the morning. They always bring bad news. So part of me is pausing because I am startled and the other part of me is hoping it will stop; as if by being quiet it will think I am not here and not ring again. I hold my breath, and even Audrey is momentarily paused against me.

The last time my phone rang at five a.m. it brought the news that my mother had taken a turn for the worse, giving me just sufficient time to race to the hospital and hold her hand for two hours before she died. Now this morning I am afraid of what news it may bring.

It stops, and then rings again; and I know I must answer, but Audrey is no longer paused; she begins to grind even more urgently against me—completing the penetration with a backward thrust.

Caught between the urgency of the ringing phone and the heat of a woman on the edge of orgasm, I feel the pressure of a slippery slope. But the decision is already made for me as I am already wilting away from responding to her. Disentangling from her requires more force than I expected, and as I reach for the phone, she shrugs away into the folds of the sheets with more anger than is necessary.

It is Una, my father's wife, and her voice is heavy with tears and panic: "Your father is missing, and I don't know where he is. And I know he is not with you."

I feel the blood drain from my face, I feel an absence of strength, and breath rushes from my lungs as if I have just run ten miles.

"Everton, Everton!"

"What do you mean *missing*, Una, it is only five o'clock."

"It was before that, but I never wanted to wake you up."

"I spoke to him on the phone yesterday."

"Yes! I did too." She pauses. "I talked to him in the morning and then I got back and he is gone."

"Got back from where?"

"I was at Holly's for the weekend."

Though I am sitting down, I am reaching with my hand to grip the sheets and steady myself. How do you respond to something like this? How do you respond? What do you say? How do you behave?

"He's gone, Everton, he's gone. And I don't know where he is." She is crying and her words are running into each other. I must calm her, I must calm myself.

"Una, you sure he is not in the back room sleeping or in the cellar or something?"

"He's gone!" Angry now and screaming.

This is 2008 Jamaica; old people are burnt in their homes for no reason at all; stubborn old men are slaughtered by gunmen. Old people living alone in the middle of Hampshire have little to protect them . . . and now my father is missing. Jesus!

"Una, it's okay, just slow down."

There is a pause.

"Una, Una!" I am almost screaming now.

"Yes."

"When did you miss him, Una?"

"I told you that already. I wasn't here, I said, I was at your brother's. His children were here for the summer. I took the children home. I stayed the weekend and when I came back, he was missing."

"But he can't just go missing so. Is the house ransacked, did someone break in?"

"He is gone to *her*! I know he's not with *you*."

"Una!"

"I don't know, I don't know." She is getting incoherent and I sense a falling away, a wilting.

"Una!"

"You better come up here, Everton."

"Una, don't do anything. Lock all the doors. Do not do anything. I am coming up there right now."

There is no lust left in this room. Audrey is already dressed. I did not notice her move, let alone find and put on her clothes.

"Where are you going?" My voice is close to a whisper.

"Where do you think?"

"You haven't even bathed. You vexed about something."

"I have water at home, and you are in a hurry. You have somewhere to go."

"Yeah, but where *you* going?"

"I don't believe you answered that." She is collecting her things now, kicking her shoes together to step into them as she drops her earrings into her bag. "I don't believe you answered that phone."

"My father is missing. You heard the conversation."

"You don't even love your damn father."

"What!"

"You don't love *me*, okay? You don't want me. You not interested in a relationship. You just love yourself. Don't believe you answered it!"

"What? You hear what I just said?"

"You don't even love your damn father!"

Is this the same woman who has been here with me since yesterday? The soft, sweet, intelligent girl, drawing lines through the outline of my PowerPoint presentation, giving me advice on how it should be shown for maximum effect? Audrey, snuggling up to me, making coffee when the night got cold, cooking dinner, and bringing wine for the evening meal? Audrey, showing patience, cuddling when I was too tired to even move— is this the soft, understanding Audrey, lying on my lap, listening while I pour out my soul to her, understanding and identifying with me, she having grown up even poorer without even knowing her father? Where did this person come from . . . and over a little sex?

"I had to answer the phone. My father is missing, okay? And you are angry about what, again?"

"Don't even make this about the sex. Don't even make this about your father. Okay? Don't even go there."

"Really! This is really the most ridiculous thing I have ever seen, okay? This is too much for me. It is Monday morning. I have a presentation in a couple of hours, my father is missing, and he could be dead in a bush somewhere. And I am being chastised because I answered the phone, to this crisis, because you did not get an orgasm. And you want me to *what*? Say it's not about the sex? How could this *not* be about the sex? How could it *be* about sex?"

She pauses halfway to the door and turns to me. In the soft light of the room, I can see the anger simmering in her eyes and beneath the softness of her face.

"Listen, Everton, you know and I know this relationship is not going anywhere. We live half an hour from each other; we work ten minutes away from each other. Yet I have not seen you in nearly a month. Last weekend it was your father, before that you got a new company to run, then last week you had to whip the company into shape. This weekend—presentation. And now you are going to Hampshire. Does that look like a relationship to you? Do you see me fitting in there?"

"But my father is missing."

"Don't!" She is so angry now it is almost as if she's going to cry. "You don't need a relationship. Or maybe you need one, but you don't need *me*. In any event, I have to leave. I have to go to work, remember? This is not about your father, okay? You damn well know this is about you and your own selfishness."

I do not chase after her as she leaves. I do not try to hold her back . . . well, not immediately, for I do not think she is serious. But now I hear the front door slam, and I am chasing down the stairs after her. I get as far as the kitchen when I hear her tires on the gravel of the driveway, and the gun of the engine as she speeds away.

I am confused, unsure, unable to focus. I try to make coffee, fill the kettle with water, switch it on, and sit at the counter wondering what to do.

Papers are scattered everywhere, just as we left them last night. The large yellow pad with all the notes I took down from her criticism is lying with the remote on the ground where we left it. Dazed, I glance around at the mess of paper she had pushed aside; the roll of taped-up leaves she made into a ball and threw, only to miss the rubbish can as she mimicked a basketball player; the smudge on the corner of the projector where she dabbed jelly in order to make me mad; the pencil shavings, the cork from a wine bottle, the remains of the ice cream on the counter where she drew her name. Everything connected, yet disconnected in its own way. Nothing making sense in and of itself—just like the words she uttered as her anger rose. *You don't love me . . . You only love yourself . . . You don't even love your damn father!*

I am suddenly struck by another strange reality. *Your father is missing.* I jump from my seat at the counter and run up the stairs, taking them two at a time. *Hampshire!* I must go to Hampshire. I must leave here now; I must go to Hampshire and find my father.

But I am overwhelmed by a strange instinct. Instead of running toward the bedroom to dress, I am being pulled by this strange instinct to the little bedroom I am planning to use as a library. Suddenly, I am rummaging through the old boxes I have stored there, first deliberately then frenziedly, digging among the confusion of old suitcases and boxes; tearing the cobwebs that ensnare me, filling my nostrils with dust; scattering papers, old books, clippings, yearbooks, magazines, graduation gowns; overturning cartons; scrabbling through books, desperately searching for a little old Bible my mother gave me a million memories ago.

Among its yellowing pages is a folded piece of paper I had torn from my high school notebook when I left home for college. The paper is so old the creases are stuck together and brown. The writing is faded but still legible. The heading jumps at me just as forcefully as the day I scribbled it there with an angry, uncertain, adolescent hand: *Ten Questions for My Father.*

I take the piece of paper and read the words over and over, each line, each question, even though they have been etched in my memory like a childhood nursery rhyme. I read them still and relive again in their fullest force the feelings that shaped them.

I don't know why I have done this, don't understand the emotions that drove me to this old Bible in this old box of memories. I can't imagine the difference these words will make when I already know them by heart, and I have no reason to believe or expect that after twenty-five years the moment will finally present itself—and if it does, that I will have the courage to ask them.

Your father is missing.

Something about those desperate words has driven me here—to this room, to memories hidden by layers and layers of years.

Twenty-five years.

And now he is missing. I feel paralyzed by an odd fear—an odd notion that I may never see him again.

Ten Questions for My Father.

I must start moving. I must get to Hampshire and find him.

TWO

I am not a selfish man. I love much, much more than myself.

I love my father.

For here I am this morning, sandwiched between two trucks on the Flat Bridge, traffic backed up on both sides. It is seven o'clock and still I am not even halfway to Hampshire. And with every honk of an angry horn, and every stop and start and stutter of the vehicles in the line, every inching forward of the traffic, I feel my career disappearing slowly behind me. So how could I be a selfish man? How could I not love my father? I am sacrificing my day for him. I am sacrificing my presentation for him. I am sacrificing a board meeting for him. I am sacrificing my career for him.

I have sacrificed a woman for him.

Three years of back-and-forth, stopping and starting, stuttering, tied together by periods of intense passion, and tenderness beyond belief. Now this, out of nowhere: *You just love yourself.* Words coming from nowhere for reasons only God knows—*You don't love me*—not making any sense at all.

And this damn ugly river sliding like a brown snake through the misting gorge that extends for miles on both sides of this slab of a bridge on which I crawl, still slithering down, slowly and menacingly. The land rising, one side green and lush, the other cavernous and bare, but both rising high—and a gorge through which the river and the road that tracks it share an uneasy alliance, slipping and sliding together like lovers entwined in some sensuous ritual—knowing, understanding, accepting that every now and then the river will gather its forces from way beyond, in the hills of St. Catherine, and thunder through it, taking everything in its wake, cutting off the north of the country from the south.

Where could he be? I have tried calling Una twice, but the phone rings out. Where could the old man be?

It is hard not to think bad thoughts. This is Jamaica, modern-day Jamaica, where it is so easy to get away with murder. Two months ago, in Manchester, a retired banker and his wife, a retired teacher, were bludgeoned to death and burned in their houses. They had lived there all their lives on a five-acre plot of land, farming goats in their retirement—murdered and burned alive. A month ago, another old man—who'd spent his life working in England, but having built a house here, returned to retire—was trailed by gunmen from the airport, robbed, bludgeoned, killed, then cast out on the street like a dog. And even now, in the news every day, old people, homeless people, emerging from the bushes and hills of Mandeville, dead, half-dead, discarded. Some wander into the sulfuric death of the bauxite red lakes, some are swept up from the streets of Montego Bay and dumped like garbage in the hills, in order to clean up for a tourist conference. It is a hard place to be old and retired or homeless.

Your father is missing . . . and I know he is not with you.

And now, this empty space, this phone ringing and

ringing with no answer. As if he has dropped off some cliff. *Missing?*

What was the last thing I said to him? What was the last thing I saw of him? What did he look like, what did he want to do? Was he smiling? What did I say, what did I say? *Later, old man, next week, I am coming for you next week.* Was that the last thing—was *later* the last thing? Did I say *later* or did he say *later*? Was he smiling, was he sad?

Did I leave my old man sad? Did I say *last weekend* meaning yesterday, day before yesterday, when I was wrapped up in the arms of an ungrateful woman, working?

Where is he?

I can't even see around the corner of this damn gorge, just the damn truck in front of me and the light blinking, indicating it is going slow as if everybody can't see that. And everything shaded in mist. And trees hanging now on both sides of the gorge: breadfruit trees along the slopes, and small cultivation with no system to it; yam curling up the vines, corn, peas, vegetation up and down—dense. Even the light posts are laden with heavy vines so that one can hardly see them, just the hint of board in some places and the electricity wires sagging out like overweight clotheslines. And the people now, slipping up and down its side like ghosts coming into view as they hit the road while the mist stirs slightly and the day starts. They are moving among the trapped motorists, hawking mangoes and oranges and star apples and jackfruits, shoving them against the glass, pushing them through open windows as we slip uneasily from the Flat Bridge and onto the road.

The truck in front of me curves away, and for a minute I am pointing straight ahead across the water, and because of the curve of the road, it seems the trees on all sides have met and I am heading into a wall of trees with the water curling, a serpentine green from deep inside it. There is a stillness and a pause—a waiting—and everything green and still, and the mist rising, drifting from the water as if it is very cold in the green dark out there, and the sky barely showing above. And for a minute, everything is beautiful as I have never remembered; everything is cold, cozy and private, yet wild, like a soft wet Christmas morning.

This must be what he sees. This must be what makes him love this place so much.

For this is his place, this is his domain; the territory he supervised while he worked for the government; all the land that is fed and silted by this river, all the land that draws water from it, all the lands fed, silted, and served by the tributaries that feed it. Everything shooting out on every side of this curvaceous, cavernous, serpentine curl. From the hills of Harkers Hall through the plains of Riversdale, Knollis, and Tulloch in the east, to as far west as the orange groves of Linstead and Wakefield and the plains of Springvale made green by miles of cane fields.

He took me there once—I now remember, yes, took me there once, a long time ago now . . . and it all comes to me right now in this place. Strange . . . but I remember.

I was at his house for the weekend, and a farmer, Hansel, came to tell him of a disease he had found in his oranges. Father decided immediately over breakfast that he had to go over the entire territory in order to provide a report for the minister on Monday.

It was Saturday morning on a long holiday weekend,

perhaps Labor Day, I don't remember. But it was one of the very few times I spent a weekend at his house. Holly had other things he wanted do, and so did Meagan. But I wanted to go with him and see the span of land he commanded on behalf of the government, and most of all I wanted to have him to myself all day.

So I jumped into the passenger seat of the fishtail car as he followed the farmer's old Land Rover, throwing dust in its wake as if it was digging a new road as it went. I couldn't have been more than fifteen, and I remember the first bar we stopped at. He introduced me to the barmaid, asked me what I was drinking, laughed, and slapped me on the back when I ordered a soft drink.

"Give him a Dragon, give him a Dragon Stout, boy turning man now. Drink a Dragon today, young boy. Next thing people come in here and see you drinking water, and I telling them you are my big son. Drink a stout."

"Aren't we going to work?"

"We are working," he said to me. "We are working, but work doesn't have to be work . . . well, not all the time."

So I had my first real drink on a dusty Saturday morning in a dirty little bar in Wakefield with my father sitting with a rum in his hand looking proudly at me and making bets as to whether or not I would throw up on myself.

We plunged through that large area west of where the Rio Cobre curls toward the St. Catherine hills, to a vast land of orange groves and tall cane fields with coconut trees standing way back in the distance. And the roads through the fields were almost always long and straight and the dust almost always thick, dry, and rising, blocking the taillights of the Land Rover ahead of us. And Father sped along the road and through the thick dust as if he did not need to see.

Every now and then, a break would appear somewhere on one side and he would swerve and swing down a long lane of trees. Then suddenly on some little hill or at some little corner would be a small farm with children running around the car and little mongrel dogs yapping at my heels.

Every little village or collection of houses or farm was no more than fifteen minutes from a dusty little corner with a bar. Some still unopened, some barely, some with no customers but a few old-timers lying on the pavement, recovering from the goings-on of the night before. Others with a couple of men sitting in a corner nursing white rum—maybe some shuffling domino pieces across tables short of players

We stopped at every bar, every shop, and almost every house along the way, where my father would engage the farmers in small talk, flirt with the bartenders, ask about their families. He may have kissed some babies, but my memory is hazy on that. Then he waded into their fields with a businesslike look on his face, slicing through the oranges to examine the cores and shaking his head; examining the sugar cane—cutting it, tearing the sharp leaves apart, till the flaking inner dust would fly in the air like powder; peering like a surgeon to where the leaves meet the skin and where the skin turns to joints; then breaking them to see the joints themselves; then nodding again or shaking his head; then moving on from farm to farm, from estate to estate, examining bananas, sugar canes, oranges, even the apples and avocados that were not being farmed for production.

Dusk caught us halfway through a little town east of Ewarton called Redwood. A little place no more than a village with a small road leading to a small square with a shop and a bar at its crest. Two roads led off to its right and left. In front, across the dusty road, a wide track led down to where I could see the tops of houses and two women walking up toward us with large water buckets on their heads.

Father parked his car beside Hansel's old Land Rover and headed straight for the little bar called George's Place. He stomped up the dirty concrete steps like he owned the building, looked across at the group of men sitting around a domino table, and shouted, "George, how things, man! You don't have anything to quench thirst in this godforsaken place?"

To my worshipping eyes he was like a god. The way he strode into the bar in the same manner he had been striding around the countryside all day—tall, broad, with his booming voice, commanding people and having them respond quickly to his smile and to the flash of his black eyes and his mouth's arc and the flesh wrinkling at the corners of his eyes. Never mind that he had taken me from my Pentecostal mother, knowing how she was raising me as a good church child; never mind that in one day he had given me more liquor to drink than I had ever even seen in all my life; never mind that in addition to that first stout, I had drunk white rum, rum punch, beer, coconut water, goat head soup, rum and Coke, and a tot of John Crow Batty—the raw overproof unfiltered rum; plus food of every kind and taste, from curried goat to jerk pork, fried chicken and ackee and salt fish—never mind that. Never mind that by the time I sat at the bar and faced my next stout, my stomach was churning with the turbulence of a boiling pot.

Never mind all of that. He was the father I dreamed of: the man who dragged life around with him wherever he went; dragged it into an empty bar with old men sitting around, desolate, with nothing to do; but as he strode in, he brought life and suddenly the barman was serving drinks, suddenly the domino game in the corner was revived, suddenly people were stopping by, peeping in and sitting down. He was a man in command of himself and all around him. And even when halfway through the Dragon Stout, I began to vomit; I tried hard to hold it in, and when my stomach rebelled, I put my hand to my mouth to stem the flood so I would be brave and manly for him. But the vomit came hard and filled my hand and spurted through my fingers onto the counter, onto my clothing, onto the floor, and onto Hansel who was trying desperately to tend to me.

"Time you son go home now!" he shouted to my father. But I wouldn't leave him that day for all the money in the world.

So I was happy and thankful when Father yelled over his shoulder from the domino table for George to give me somewhere to lie down. "Boy must turn man," he laughed. "My big son that you know, boy turning man now. George, find somewhere to put him to lie down and give him a little rum to hold his stomach."

Then George called a woman from somewhere inside who stripped my clothing and gave me old trousers and a T-shirt and put me on an old bed in the back. Then she gave me a mixture of rum and something very sweet that put me to sleep almost immediately.

When I opened my eyes, it was past midnight and I was in a different bed in a different place. This was a nicer room, with a bed with sheets stiff as starch and a clean hard smell. My stomach was burning as if someone had lit a fire inside me. Somewhere outside I heard singing. I opened the curtain, looked out, and saw a large yard with trees and flowers with a walkway on one side that led to an open gate. Through the gate I could see another yard across the road where part of a large tent showed.

Father had found a wake and he was over there singing his heart out, paying tribute to someone he may or may not have known. In the short time since he'd hit the town, he had even found someone to put me in a clean bed, medicate me, wash and dry my clothes, and hang them neatly on a chair next to me.

A woman came and told me my father had left instructions for me to dress and join him as soon as I woke up. "How you feel?" she asked.

"Not so bad."

"You feel terrible, don't it?"

"Little bit."

She laughed, shook her head, and gave me some hot soup to drink. But though soothing to some extent, it did little to calm the storm inside my stomach, and I began to retch again as I tried to fight my first hangover.

"What a little boy like you doing drinking so much rum?" she asked me, wrinkling her nose at the stench of liquor coming from inside me. "Drink this."

Whatever it was, it was so bitter she had to hold my nostrils for me to swallow it.

"Now lie down and don't move," she said.

I did. And did not.

The next sound I heard was my father as he shook me and teased me. Why had I come to country and slept through the whole night? "Come, rise and shine," he said. "We have to bathe and finish the inspection."

"What time is it now?"

"Soon five o'clock."

"We not going home?"

"We'll go home later, after."

"Where is Hansel?"

"He went home last night."

"But Aunt Una!"

"We are working."

"But what is Aunt Una going to say?"

"What must she say? We are working! If what we doing important, a little waiting won't hurt her. It is the choices we make. You will learn that life is like that sometimes."

And so he led me, with George and his woman, through the town and down the little hill where I had seen the women bringing water on their heads. It was still dark, but my stomach was normal again and I was as hungry as if I had not eaten in weeks.

We got to a crystal spring that my father said was the main tributary of the Rio Magno. It was barely more than a trickle from the hills but we were led to a deep pool where the water was sweeter than the filtered water they sell in Kingston, so clear the sides reflected deep into it and through the predawn mist curling there.

Father stripped naked in the early morning, walking carelessly into the water as if into some sort of baptism. I stood staring, amazed that he could be so casually naked, then looking around to see that George too was naked and all his wife had on were thin panties. Her breasts hung down her chest like small palms turned inside out. I was standing there, mouth agape, feeling shy, wondering if I would measure up to my father.

"You afraid of the water?" Father asked

"No, not really."

"Well, come in."

And finally, still clad in the shorts George's wife had washed for me, I slipped from the unassuming graveled beach into the harmless, transparent water which suddenly gave way to a deep pool that reached my shoulders; it was icy cold and everything around and above was intimate and cozy—a thin fog misting, flitting, and tangling with the dark foliage that covered the steep slopes of the hills around us, just as this Rio Cobre valley now surrounded me.

None of my friends had a story like that, ever. Not through high school or college; none had a story to rival that weekend I had *trampoozed* through the, hills, valleys, and plains of St. Catherine with my father.

We did not get home until close to four o'clock Sunday afternoon, the time it took to do the rest of the territory. And though the routine was the same, though we stopped at almost every farm along the way, and though there was more food on offer, we ate a little less. Yet the drinking was the same. There were fewer bars open on a Sunday, though, so by the time we got home I was less filled and less drunk and a little less sick.

We still had space for Una's Sunday dinner. And he still found time and energy to drive me back home to my mother's that evening. And when we got there, we sat in the parked car outside the house for about fifteen minutes or so while he talked a bit about my career and asked what I planned to do with my life.

"You enjoy yourself this weekend though."

"Yes sir, but me vomit up."

"Don't worry 'bout that. Boy your age shouldn't learn to hold liquor too well. You don't want turn rum head or nothing like that."

"Yes sir."

"You see how you old man have to work hard for a living though."

"That no hard, is just drive and drink and eat and get drunk."

"Well, the lesson for you here is not how hard you work, son. Is how much you enjoy you work. That is the thing. You don't see I finish that entire farm on them? And right away I understand what causing the problem, for the people them find it easy to talk to me. So now I know what to do and what they have been doing wrong. You never pick up that?"

"Ohh."

"So what you want to do when you grow up?"

"I don't know yet."

"Well, at your age you should have a very good idea. You must start thinking about that now. What are you good at? What do you like to do in school?"

"Everything—well, I try to get good grades in everything."

Then he laughed, reached into his pocket for some

money. "You not easy. This is yours, don't show you mother . . . Whatever you choose, make sure is something you like, something you enjoy . . . that mean something to you . . . so when you make sacrifice, stay out and make you wife vex, it still not matter. You understanding?"

"Or my mother?"

"Well, if you want tell her about everything, is your business. As far as I know, you come spend the weekend and I bring you back home. Come!"

The Pum Pum Rock shifts by slowly across the river to my left. With the traffic's pace, I can't help but glance at it. Even now, as early as this, in this traffic jam, people are still stopping to take pictures of this perfectly formed vagina in the rock. Some stop just to point it out to their friends and children.

One man is fighting his way down the slope of the river, carrying his son. He gets there and is met by a hustler of a guide in a sleeveless undershirt and shorts, who pilots them both, him and his son, across a shallow section. Then they are scrambling and crawling up the bank to the rocky edge where he finally places his son in the middle of the cleft of the rock, resting his child's head on the smooth, hard clitoris. Then both are leaning deep into the crevices of the flaring dark inner portion, as the guide backs away, down into the shallow water to take a picture. There is laughter and cheering all around. Everyone finds it funny. I can't help but smile myself. And wonder what hand of nature could have sculpted a vagina so perfect and brilliantly detailed in the hard face of a rock.

Thank God the traffic finally begins to move. I shake

the image from my head; a perfect vagina is not an image I want in my mind right now.

I try to get Una on the phone, but there is no answer.

I try to get ahold of Holly to hear what he knows and whether or not he has called the police, but my brother's phone is busy. Or perhaps he just switched it off. He has been known to do that. Maybe I should have called him earlier, or maybe I should have gone to his house in St. Jago Heights before I made the drive down here all on my own. I don't know, I am a bit confused this morning; Una called me and I made a promise. It is now my responsibility to fulfill that promise and find out what has happened to my father no matter what the cost. I have to go. So what if my career is on hold. So what if my future is on hold.

I made the decision that was right.

Now the traffic is moving and if I hurry I might make it to Hampshire by eight thirty. But my workday is dead—I will not make it back in time. I try to push my job from my mind. So what is a job anyway? Corporations can wait. Opportunities will come again. *There is always a better deal* has been one of my mantras in sales meetings and negotiations. "But not in sales, not in sales," I tell my staff. There is always a better deal for us, but never for the client. We are the only deal they have.

Not in sales, not in sales.

"Dorill," my manager recently said, "you were born for this."

"No," I replied, "I am born for everything; this is just a part, sales is just a part."

Now they have given me my own brand, my own line. They went out and bought a snacks and bottled water company and gave it to me to run. This is not sales anymore, this is marketing management. And now this, my first board meeting, the first board meeting when I must present my plans and projections for making this company the number one on the island. After years of dreaming, months of planning, nights of sweating, days and days of planning and phone calls and studying, now after all of this, I must let it go and take care of my father.

Now, suddenly, at this moment, at this crossroad, just as the Pathfinder enters the first roundabout at the end of the gorge, I am assailed by uncertainty and confusion, and I am being blinded by tears. Suddenly, I am fighting tears of despair and anger as if all the events of the morning are catching up with me. Halfway to my destination and I cannot hold them in anymore. Hard tears too, not sobbing ones, just hard blinding tears, clear and unaccompanied by any sort of emotion, like rain while the sun still shines. Hard tears burning my face and filling my lashes, tears I do not need to wipe away. And even as I blink them away, I find that the car has gone around the roundabout twice without exiting.

I must be a mad man, thinking like this when my father is missing and may be lying dead in a ditch somewhere. I must be a madman thinking this way, in a time like this, in a country like this, where old people are murdered in their sleep and nothing seems to come from it. I must be a hard, selfish person to think of my career at a time like this.

But I am not thinking of my career by my own will; the thoughts are flooding me even as I try to push everything from my mind and focus on my love for my father—on my duty as his eldest child. I am trying, but it is upon me, this feeling, this desire to save myself and my career. I am confused by the emotions and I am blinded by my tears.

Brakes screech behind me, horns blow from all sides. I am still in the roundabout and I am now endangering other motorists around me. I swing to the soft shoulder near Juici Patties, and I hear even more screeching of tires and cursing motorists. The vehicle lunges over the curb wall and stops on the soft shoulder. I press my hands to my face, lean into the seat to calm myself.

My hands are trembling. *There must be a way out of this, there must be a way to save us both.*

But there is no way, at least not at this time. I can't call and stop a board meeting. People have come from Trinidad and Barbados for this meeting. And I can't leave him there lost wherever he is. He is my father and I love him.

But there is always a better deal.

But not in sales. Not in love. Not in "Father."

But there is always . . . What about Holly? Holly. Maybe Holly can help. He has big house in St. Jago Heights. The traffic is thinning—he could make it here in no time.

I dial my brother's number. This time he answers.

"Holly!"

"What's happening, Eva?"

"You heard anything? You know that Father is missing?"

"Mother called. She says you are taking care of things, and that you going down there. So I should be asking *you* that."

"I am not there yet."

"You don't reach yet, where are you now?"

"On my way, but Holly . . ."

"Well, all right, fill me in. I have to move, Eva, I have to move."

I have never really liked my brother. Mother said it was because I was jealous for my father's attention. But I am not sure. I don't like the way he always looks out for his interest first. As if he was trained to look out for himself because his needs are more important. And not to mention his "Ivy League" University of Miami education, his fancy orthodontist doctor title, his fancy private practice, house-on-the-hills, better-than-people attitude. I am not even aware how I hate him, maybe because he always had my father, every day, every minute, he had him, living in their fancy house, going every day to high school, passing my home every day, sometimes driven by my very father, while I was on the bus, sometimes not even having bus fare. All the privileges, all the favors, all the fathering he needed. And every time there was something to do, they would always find a way to call me and I would come running.

And now today, I must sacrifice all that I have worked to achieve.

Everything, everything I worked for to this day.

I ring Holly again. "Holly, you hang up on me. I wasn't finished."

"Sorry, Eva, but I trying to get out of the house, kids to go to school and so on."

"Holly, I need your help. I have a b-board meeting and I will not be able to m-make it in time . . ." I am stuttering.

"What you mean?"

"I need you to go to *your mother* for me."

"How you mean? Me?! Go?! I have to take the kids to school."

"Holly, you have a wife."

"But she has to go to work. I have to go to work."

"Holly, is your practice, and there are two of you. I have a board meeting."

"What kind of meeting can be more important than the well-being of your family, Eva? Some things need prioritizing. It is your father we're talking about here."

"Holly . . ." I pause and almost bite my lip. "You don't have to tell me that. Everything depends on this meeting; people are coming from abroad, I must make this meeting."

"But is you father—they will understand."

"Holly, I will take care of this. All I am asking is for you to go there, see what is happening, do what you have to do, call the police. Then, as soon as my meeting is finished, I will take over. Just the first part, Holly."

"Boy, Eva."

"Holly, *your* mother." I pause at that for effect. "*Your* mother needs you to come now. I must make this meeting."

"So what time the meeting going done?"

"Ten."

"Boy, Eva, I don't know . . . Okay, I will see what I can do."

"Don't just see, Holly, I need you to do this, I need to be sure you are taking care of this."

"All right, all right," he shouts in my ear, "go to your damn meeting, all right!"

"Thanks, Holly." But already the line is dead.

I do not mind that; I am already thrusting the Pathfinder to join the traffic. Gravel is flying in the air, dust is spiraling high behind me as I swing hard into the roundabout and point my nose toward Kingston.

I have meetings to do, I have a career to save . . . I am running out of time.

This is important, and even Father has said that decisions can be justified if the cause is important enough . . . or something to that effect. Again, for some unknown reason the hard tears are back, they burst through my lashes even as I try to blink them away.

This is not selfish, this is not selfish.

I am not a selfish man. I love my father.

THREE

The traffic fights me like a pack of snarling mongrels, as if trying to frustrate me into turning back. At one point it gives me space to move, then at another spot it hems me in, cutting my space to nothing, forcing me behind trucks and corners I cannot see around. It is heavy in spurts, every now and then there is a break, but the taxis are out in full force, overtaking everything, converting the one lane into three in their ungodly haste to Kingston. I cross the Flat Bridge freely, but Angels is backed up. By the time I get to Spanish Town, the highway is closed. I take the back roads through the cane fields of Bernard Lodge, but there is an accident somewhere blocking everything. I have to reverse and swing through Portmore—all the way the traffic fights me. And each time I have to stop and wait is an opportunity for me to curse myself for abandoning my father or remember the woman who left me and the words she spoke and the guilt and emptiness she has filled me with. But then the traffic would thin again, I would press the gas and work would loom closer and I would feel I am doing the right thing.

So I am here now bursting through the glass door to my office at fifteen minutes to ten. I am greeted by my assistant Trudy, with a cup of coffee and a sober smile. I had instructed her from the car and her smile tells me things are as ready as they can be. She has printed the outline of the presentation for the board meeting and it is already in the conference room.

"I couldn't make the changes to the outline since Friday, sir."

"That's okay. It's just the fine-tuning of the details that got screwed up."

"Oh well, not to worry, you can handle that. I have seen you handle worse."

"Sure."

The conference room swirls as I enter. The desk and the chair behind it seem farther away than I remember. My hand is trembling and the coffee spills as I sit. I can almost feel my brain sweat.

Where in hell could he be?

I need time. This is not my style. I need half an hour to sit and reflect, go over my notes, drink my coffee, eat a salad, and take deep, slow breaths. I need time. I need my peace and quiet before my storm. But I do not have that now. My notes are undone; my mind is all over the place; I cannot focus on the paperwork in front of me. And I must make the presentation of my life to a room of men who do not accept excuses.

As I sit down in this room of powerful men, I feel as incomplete as my presentation. Something tells me that to be successful here, I will need to work harder than I had planned. And it is not the room; I have been here before. It is not the powerful men, for I have met each board member at sometime or other in my ten years here. It is something in my head—as if the whole morning has been a process through a washing machine. As if the space around me has a different aura than the room. I feel I am in a bubble—as if I am seeing everyone, but the feelings that wrap me are different from those around me, so my reactions as they greet me are informed by an immediacy that is veiled. I am there but separated, and though the conference room is solid and firm and sober, my immediate space is opaque and spinning around me.

But it does not matter now. However it feels, I must be ready. *But is this nervousness I feel? Me?! Nervous?! The man who said nervous is good was an idiot.*

"Meeting is called to order."

Mark Seymour, CEO, head of the Reggae Royal Beverage Company, my boss, begins the proceedings. He makes the introductions and the opening jokes. Time goes by in a blur. He taps my arm to tell me I have a minute to go.

"Gentlemen," he is saying, "as we decided, because we expect the majority of this meeting will be about our new acquisition, Rio Grande Snacks, we will just go right into it. The other matters we may take up later if there is time. And of course our director of operations for that company is Everton. So I will just hand over the meeting to him."

I have only said good morning and pointed to the documents in front of each board member when the phone rings. Something tells me that the telephone is not done with me for the day. My head begins to buzz as the secretary points the instrument at me like a blunt weapon.

It is an hysterical Una. "Everton!"

"Yes, Una."

"I have been calling you. Where are you, Everton?"

"Holly not there yet?"

"Holly has to work. I don't see him. Where are you?"

"Una!"

"You said you were coming. Where are you?"

"Una." The phone is no longer at my ear

"Everton, Everton. You dropped the phone."

A strange voice: "Everton . . ." A hand on my arm. My CEO. "Everton, is everything all right?"

"My father is missing, my father is missing."

"What you mean?"

"He just disappeared and no one knows where he is."

"When?"

"Since perhaps yesterday . . . last night."

"So what you doing here? What you doing here? Go deal with that."

"My . . . my . . . my presentation . . . my job."

"What you doing here? This can wait. Go. Go find you father, man."

I stumble to my office, trying to act normal as I hasten through the hallways of the executive block to the glass door that bears my name. I feel like a fool who has condemned his father to hell. But on the other hand, I feel the load of the meeting lifting from me. I now have full permission and freedom to go to Hampshire and sort this thing out.

My assistant greets me with concern on her face. "We forgot something?"

"No. I have to go and find my father."

"Oh!" She pauses. "Audrey has been calling, wants you to call her."

"Really." My sarcasm is almost acid.

I slam the door behind me, then collect my bag and look around for the few things I had taken out of it. But there is nothing to pack. *I must go.* I am turning for the door when the phone rings again. I stare at it, puzzled, annoyed. *Jesus Christ, why can't the phone just leave me alone this morning?*

"Hello!" I am shouting into the instrument of bad news.

"Hello. Mr. Dorril, please."

"Holly?"

"I am holding for Mr. Everton Dorril."

If Trudy has a weakness, it is her tendency to put through calls without first telling me who is on the line, especially when she is excited.

"This is Everton Dorril," I assure the strange voice.

"Oh, Mr. Dorril, this is Sergeant Grant of the Spalding Police Station."

The words are like a cold shaft down my back. I gasp and straighten with the shock of it. "Yes?"

"I am calling on behalf of your father."

"Yes," I shout into the phone, "you have seen him?"

"Yes, we have him here."

"May I speak with him?"

"He tried to get you several times. I am trying for him now . . ."

"But may I speak to him?"

"Let me check. You know, sir, I don't really think so. He says you must just come."

"Is he all right?"

"Apart from the accident?"

"Accident?!"

"Him run over a cliff with the car. You better come now."

"A cliff? Where you say this is?"

"Spalding, Spalding Police Station. I think you should come as soon as possible."

FOUR

Spalding!

SI am rushing through the large glass doors that separate the head office from the streets. The world outside is a blur of faces and a multitude of colors. Something falls from my hand. It is my cell phone. I drop to my knees to grab it. It is clattering down the wide steps to the open Holborn Road. I am losing my balance. A woman gasps, legs scatter from before me. I am on my belly now. The phone bounces high and lands hard on the last step. The battery breaks away.

I stretch my hand to pick up the pieces, and by the time I collect them, I am sitting confused on the steps, on the edge of the street in the middle of New Kingston.

"Everton, what's happening?" A bewildered voice at the end of a hand that is reaching to help me. "What happened, man? Mind the phone kill you, man."

It is John, the customer service guy. Our eyes meet, and I see him recognize that all is not well in mine.

"You all right?"

"Yes," I tell him. "My father, I have to get to my father."

"Okay, man."

I am off, the pieces of the phone sliding into my pocket, my keys in my hand, and I am racing down the street to the parking lot.

Spalding.

The day is hard against me. The sun is moving toward twelve o'clock, and the heat bears down upon my head. The parking lot is heavy with traffic as the lunch crowd has also taken their cars to the streets. For a minute, I forget where I am parked.

I must stop. I must bring order to the world that is spinning around me. I must check this panic.

The van, where is the van?

The dark blue Pathfinder is right where I parked it, where I always park it. It is in my reserved parking spot on the eastern edge of the lot near the fence where the evening shadows will cool it by the time I am ready to go home.

But now it is almost noon, and the heat is trapped inside.

I am moving before my seat belt is fastened or the blast from the air conditioner rushes from the vent to flood my face. But the parking lot is full and the vehicles crawl like snails. I have rushed, scampered, and fallen in panic, but still it will likely be late when I get to Spalding.

Spalding. Where the hell is Spalding?

I am suddenly aware how unnecessary my haste and panic have been. How ridiculous I must have looked. I had dropped my office phone, picked up my cellular from the desk, raced by my secretary, crashed past whoever may have been in the hallway, rolled down the steps onto the street, made a complete fool of myself, and now I am nowhere further along on my journey than if I had paused, taken the time to plan my moves, made a few necessary phone calls, ensured I had enough money in my pocket, found out where Spalding is, and strolled leisurely to the parking lot.

I should have at least called Una to tell her I have news—that I have found him and am on my way to get him.

But I am like that. I think first of solutions then solve them before I find out what they may cost or whether they were mine to solve in the first place. On those rare occasions when we get together, Holly will occasionally tease me that I could never make a modern doctor. That I would treat the patient before I realized they could not pay for the medicine. "You would go bankrupt as a doctor," he has said with a laugh.

And Father tells me that people with good hearts are always bankrupt, but a good heart is a good thing. Oh, Daddy, he always has those sayings that seem to double back on themselves and mean so much. *A good heart is a good thing.* Or his all-time favorite: *Life shorter than you think and longer than you believe.*

Now I am chuckling. I wonder what he is doing in Spalding.

I put the battery back in the cell phone without stopping the car and call Una. Her phone is busy.

The traffic is giving way and the light to Half Way Tree Road is amber. I press hard on the gas. The van leaps at the tail of the vehicle ahead and we go through as one. All the calm and lull of the past minutes are behind—the urgency is upon me again as I swerve and skid through the narrow streets toward whatever has befallen my father.

I am thirteen years old again, charging down the corridors of the Kingston Public Hospital to a cold room where he lay unconscious among a tangle of tubes, his foot in a cast and his face bandaged like a mummy. My mother had left a message at the principal's office that he had been in an accident. She figured that since the hospital was close to school, I could stop by on my way home. I got the message at lunchtime and raced out of school without returning to the classroom to retrieve my bag.

I got to the hospital two hours before visiting time and waited there on a bench and fretted till the nurse got tired of me sitting there so sad and let me in an hour early.

He was traveling officer for the Ministry of Agriculture at the time, and his car had collided with a tractor somewhere on the Tulloch Estates. He had broken a leg and severely sprained an arm. His face had smashed into the steering wheel and though no bones were broken, the skin had torn and his whole head was swollen and bruised.

When I saw him lying there with his foot in a cast and his face bandaged up, I thought he was dead. And I will always remember the fear I felt when I thought I would never hear him call my name again.

"He's sleeping," the nurse had said.

"Oh," I whispered in wonderment, and sat down to just stare at him.

When he woke, I screamed, "Daddy!" and I remember how startled he was, how his head snapped up and his eyes fluttered as if they did not recognize me for a moment. And how they settled and rested on me, and how his head dropped back onto the pillow as he whispered, "Oh, it's you. What you doing here?"

"Mamma said you have accident," I replied excitedly.

And he stared at me then, with those eyes through

the bandage. And I did not see the feelings on his face, but I saw the glint in his eyes. I leaned back into the seat, and we stared at each other. And while I did not know what to say, I remember how happy I was that I had him all to myself.

For though I had visited his house to spend weekends with him, it is the times we spend alone together that I cherish the most. Holly is about four years younger than me and Meagan is two years after that. And I always felt it unfair that I had to share him and then go home, while they could have all they needed of him.

But that evening I had him all to myself again. And we sat silently, till he asked about school. I told him I had exams, but that I had run and come the moment I heard he was hurt.

"Where is your bag?"

"I left it," I said. And he had chuckled and rocked his head and changed the subject to ask if I could see how the old man mashed up.

I asked him what happened and he sighed. "Too much haste. I try rush back to catch the bank—too much haste. Never try and pass a tractor on a narrow road. Tractors don't use rearview mirrors, they don't use indicators, and they don't hear horns."

Una arrived close to five, an hour into visiting time. But Holly and Meagan never made it till two days later. I was there every day after school to sit with him. Soon I knew all the nurses and was pleased to overhear one whisper to the other how I really must love my father.

I have often thought about that time, those evenings sitting there with him, those days at school, and the pride I felt when I would tell my friends that I could not play cricket that evening because I had to go and look after my father. And then I would go to the hospital and just sit with him and say nothing.

Then one evening he asked if I had done my homework yet. And I had pulled it out and completed it there in the hospital. And that was the first time he ever looked in one of my books. The first time he ever commented on my schoolwork or made a notation on my homework. He was sick and laid up in bed with his foot high in the air in a heavy cast.

He was in the hospital for about a month. And when he left, I visited a few times at home and spent another weekend with him. But it was never the same; time petered out and I returned to my routines and friends and games.

It must have been a year after that that I saw him. He must have been well for some time, for there was no sign of his injuries and his walk was just as I always remembered it. There was no evidence of the accident on his face. I can't remember why he came, but it had to do with my mother. I arrived home from school to see him there at my home. He was heading out and we met on the veranda.

"Daddy!" I screamed.

And he had squinted at me and smiled his dimpled smile. "How my big son?"

"All right," I remember saying. "You get better."

And he had laughed, "You can't come look for the old man sometimes?"

"Yeah," I said eagerly, "yeah."

"I left something for you with your mother." He

smiled, rubbed my head, and walked through the door to the gate.

It was money to buy a cricket bat. And I never had the chance to tell him thanks, for I had chased so quickly through the door to see what he had left and he had slipped so quickly into his car to go to his family.

I am thirteen again, charging down a corridor to find him.

Spalding.

The word is hard and weighted, stays on my tongue and burns into my brain with the residual fire of hot chocolate tea. It is a small town to the northeast of Mandeville that sits like a snake's eye on the curve of a meandering black line on the map I have bought. Somehow I had imagined it was spelled *Spaulding* with a "u" in it.

"Take the right turn before the next gas station," says the man at the stall of oranges.

"But how will I know . . . ?"

"If you reach the gas station, you gone too far."

I am past the gas station. I have gone too far. I curse.

The gas station is old and dirty. The sign says something like *Texaco Williamsfield.* But I am beyond that now and my tires are screeching into a turn as I spin around and seek the road that leaves the main one for Spalding.

I have been on the road for two hours now, and I feel the length of the drive in my eyes.

The country is lush and green around me, the hills are many and far apart, the blue and the green patch together in a lush tapestry of mounds, valleys, and massive hills rolling into the deep blue sky. It's bauxite country and the large sign tells me that Kirkvine Works is the factory with the well-kept lawn that is rushing by. The dark brown smoke that rises from its far corner tells me where its kilns must be. Everything is cleaner than I expected. I wind the windows down, and the breeze is cold and fresh against my face. It strikes the drowsiness away. The road is long and curves upward, the surface is beautiful and good. The hills are dotted with nice houses, and a large church sits in the middle of a hill off to my right.

I see things, but the details are flashes of green. I feel the force of the breeze, but I do not catch the essence of it. The beauty around me is a passing one, for I am filled with fear for my father.

The Pathfinder likes the road as it makes the hills flat and cruises the grade like the straights of a Kingston street.

I crest a hill and I am there—in a clean little town that spills onto the streets. Suddenly the road is curving away over a small bridge. The hills and the space are opening up to me again. I am through Spalding before I get my bearings.

So now I am here. And my heart is filled with fear and trepidation. I have been on the road for three hours. I have driven eighty miles. The police station is at the northern end of the town, across a narrow street from the Spalding Presbyterian Church whose large structure and immense courtyard contrasts starkly with the sizes of other things I have noticed in the few minutes I've been here.

I park in the churchyard, then step from the car and peer up at the high steeple.

I am not a Christian. I wanted to be baptized once, but my father put paid to that idea. I have not prayed in years. But I whisper softly that I wish He would spare my father.

I cannot say that the panic has left me, rather it has become cold and hard and still. And as I close the door and face the little station across the road, I feel a drag on my feet for the first few steps. But I am on my way. I cross to the little station where I know there will be things I will not want to hear.

Thirty-seven years old, and my first time in a police station. I do not know what to expect. It is a quiet place. There is a large counter and a policeman is sitting at the center of it with a large book in front of him. A police-woman is at a desk behind and off to the right. A door joins the left corner of the counter to the wall. Another large policeman leads a woman out through it. I stop at the counter, brace myself, and wish the officer good afternoon.

"Good afternoon, sir," he responds. "How can I help you today?" He is pleasant enough.

"I am looking for my father . . . or Sergeant Grant. My name is Dorril, Everton Dorril. A Sergeant Grant called me . . . said my father has been in some kind of accident—ran over a cliff. I have come to get him—"

"Oh." If he had not interrupted, I would have mum-bled on till my tongue fell out with nervousness. "Mr. Dorril, ohh." His mood is less formal than I expected— less serious. He is dark and his smile reveals false teeth in the front. He stands and I can see that he is a tall man. His uniform is neat and his belt buckle shines. "I am Grant," he says. "So you come for your father?"

"Yes."

"A nice man," he shakes his head, "a real nice person."

"Can I see him? May I see my father?"

"Oh yes, he is in the rec room."

"The wreck room?"

"Yes, just go through that door, then turn left, and cross the yard to the little building behind. You will find him there."

"The wreck room! But why not the hospital?"

"Why, you think him dead? I tell you something," he laughs and sits back down, "any side him sleep on last night, you make sure him sleep on that same side tonight. Nice man."

I stagger through the door, my head harboring images of a room filled with wrecks—men with broken bones, men in handcuffs too sinful to move; visions of an old man suffering, broken and lonely. Why hadn't they taken him to a hospital? Only Jamaican policemen would come up with a wreck room—a place of torture for people who break the law, and break themselves in the process.

I shove the door wide and enter a spacious room, a polished space with tables and chairs scattered around. I see a lone counter to one side. To the other side, a large group of men are surrounding something. There is raucousness here and loud sounds. There are shouts. I do not see my father, but I hear his voice. I hear his screams. His voice is loud and high above the rest. But the sounds I hear are not consistent with my expectations. These are sounds of tournament, hard shouts of combat, voices raised in exclamation, and my father's voice, the loudest of all, is one of victory. Then I see him, fit as a fiddle, shouting at the top of his lungs, laughing in the face of the man beside him, having revealed his winning hand of dominoes only to slam them one by one with a sound like thunder on the table before him.

FIVE

If Father had not seen me, I would have turned from the room, jumped into my car, and left him there, playing dominoes with his new friends. That is how angry I am. But he catches my eye and leaps from his seat to fling his hands around my shoulders and introduce me as his big boy who has come to pick up the old man. And even then, all I can muster is a short nod at the crowd and a sober, cold, stony look at him and one word: "Come!"

But we cannot leave immediately because there is some paperwork for him to complete. He crashed his car nearly twelve hours ago, has been in Spalding all day, and still has not completed his full report.

"We did not have time," Sergeant Grant says, remaining always cordial and always smiling. Then we have to go to the hospital where Father has a man holding space in a line for him. Even so, we have to wait another hour to see the doctor to find out about whatever hidden injury he may have from his accident.

Then we have to make arrangements to get Father's car from wherever he crashed it so we can be back in Kingston before night. Sergeant Grant again takes charge of that. He knows a man in a district close by, called Silent Hill, who has a large truck and a wrecker. He spends ten minutes on the phone and then returns to tell me the man will be here with the truck in an hour. So I wait while Father drinks and plays dominoes with his friends in the *rec* room.

After an hour no truck has come. "That is how he is sometimes." Sergeant Grant seems unruffled. "Always a little late."

After another hour, Sergeant Grant informs us that the man has called to say he had a breakdown and cannot make it before tomorrow. "Not to worry," the sergeant says, "there is a man called Small Man just down the road with a smaller truck that should work just as good." He sends someone on a bicycle to call him; says Small Man is old and does not like cell phones but is dependable. After another hour or so, the guy on the bicycle returns with the news that Small Man was not at home and his wife said he went to do some work at the bauxite factory and would "soon come."

So it is late evening before we are on our way with nothing but a promise that we will be retrieving the vehicle first thing in the morning. And even now, sitting in the cabin of my Pathfinder, my voice cannot find a path through my anger. So there is silence in the car. I am angry not just for being dragged down here for nothing, wasting my time, interrupting the most important morning of my career—I am also angry at myself because I know I cannot be mad at him for long. I know that once the silence is broken, once I begin to speak, this emotion will disappear like mist against the sun.

Father reaches above and turns the reading lights on. A slim book of poetry appears in his hand. He reclines his seat and adjusts the lights to suit him and taps his

breast pockets for his glasses. I hope he left them in the
police station in Spalding.

"Turn here," he says.

"What?"

"Turn here, if you're going to Mandeville, that is."

I just grunt at this. I am passing the turnoff quickly.
But the brakes are good, it is a country road, and there is
no vehicle behind me. I reverse and swing right.

It is one of those evenings when the sun plays hide-
and-seek with the clouds till it runs out of luck. The
clouds quickly give way to the densely forested hills in
the distance and all that's left of the brilliant sun is a
pale yellow glow that rims the hills but barely touches
the skies.

Night comes quickly and is cool.

We are closer to the large bauxite plant than I was
on my way up. The large kilns are visible here and the
brown-white smoke curls into the sky. The air on this
side has acid in it and it burns my nostrils and bothers
my eyes. I wind the windows up.

"You don't like fresh air, no?"

"It is pure acid out there."

He grunts and straightens the small spectacles on his
face. I guess he feels that he is gaining ground and is in
control of the silence now.

Another layer of darkness is added with each corner
I take. Now it is pitch black. I must drive slowly—I do
not know the road and country people do not drive on
their side all the time. They take their corners wide and
their lights are stuck on the high beam. I will need time
to get used to this.

"Blow your horn when you approach the corners."

He barely looks up. "We're coming to the red lake now. You ever seen the red lake?"

Red lake—I have heard of it somewhere, a valley where all the acidic residue of the bauxite-to-alumina process is stored. But who cares about a damn red lake. *He could have at least made a phone call.* I press my horn hard and swerve into the bushes, jamming on the brakes as two cars approach at top speed, one on the tail of the other like drivers at Dover Raceway.

"Press your horn before the corner, not when you're halfway through it."

"I have driven in the countryside before."

"Suit yourself."

"But they should see my headlights—the night is dark enough."

"Not all the time." I feel him turn to me. "Man can't drive vex at night."

Vex, you don't see vex yet. I am sure there is a soft smile and the slightest dimpling of his face. But I cannot turn to see, for another sharp turn is coming. Headlights are dancing and I must press my horn and pray.

"The key to driving at night on country roads is to dim your lights when you see a bright one coming and then hold your corner. Just watch *your* edge of the road."

We hit a long stretch so I glance over to him now. "Dim my lights?"

"Not now, when you see the other driver coming with his bright lights on. Dim yours and hold to your side."

"Dim my lights? On this road, while he is on bright!"

"You will see better." He drops that with a do-whatever-you-wish tone, switches off the reading light, puts the glasses away, and rests his book on his lap.

I hear a horn approaching. I see brightened head-lights speeding toward me. I dim my lights for the hell of it. He is right, I see much better. I hold my edge of the road and as the truck passes, I do not have to brake or swerve as madly as I did the last time.

"Red lake up the road," he says. "You should stop and see it. Couldn't tell when I see the red lake. It is beautiful at night."

"Well, we're not stopping tonight," I tell him. "I am tired, and it is too late, and the place is too dark." He needs to know he did something wrong. I glance from the road to him momentarily. He still has that do-what-the-hell-you-want look on his face.

"Watch out!" he yells.

Out of nowhere on the periphery of the lights a dark form of a man is rolling from the hillside. I brake and swerve instinctively, pushing the face of the van into the bush. The van stands on its nose, catches a skid, and stops with its face halfway into the shrubbery on my side of the road.

"You hit him?"

"I don't know, I don't think so." I am slightly dazed.

"Where is he?"

"Is it a man though?" I try to catch my breath and press my hand against my chest to still the heavy pound-ing there. "Where are you going?" I ask him as he pushes open the door.

"Get your flashlight and come. And put on your haz-ard lights."

Father has already disappeared around his side of the van. I find the flashlight and make my way quickly over. It is dark and cold outside. We have stopped at a very lonely spot, close to the place the figure emerged from the slopes up through dense bush.

It is a man and he is sprawled at the edge of the road behind the van. The swerve of the tire marks show that I barely missed him and only because his shirt was tangled on the barbed wire that runs along the fence of the property he rolled from. In the headlights, I see he is about my father's age. He is covered with red mud from his bare, chapped feet to his matted hair. His face is chipped and burnt, his lips are cracked. One eye is closed and the other is too swollen to open properly.

Father reaches down to check on him and lifts his head. "He fell in the red lake."

"Don't touch him." I reach down to pull him away and am hit by a smell so foul, I have to cover my nose. "Don't touch him. What you touching him for?"

Father straightens and brushes his hands together like a man ready to take charge of a situation. "He fell into the red lake. We have to get him to the hospital." He takes the flashlight from me and walks beyond the man through the bush.

I chase after him. "Where you going?" I demand.

But he is making his way slowly through the bush, retracing the path of the mud-caked man.

"Where are you going?" I grab his hand. "Where do you think you're going?"

"Come, man, we have to check," he says.

"Check! You are not going one step farther. I don't need to find out what happened up there and neither do you."

He stops and turns to me. I see excitement in his

face. I see light in his eyes and am reminded of that evening some weeks ago when he took off after a mighty explosion in his backyard. While everybody else was terrified, he took charge and ran down to the source of the terrible noise. The explosion turned out to be a wine bottle from his makeshift distillery carved into the hillside of his massive yard. But this is a different night in a different place. It is a pitch-dark night, in the bushes of Mandeville, on the trail of a mysterious man who fell from nowhere. This is not his backyard, this is open-road Jamaica, and he will go no farther up that hill if I have anything to do with it.

"Give me the light." I grab the flashlight from him.

"There may be other people out there. You don't know what happened," he tells me.

"Exactly! You come. And Daddy, I am not asking you this time. We don't know what happened. We do not know where he came from. There may be danger up there. Come. We will report this to the police."

We are the same height, but he is slightly uphill so I am looking up to him. Still, he sees the sternness in my eyes. He relents and we make our way back through the bush.

The man has found enough strength to drag himself to lean against the wheel of my vehicle. I step across his feet, play the light around the van to check what damage has been done. The front bumper is resting lightly against a large tree but there are only a few scratches made by the thick bush.

I return to find my father in deep conversation with the man on the ground—if it could be called conversation. For my father is the only one speaking, and the man is panting so desperately he is hardly finding enough strength to breathe, let alone talk. I am standing above them, and all I can do is shake my head at the stubborn old man cradling the smelly muddy one as he tries to comfort and extract information. I know what is coming next. He came out of nowhere. We don't know what he did, don't know where he came from or what trouble he may get us into. But I know Father will insist that we take the smelly, dirty man with us. Man falls out of the night, out of the pool of acid and into our path, half-dead and mysterious, and my father has adopted him and all his circumstances.

I am afraid that my father is in a mood of adventure I do not recognize and that nothing good will come of it. I am worried that another body will roll down that hill at any moment. I am terrified that whatever caused this old man to roll down might come chasing after him.

"What now?" I ask my father. "What now, old man?"

"We can't leave him here," he says stubbornly, "we can't leave him here."

So I drag this man, dirty and stinky, rancid with the acrid smell of bauxite acid and urine; body slippery from layers of dirt and muck, hair plastered with all kinds of grease; stench so high I have to pause twice, put him down, and step aside for fear of vomiting. I take him and I put him in the back of the van. My father climbs in beside him.

Even after winding all five windows down, and taking the van to seventy-five on the dark and winding country road, the stench lingers here with me like burnt flesh in an enclosed kitchen. It is on my skin, it is on my clothing, it permeates my very existence. My nostrils are flaring and my old asthmatic sneeze is coming on.

God, I can't wait to get to Mandeville and deposit the load. I cannot wait.

"You know where the hospital is?" I ask.

Father raises his head from talking to the old man on the seat. *God, how can he stand the stench? How can he cradle his head in his lap like that, as if he knows the man—as if he is a baby or an injured pet?*

"I asked if you know where the hospital is."

"Just drive into the town center, man. I hear they have a new one now. I haven't been here in a while."

It is a long time for me too. But why bother telling him that.

My father never gave me a pet. I asked for a dog; he told me a dog would bite people and get me into trouble. I asked for a cat; he said it would aggravate my asthma. I asked for a goat; he told me he would raise one for me on his farm when he bought one since goats don't do well in urban areas. And what would I do when they have to kill it to make curry goat? He never gave me a pet. My mother said it was because he was not convinced I could take care of one. After a while I figured he just didn't want to make commitments to me that would make him have to come on particular days. He didn't want to schedule me so I would expect him at promised or set times. Promises bring disappointments, disappointments bring explanations, explanations show weakness.

He preferred to just pop in at his leisure.

After a while I must have grown to accept or even

prefer that he came without schedule. For the surprises were good, and as Mother would say: "Long-to-see better than tired-to-see."

But I always wished I had a dog.

The road valleys then slopes gently up to crest and merges into the Winston Jones Highway. Mandeville is across the road.

At this time of night, Mandeville looks like a sleepy, expensive housing development. It is a town, more suburban than country. The houses are large and tastefully designed, the lawns are manicured, and the yards are big and open. There are few fences and there is an expansive beauty about the place, yet tight and cozy. A sign points to *Town Centre*. I turn left as it is directing. Mandeville is also a town of hills and valleys; half the time one is going up or coming down, rising onto a small plateau or cruising down a gentle hill.

I am now facing a town center with a sign that welcomes me to Mandeville, a sign made of iron in a park that rivals the hundred-year-old one in Kingston proper.

Straight ahead are old buildings that match the park but on either side of the square are brand-new banking and insurance buildings.

"This is the town square," my father tells me from the back. I do not bother to tell him that I know. "It hasn't changed much at all. If I am not wrong, the police station should be right down there so." He points directly across the park. "If they haven't moved. Let us stop over there and ask where the new hospital is."

The police station is tucked away off to the side of the road a bit under the park. I bring the Pathfinder to a halt. As soon as I switch the engine off and the air-conditioning dies from my face, the stench hits me again with a mighty force.

This is a bigger station than in Spalding. There are more policemen milling around and more cars are parked in the yard. As I alight, a swarthy, well-dressed policewoman approaches.

"You can't park here," she says. "Parking is on that side."

"I just want to ask directions," I tell her.

Her nose wrinkles. She must have smelled the stench of the man on me. "Yes, but you can't park here. Please move the vehicle."

"I am not stopping. I just want to know where the hospital is. I found a man on the road. He must have been beaten. He is in a bad way."

"You found a man?" Her eyes become alert, suspicious.

"Yes."

"What kind of man?"

"An old man . . . he looks injured, as if someone beat him. As if he was in the red lake or something. We need to take him to the hospital."

"Where is he?"

"In the back."

She steps away from me slightly. I almost feel I should raise my hands above my head. She then walks half a pace toward the vehicle where my father cradles the man in his lap. Her interest is piqued. "Turn on the light. Let me see."

I reach inside and turn the roof light on.

"Hmm . . ." She looks inside and takes in the scene there. I know the stench has hit her, but she seems unaffected. She turns her head from the car and lifts her voice toward the station: "Sarge, they found another one."

Suddenly there are five cops around the van with a thousand questions.

"Then why you never carry him to the hospital directly?" one of them asks, "Why you have him here?"

"Who are you, sir?" the one called Sarge asks. "Don't you see this is a police matter?" He turns to me. "We will take him from here. You need to fill out a few forms inside."

I thank God for sergeants and motion to my father to give him over.

"This man is sick." Father seems reluctant. "This man must go to the hospital now."

"Don't mind that, Daddy," the sergeant says. "We have a special vehicle for that. Plus, you gentlemen must be tired. Just fill out a few forms and then you can leave." He turns in a businesslike manner to two of his colleagues. "All right, take him out. Where's the truck? Take him out and send for the truck."

We spend half an hour inside. By the time we are finished, the excitement has died down in the station and the general routines seem to have settled back in. We learn that the man has been the third one discovered that night. They are street people out of Montego Bay who have mysteriously found their way to the mud lake in Manchester.

The sergeant, named Clark, who takes our information is a nice, talkative, respectful man who divulges that this is not the first time it has happened.

"What do you mean?" my father asks.

"Not the first time we find them up there."

"But how they walk so far from Montego Bay to Manchester? And how did they get to the red lake?"

"They are madmen," I tell my father. "Madmen do mad things. Stop pestering the sergeant."

He hisses his teeth and gives me a long reproachful look. "I don't see how people can walk that far."

"Who say they walk?" the policeman replies. "Who say they walk? Is dump they dump them. Don't say I say, just sign right here."

"Dump them?" Father is bewildered.

"Well, don't say I say." The policeman retrieves the book after we sign. "Don't say I say. But I hear they have a big tourist conference down there. Every time they have a big conference in Montego Bay, they clean up the street people and bring them and dump them in the red mud lake. Can't embarrass the tourist. But I never said so."

"You will never learn anything," my father says to me as we turn to go. "Not if you in too much haste and don't have time for nobody and nothing."

"What is there to learn?"

"Nobody cares about old people, that is the problem. This country getting too hard—nobody cares about people anymore."

"Daddy! He is madman."

He hisses his teeth and turns away.

So we are standing outside, and the wind is cold and fresh against my face. I feel hungry and my mind is returning to the KFC I saw down the road.

"I tell you, we should have taken him ourselves," my father says disgustedly.

"What?" I follow his eye and I gasp. For that is all

I can do, as the old man is still lying crumpled on the steps that lead to the police station.

"You're not taking him to the hospital?" I call to the first officer I see. The swarthy policewoman is standing over to the side of the door. "Excuse me, I thought you were taking that man to the hospital."

"Sir . . ." she looks at me with a stern, patient glare, "we are taking him."

"But he is lying on the steps outside like garbage," I tell her.

"We are waiting on the truck."

"But there are a dozen cars." I point around me.

"We will take him," my father tells her. I don't want to go that far, but I dare not contradict him.

"We are taking care of it." She takes a menacing step toward us.

I pull my father away. "Come," I tell him. "It is a police matter now, come."

But he is a stubborn old man, and he is raising his voice angrily: "This is a tax-money car, they are all tax-money cars. You are afraid he will dirty up the tax-money car? It's not your car!"

"Come." I wrap my arm around my seething old man. "Come, Daddy, come!" I force him into my van and we drive around to the First Caribbean Bank, where I stop at the ATM.

Cash in hand, I return to find my father gone. But I know where he is. I leave the Pathfinder and walk across the square to the police station where he is shouting angrily at everybody in uniform. The swarthy woman is before him with the sergeant at her side. Other policemen are milling around, and a stranger is restraining my father. I replace the stranger's hand with mine and whisper into Father's ear, "What happen to you, old man? These are policemen. They can lock you up."

"All o' you wicked. I am going to write to the minister," he is saying. "Wicked people. Taxpayer car and onoo make the poor man dead before onoo take him and dirty up the taxpayer car. Make him wait on some dump truck onoo know not coming. Nobody in this damn country care 'bout old people. Nobody care 'bout old people!"

"See the truck there, Daddy," I whisper as a battered police vehicle rumbles toward us. "The truck is coming. You don't see the truck coming? They are going to carry him now."

He turns to me and drops his arms. His mouth works, but no words come. There is a sudden silence.

"See the truck come, it late, but it has finally come. See, it is here," I continue to point.

"Come, you damn fool!" my father yells at me, and storms toward our van. "Come."

Suddenly I know the fool I have been. For as I turn to leave I see that the old man who was once folding himself, hugging and suffering upon the steps, is now awkwardly sprawled, his hands by his side, and he has rolled halfway down from where they had put him. His body is all askew and his lifeless eyes stare blankly into the skies.

SIX

The place where my father wrecked his car resembles a scene from *The Fugitive*. A ravine, as deep as a football field is long, runs along the edge of the road for several miles. It has a steep rugged face with large trees, thick shrubs, and bare jagged rocks. All that lies between the badly paved country road and the edge of the precipice is six feet of dirt. All that saved my father from death was a large cluster of bamboo trees halfway down the treacherous slope.

His car is on the hill, anchored precariously in the bamboo roots. It rolled over twice to get there and now rests on its top. From the end of the front door to the rear bumper, it hangs unsupported, while the front is buried in the roots of the bamboo cluster. A fat bird could land on the bumper and send the vehicle tumbling the rest of the way down into the valley.

As we stand here, the valley is still shrouded with mist and it is cold though my watch tells me it is after nine. Father says it rained last night. I slept through the rain, and the morning must have slept late too, for the sun is certainly taking its own sweet time.

"That wrecker can't pull it up! The crane too small." Sergeant Clark is all business this morning. The two men from the small wrecker flank him.

"So I see," I answer. I could have told him that the

moment I got here. I am afraid to ask if this is Small Man or the man from Silent Hill, or maybe Smaller Man by the looks of the truck.

The sergeant scratches his head. "What you need is one of those big bauxite cranes to pull it out. It is going to cost you some money. But that will be the only way."

The wrecker man says that he could arrange the whole thing. "Sarge did not tell me, I would bring a bigger crane-truck with me."

"Couldn't you just hook it to that truck and pull it up?" I ask.

"That would mash up the car," the policeman says.

And now the dilemma: if they get a bigger crane, it will probably cost the price of the car to pull it up that ravine and the same amount to tow it to Kingston and then to fix it. My head begins to throb.

I do not have time nor am I in the frame of mind for negotiating this morning. These country people treat everything like market day. They are hemming me in, scratching their heads, eyeing my SUV. *The old man have rich son. Charge him, man, Kingston people have money.*

"How much to take the whole thing to town and leave it?" my father asks, his eyes glinting, cutting to the chase. He is finally emerging from the silent brooding mood that has held him all morning.

"Well . . ." Small Man scratches his head, "what you think, Sarge?"

"Well, you are the wrecker man," the policeman drawls.

Jesus, at least they could be more original.

"I'll give you ten thousand," my father offers without

a blink. "Ten thousand and you drop it off at a garage in Linstead till I pick it up in about two weeks."

"Ten thousand! Gas money that," Small Man exclaims.

"So!" I join in.

Twenty minutes later and we have reached a consensus. They will pull it out and haul it to a garage in Linstead for twenty thousand dollars.

As soon as the man asks for a down payment, my father adds a condition that he wants his suitcase retrieved from the car.

Small Man's assistant says he could do it for a thousand dollars.

So we stand quietly off to the side as the man from the wrecker climbs carefully down the slope at the end of a rope played slowly out by the wrecker's gantry. I cannot imagine what is so important in that suitcase to risk a man's life for. I do a mental tally of my current account; I should be able to get the down payment with my ATM card.

"Let him work for his pay," Father whispers to me.

"Is money in there?" I ask. "You have money in there?"

"There is a little," he says through the corner of his mouth, "a little small change."

The man is at the car and his partner shouts down that he should just break the window. But he ignores this advice and tries to open the back door.

"Don't touch it," the sergeant shouts down, "just bust the glass!"

My father seems not to care what they do. "Ask him if he sees the suitcase," he says to the policeman. Then he directs his voice down the hill: "Can you see the suitcase?"

But the man is ignoring everyone. Maybe because

he has discovered that the car is much more securely lodged than we expected. He has managed to open the rear door. Half of him disappears inside and then he re-appears slowly, burdened by a large suitcase.

Then it hits me. "Daddy, what do you mean 'bout two weeks?"

"How you mean?"

"What do you mean when you say that you will pick up the car in two weeks' time. What are you doing with such a large suitcase in your car?"

He tells me not to worry myself. Then he is silent beside me. In fact, except for the brief exchanges of a moment ago, all morning he has been strangely quiet and into himself, reflective even.

Not much has passed between us since we left the dead man sprawled on the streets last night. I tried to buy him dinner, but he said he was not hungry. As soon as we checked in, he went to his room and closed the door. I know he was shaken by the death of the old man, so I went to check on him first thing this morning. When I got to his room, he wasn't there. Before I had a chance to panic, however, I spotted him on the street walking slowly and pensively from the direction of Mandeville.

"You must try to walk at least a mile each morning," was all he said to me as he brushed by into his room. And later on the drive back, I noticed that as we passed the police station his face fell slightly and sadness seemed to creep over him.

I raise the back of the SUV so the man can place the suitcase there. My father seems to tense a bit as he opens the latch of the suitcase, but I have already decided I want to see inside. There are clothes in there, about two weeks' worth I guess at a glance. There are gifts inside. I see bottles of his pimento wine.

He digs around for a leather pouch and his fingers tremble at its zip. I reach to help him, but he snatches it away even as he is pulling the money from inside it. Papers drop into the suitcase and a picture falls onto the floor of the van. He is unable to get to it before me because his hands are full with the pouch and the money. I pick it up quickly. The picture is old but in excellent condition, and I see a beautiful, sexy young woman staring back at me.

There are more things to notice now than I can digest, more things to take care of than can be done in an instant. The photo has distracted me and so have the contents of his suitcase, so I am unable to monitor his transaction as I'd like to. But he is his own man. He concludes his business quickly and efficiently. I watch him calmly as he finishes what he is doing and folds the remaining dollars into his wallet. I want to ask him why he has so much money on him, but now is not the time. I hand him the picture so he can put it with the rest of the spilled contents back into his pouch.

"You want to explain this, old man?"

"Explain what?"

"I have a sister I should know about?"

He laughs dryly.

"What is so funny?"

"That picture is over thirty years old."

"Who is it?"

"A friend I have not seen for thirty-five years."

"Oh . . ." I laugh sheepishly and turn around. "I figured you had a thing on the side or something."

"She is no thing on the side." His voice is almost stern but with a longing in it.

"What do you mean, Father?"

He hisses his teeth and walks away. "You're acting as if you don't believe the number three thing all along."

"This is number three? There *is* a number three? This is the woman Una has been calling number three all these years? You have a woman on the side, number three in your relationship? You have been in love with this woman for thirty-five years? This is why you ran away, to chase after a woman you have not seen for thirty-five years?"

"You never knew? Stop acting as if you never knew. I hear you and Una talk 'bout it. Stop acting like you don't have any sense."

Jesus Christ! Sixty-seven years old! So many times when I would visit him at his house in Hampshire, I would find him sitting off by himself looking into space with a soft smile on his lips; or maybe in the middle of some conversation, his mind would just wander off with a longing in his eyes, and Una would nudge me and say, "Him gone to her again."

"Who?" I would ask.

"Number three."

After a while, I became part of the joke and started to make my own private comments. But never in a million years did I think there was anything to it.

Now this.

"I was joking; I thought you guys were joking; I thought this was just a private joke about you wandering off in your reflections."

"Cho!" He waves a dismissive hand.

Sixty-seven years old and my father has packed a grip, left his wife, and run away after a woman he has not seen for nearly four decades. *Sixty-seven years old . . . thirty-five years.* You never hear these things in conversations sitting on his veranda sipping pimento wine. He tells me this on the edge of a cliff, on a lonely winding country road in the middle of Manchester, where he has no right to be driving alone in the first place.

He must be mad. What does he take me for? Who does he believe I am? That he suggests that I believed this number three business. *Number three . . .* that this joke between him and his wife was not a joke all along and that I knew or believed it, and tolerated it and respected him still, all this time. *Me!* What does he take me for?

Even as I reel from the enormity of his statement—the revelation of it, the accusation of it—I try to remember if there had been any clues in the past from which I should have concluded the truth of this thing. The last time on his veranda, I had confronted him and he had not responded. Should I have concluded then that this phantom of a number three was real? And the many times, I suppose, Una had mentioned it, should I have been listening more closely? Her hysteria on the phone when she sounded more jealous than concerned: "He is gone to her! I know he's not with you."

My God! What kind of game can two old married people play and why have they chosen *me* for it. How do you love a woman who is but a shadow in your marriage . . . for thirty-five years?

My watch says two o'clock. The day is dead.

The side man is wrapping the last of the chain onto

the barrel of the crane. He seems quite pleased with himself, having just risked his life to retrieve a grip for my father for a good fee.

In five minutes of bargaining father had summed up what the man's life is worth and had his way with him. Father has a way of making people do crazy things.

Is this how he sees me? Does he think he has the measure of me, that he knows what makes me tick? Is this why he throws this thing at me now? Does he think he will now have his way? He is making a sad mistake!

The back door of the van is still open. The old suitcase is still half-open. I lift a bottle of pimento wine from it, caked with the dirt that had hardened around it from his cellar where he buries them to ferment. Is this trip all about a woman?

I feel him brush by me.

"So, you are leaving Una? What are you trying to tell me?" I say this to the side of his face. "You are leaving your wife for this woman you have not seen for thirty-five years? Suppose she is dead."

"She is not dead."

"Suppose she is married and has grandchildren."

"Does it matter?"

"Do you think the woman you're going to find is the same woman in this picture? Do you think she looks like that?"

"Does it matter?"

"What?"

"What does it matter, Everton?" He gestures for the bottle in my hand. I make no effort to pass it over. "Just say," he continues, "I am taking a break to go and look for an old friend, all right."

"But that is not what you said. That is not what you meant when you spoke just now."

"What does it matter what I said or what I mean? Stay with me. Spend some time with the old man."

"Me! I am not going anywhere. I am not going on any quest with you. You are not going anywhere. You are going home, with me, this evening, to your wife."

"Take a break," he says as if I had not spoken a word. "It would do you good, take a week off. Spend some time with the old man."

"Are you listening to me?" My voice is rising. "You are not going anywhere. I am not going anywhere. We are going home now! Back to Una—your rightful wife. Stop this foolishness now, Daddy!"

He pauses his activities, turns his face to me, and for the first time in my life I realize I do not really know this man I call my father. His face is all composed; his eyes are hard and unwavering and he is steady as a rock before me. There is a force in him I have never seen—as if age has made him stronger and when he gets to a hundred he will be powerful enough to lift the world. His voice is just a hint above casual, but it balls the space before it into a savage punch.

"Don't tell me what I can or cannot do. You have no control over that."

I find I can't hold his stare. "What about Una?" I ask. "What about your wife?"

"She was fine the last time I saw her. Don't let that bother you."

"She was hysterical when I spoke to her. You need to talk to your wife."

"I will talk to her when I get back. I am not going

back there now. It is like a damn prison. I want some damn space. This is something I have to do."

This is new territory for my father and me.

I have never been close enough to his business to get into it. We have lived in separate worlds all my life, and have come together in convenient patches of time. Funny how I describe them now, for those times, to me, were the most beautiful moments in the world. From a week of summer to glimpses of him as he exited my mother's door and the sound of his voice on the phone. Times when I was old enough and would visit him on my own, or invite him to my apartment for the weekend and take him to a play or a concert. Those snippets of time have been the moments that string together the mundane drudgery of my everyday life.

But now, as I stand here unsure of how to breach this space in which we now exist, I have to say that those were only patches of time, cameos in a grand performance. For now I stand with this man that I have lived for all my life, who has been my universe, and it seems I do not know the essence of him. I do not know the next word to say.

But I must assert myself. For I too have priorities. I have a presentation to make, a brand-new plant to whip into shape. I know my boss gave me time to find him, but they expect me back. I have made plans for my time off this year—a trip to America to see Venus Williams play in the US Open—and every day I spend with him, I lose from my vacation. I do not have the time to give, the time that he needs. And even if I could, I would have to return to my office and negotiate with my bosses. It is not as easy as he thinks and he must respect me for that.

"I cannot just leave with you like this, Daddy," I tell him. "I can't just leave. I am an executive now. I have responsibilities. You got up, packed your bags, and ran away. You can do that because you are retired. I had to run out of the most important meeting in my life for you. I have already lost two days. I can't just pick up and leave. I am an executive."

The click of the latch on the suitcase is as loud as thunder against a granite mountainside. I hear its thud on the ground beside me.

"Well, you can just leave me here."

"I can't leave you here. You damn well know I can't leave you here."

"You know, Everton, I'm your father. This has always been your weakness. You are never really sure of what you could or could not do. You are too afraid . . . afraid of risks. Now, why do you think you cannot leave me here?"

"I cannot leave you here because you are my father. I am responsible for your safety. I couldn't leave you here."

He laughs loudly, infectiously, and gestures around. "This, you see all of this? This is my country. Do you know where you are? When I was young, in my twenties, this was my playground. I know every nook and cranny around here. I know the dip and swell of the land, the rise and slope of every mountainside, the trail of every river. I know every landowner. This is my country. I could not leave *you* here because you are afraid to take chances and be adventurous. But me, just leave me here. This is my country."

And now, this anger that I have tried so hard to hold

in check is getting the better of me. "So that is what you want? You want me to leave you here with your grip on the roadside? That's what you want?"

"Yes. I'll be fine. It is just twenty minutes from Mandeville—before you can blink someone will pick me up and I am on my way."

"That is your wish, Daddy? I want to make it very clear that you gave me this instruction."

"Give me a paper, I will sign it."

"This is your country. You want me to leave you here with your grip? Make sure, Daddy, make sure. This is what you wish for? This is what you want? You are going to get it, old man, you are going to get your wish."

"Now you are starting to sound silly, son. Just do what you must do."

"All right, all right!" I walk away from him without another word. I slam the rear door of the Pathfinder so hard the whole van shakes. I open my door and can hardly see to sit down through the blinding rage. I floor the gas before the key is through turning and I am on the road so fast I have to brake to avoid joining my father's car down the precipice on the other side. My reverse is better and now I am moving forward again and my tires screech as I head down the road toward Mandeville.

Where did God get a man like that? And why did He give him to me for a father?

I don't know who I am trying to fool. There is no way I am going to leave my father there alone. And I am sure he knows it too.

I am less than five minutes down the road when I slow at the next crossing, make a U-turn, return to stop at his feet, and tell him to get in.

But he does not. Instead, he pushes his face through the window. "I am not going back."

"Get in," I repeat.

"So you decide to spend time with the old man? I don't want you lose your job."

"Tell you what," I say. "I will give you the rest of the week if you talk to your wife."

"I don't have anything to tell her." He walks back toward the suitcase on the road.

I hop from the van with the cell phone in my hand. "Here," I tell him, "talk to her."

"She's too miserable. What will I tell her? She'll never understand that I am doing what I must do."

"I don't care, Daddy. You take that chance. I am the one you say is afraid. You're always sure. You talk to her. You want me to come with you? Well, you take this phone and you talk to her, you set her mind at ease. Show some respect to someone who has loved *you* for thirty-five years."

So he takes the instrument from me and tries to calm his hysterical wife on the other end of the line. "Everton and me going to see the country, man. Boy decided to spend some time with the old man . . . Never meant anything . . . You weren't there . . . No, I didn't wait till you left to run away . . . Just decided to take a little time. Everton is with me . . . Yes, I have it . . . I will come back next week."

I move away. The conversation fills me with the guilt of intrusion and the feeling I am letting Una down. I cross the road to the edge of the precipice and peer down to where the car lies tangled in the cluster of bamboos. He is lucky to have survived that crash unscathed. After an escape like that, any other man would have changed his mind from whatever adventure he had planned. Any normal man would have rushed to return to the arms of his family. My father instead grips more tightly to what-ever reason he has for fleeing.

And now I find myself feeling curious. I would like to see this woman. I would like to hear this story.

Thirty-five years . . .

Why did he marry Una then?

SEVEN

So here I am. It is Wednesday morning and I am ready to do this thing with my father. I still cannot understand how I allowed myself to be conned into this. But I have made him a promise and I am here, for what that is worth. Of course, I had to lie to my boss about a nervous breakdown my father is having, how he went for a drive, crashed over a precipice, and is not himself. But it bought me the few days I promised him and now I am here. And in any event the story is not far from the truth. In fact, I cannot say in all honesty that my father has been himself for the last few days.

We are sitting at a concrete shed by the side of the road where he wants to buy me breakfast. It is seven a.m. and there is no one here. A slab of a counter separates the concrete stool from a space beyond, rimmed by a long, large fire side. The stale smell of the food from the night before hangs around us. Behind, the land drops away and disappears, so we seem to be on the edge of a massive valley that expands to show the entire southern plains. I can't believe he dragged me away from my continental breakfast at the hotel for this.

A little old man emerges out of nowhere as if there are steps on the sides of the cliff's edge. He is tightening a dirty black belt around washed-out jeans. He has no shirt on.

"We don' really open yet, you know." He smiles cautiously at us. "We don' usually open till round nine or so."

I smile to myself, prepared to leave.

But Father is not at all bothered. "You don't have anything there you can rustle up for us? My son here never have roast yam yet."

"Well . . ." The man scratches a dirty head. "Well, I could see what I could rustle up."

"Some nice St. Elizabeth yellow yam, man. You don't have any soft St. Vincent yam and roast salt fish and so?"

"Well, I could see what I could do if you willing to wait."

"About how soon you think—hour, half an hour?"

"'Bout that. And I have some cabbage too and a little ackee."

"Ackee?" My father's eyes light up. "But I didn't know that ackee would be down here this time of year."

"We have a little tree on the hillside round the back behind the house."

"Then that is the thing." My father smiles and slaps me. "We will wait the half hour. This is my son, you know. First time this side of the country in years."

He has been treating me since last evening. Took me to a store and insisted on buying me clothes for the trip. Polo shirts of colors so loud you can almost hear them scream across any space I enter, Levi's jeans, and sneakers with too many reds and yellows for my liking. But I sneaked behind him and bought a couple of T-shirts as insurance against his style. I wear one now, a shirt the color of the sky to match the blue of the jeans he gifted, though I still can't find the courage to wear the ugly sneakers.

"The clothes look good on you," he says as we wait.

"Thanks. The old man has taste."

He laughs at that. "You too stubborn."

A woman disembarks from a car. She makes her way toward the corner and sits with a frown on her face, then shakes her watch and looks up at me. "Excuse me, you know what time?"

"Seven thirty," I tell her.

If she thanked me, I am not aware, though her manner suggests she has nodded graciously or something. Not too bad looking either. She is wearing a pair of waistless jeans and a small sky-blue shirt that stops at her navel. Her stomach is flat and deep. She has a strong face, a nose just shy of big and rounded at the tip . . . lips as if she is about to pout . . . false braids falling almost to her shoulders.

She sees me looking but ignores me. There is a weary sadness about her.

Father elbows me and nods. I raise my eyebrows in acknowledgment. I'm not happy enough with him yet this morning to do the buddy-buddy girl thing he is seeking.

The shirtless man in the dirty jeans has reemerged. He begins to fuss with the long fire side. I stand to move away before the mix of dust and stale food make me sick.

"Where is the bathroom? Where they wash their hands, Daddy?"

"Who are you talking about?"

"The people who work here—him." I nod at the old man. "Where do they wash their hands? Where are their toilets? They use the bush? When they use the bush, where they wash?"

He ignores me of course, stands, and then moves across to where the young woman is sitting. "How you look so sad this morning?" he asks her.

I cannot believe this one. Why do I fear that the next statement will be, *This is my son*.

"You look like the Vassals from down Alligator Pond," he adds.

The smile escapes her like a precious, private thing. She catches herself and retrieves it quickly.

"You such a nice young lady," he continues. "Tell me what you doing up here?"

"Waiting on somebody. You see a red car stop? How long you up here now?"

"Not too long now." He sits beside her, stretching his legs toward the street. "You would have to ask my son, him notices everything. I'm getting old. You sure you not a Vassal or Turner, then?"

She smiles longer now. "No sir, I come from Ballards Valley way. I am Thomas, Angela."

"You know that *Angela* is Spanish for *angel* . . ."

He is acting more like a man on vacation than someone who is seeking a long-lost love. There is no urgency in him. He has not told me where we are going or when we intend to get there. I had expected that once I agreed to go with him, we would have been halfway there by now, would have spent last night hustling from Mandeville to get to wherever this woman may be. But it seems my submission has been an excuse for him to shed whatever urgency his quest may have had, as if I have given him years and not a couple of days.

So after he spent last evening shopping for me, he went for a long walk around the adjoining golf course. I took the opportunity to have the vehicle cleaned. I am not sure what time he got back. I had eaten, had a drink at the bar, and gone to bed early. This morning he woke me, said he was headed out to the golf course again. He invited me, but I declined. Now it's close to eight o'clock and I still don't know where we are going or when we will get there.

So here we are, missing my continental breakfast at the hotel, at this awful-smelling jerk pit with no toilet or bathroom in sight, with this little man as stale as the fire side he is trying to stir to life, *rustling* up something for us to eat. And instead of discussing the trip with me, my father is over there at the edge of the road trying to steal smiles from a young woman like a pickpocket.

I leave him to his endeavors. Somehow, I now feel a bit guilty for ignoring Audrey's calls. She has left four messages on my phone since yesterday, but I have not even listened to them. My anger and resentment toward her is dissipating a bit even though she was wrong; we had come too far together for her to say the thing she said. There are places you do not go, things you do not say, lines you do not cross however angry you become. For they are like bullets fired in the air, which you cannot take back and you have no idea where they will fall or the damage they will cause. We have quarreled before, and I am accustomed to the wounds her tongue can make, but she has never crossed the line before in the way she did that morning. "You don't even love you damn father." And over an orgasm at that.

How could she say something like that . . . in that ugly way?

I head toward the other side of the shed where it hangs onto a concrete building with a sign saying *Hill View Hide Out Restaurant & Bar*. There is no wall here and I have an uninterrupted view of the valley below.

I look out onto the plains of St. Elizabeth and everything beyond: from the sea that peeps between hills way off to the south, to the smoke curling from the rusty red compound of the bauxite plant that sits square in the center of everything. It is a massive, sprawling valley.

Though it's close to eight o'clock in the morning, the sun has not yet made its way up the hill to where we are. But down in the valley and way over to the plains, I can see its shadow shrinking its way eastward. And as it comes, slowly, creeping, there is a moment when part of the valley has a hint of sun, and part still sleeps quietly and peacefully snuggled into the gray bosom of the morning.

My wallet is in my hand and I do not know how it got there. But it is there, and protruding from an inner pocket is the yellowing edge of a piece of paper. I take it out gently, unfolding it. Its creases are almost as brown as the land around me as I open it. *Ten Questions for My Father*. Here this morning on the edge of the precipice, the old writings of years ago, drawn by the tentative hands of an uncertain adolescent, still hold. *Ten Questions for My Father*.

When I am away from him, I do not remember these questions. And even if they come to mind, I usually discard them. I have formed my own conclusions about them, provided my own answers and justifications. I am a man now, I tell myself. I have gone through the years when the questions would have mattered. For any son may find more questions for a parent than can be answered in two lifetimes. And no span of life is able to resolve all the stories that fill them. That, I tell myself, is the reason for forgiveness . . . it fills those gaps of unanswered questions.

The questions came from a suspension I had from school for fighting when I was twelve. My classmates and I had been teasing each other under a big tree in the schoolyard at lunch break and I had been boasting about my father as I usually did. But my best friend, in trying to win the argument, shouted out that I was lying because I could not even remember the last time I'd seen him. "Your father not even come look for you," he had sneered.

It was a secret we shared and he'd betrayed me.

I gave him such a beating, I was suspended from school for two weeks.

It took my mother two days of insistent badgering to extract the reason for the fight from me.

That was after my father had come. He drove up in his brand-new fishtail car on his way from work to his house in Sydenham and threatened to beat me till I had absolutely no backside left. "I went to school for fifteen years and never get detention. You are twelve and get expelled for two weeks. Two weeks."

I never told him the reason for the fight, though he asked repeatedly and slapped me so hard I almost fell to the ground. But people said I had a devil in me then, and a sullen silence that could infuriate the Lord Jesus Himself. So I never told him.

But my mother had a way of getting things out of me and after two days she succeeded. When I finally told her, she gave me a long, measured look and said, "Some things you must let pass sometimes or you won't have many friends."

But as I said, I had a devil in me. I drove my mother to the edge of madness. I never got suspended again, but I romped at school till my clothes were so dirty that my mother cried when she washed them. I stayed out late after school with rowdy friends when I knew she would be worried. And I would refuse my chores and leave them half or badly done. And worst of all, though she often forced me to go to church, I would stay outside and hang out as if I were on a school break.

I drove my mother to the edge of madness.

Then one day she took me to the pastor, and right there in his office, in the middle of asking for his help, she broke down in tears. "He hates me, pastor. He hates me. I try my best but I don't know why he hates me."

The pastor nodded his head, looked gently at her, and asked her to excuse herself so he could talk to me alone.

When she left, he leaned back in his chair and peered across at me; my shirt buttoned haphazardly, shoe laces untied, dirt on my face, and it was only halfway through Sunday morning.

So he looked at me, and instead of preaching or sermonizing, which I was prepared for, he threw a large Stagga Back at me, speaking as I caught the large candy. "Women are like that, they get hysterical sometimes." Then, as I contemplated the large gummy sweet, he leaned forward over his desk and trapped me with the softness in his eyes. "It's your father, isn't it? You have a lot of things you want to say to him, don't you?"

I remember feeling as if a hand had reached inside and touched my most tender part. I jumped as if stung by a bee.

"Is so men stay." He leaned back in his chair with a friendly, victorious smile. "That is how we are, men. Well, some men . . . some fathers stay so. Me, if I see my father now, I wouldn't recognize him, probably only saw him one time in my life and it was a stranger who pointed him out to me on a bus one day . . . *See you father there!* But I don't make that cause me to destroy myself. The most we can do, people like you and me, is try to be better when we become men."

I remember squirming in the seat, sullen and silent. I could not sit still or meet his eyes.

"Tell you what you do." He was leaning forward again. "When I was your age, nobody really understood me either. And sometimes, to tell you the truth, I never even understand myself. But it is all right. You are a good boy and you will be okay, you will grow it out. But you can't go around angry like that, because you poor mother don't understand and will think is she you hate . . . and you don't want to distress her. So tell you what you do. After church, when you go home, sit in your room and write down the ten most important things you would like to ask your daddy. Keep it as your secret, and when you get a chance, give it to him. Mail it too if you want. Or just keep it as your own secret—or, if you really feel you strong enough, call him one day, tell him you want to talk to him, and read them to him."

"Ten questions?"

"Yes, ten questions."

So I went home and wrote the ten questions down, and my whole life turned around. I can only recall one major fight afterward, but that is another story. My mother said it was the pastor's prayer. But I knew it was the weight of the responsibility of the ten questions I carried around in my breast pocket everywhere I went. And the hope that I would one day do what I wanted with it. And somehow, too, those questions ensured I was good, pinned me down against my pride. For to be angry at anything else now, to me, was a sign of weakness I could not admit to myself or to anyone . . . so ultimately, then, in a reverse kind of roundabout way, the ten questions were my source of strength and resolve as I moved through my teenage years.

I never asked my father those questions, never showed a soul the list. I tweaked it over the years, removing childish questions as I grew, changing one, honing another. But somehow, this list, this old original list written by uncertain teenage hands, feels more powerful and fills me with more emotions than any version I hold in my head.

"Memories? Old memories?" He is beside me now.

"Yeah."

"What is that you hiding?"

"Not hiding anything. What is in my wallet is my business, old man."

"You ever seen anything pretty so, boy?"

"What?"

He points ahead as the morning creeps up the hill and the valley brightens and the clouds and mist roll toward the colder, darker side. The land below me has more yellow now, and even the hills way over in the distance are changing in the face of the coming day.

"You have a point there, old man, it is amazing."

"You know where you are?"

"Manchester."

"Yes, but where? This is the Spur Tree Hill, boy. There is no other view like this anywhere else in Jamaica. And I should know. I travel everywhere."

"I must admit it's beautiful."

"See! And we not even start off yet. Suppose you had gone back."

"Ahh," I wag my finger at him, "I said a couple of days. No more."

"Come." He slaps my back. "The food ready."

"Already? How long have I been standing here?"

"Is so beauty stay, man, it kills time. Come."

The young woman is sitting between us. And why am I not surprised? My father introduces her as Angela from Ballards Valley. I see now that she is younger than she appeared from afar. Though her movements are assured, I am certain she is not more that twenty-two or so.

A dish of ackee and salt fish and a bit of roast yam arrives. I look suspiciously at the butter draining from the heart of the yam. It seems to me that the vegetable could do with a little more scraping or a good peeling. The roasted salt fish still has the black of the grill on it. A large bowl of mixed vegetables and a big black pot of steaming chocolate tea complete the offering. The spread will not win a beauty contest, but it smells good and my mouth is watering.

Father reaches quickly for a fresh broccoli spear,

spins it in his hand, and smiles before crunching down on it. He then pours himself some chocolate tea and pushes the pot along the counter. I am the last to taste the food, and I crush the butter-soaked yam into a serving of ackee and, on swallowing, immediately forget how dirty the man is who cooked it. I glance up to see everyone staring at me. I nod to the man and his smile broadens to show bad teeth.

"Try more of the roast yam." He pushes the plate across to me. Butter drips to the counter. I taste it. It is beyond belief. I try not to look too pleased as my father passes a blackened piece of cod fish to me.

"First you eating roast yam and salt fish, don't it?" This comes from the woman beside me.

These are the first decent words between us since I sat and nodded to her at my father's introductions and my mouth is too full to respond. I nod to her and the hot butter runs down my chin. I bite into the yam; it holds its heat and delivers it to me slowly. My mouth burns but I dare not spit it out and embarrass myself.

"Don't bite too much, it will burn you," she advises.

"You always take a big first bite." My father smiles proudly at me and then nods to the man. "Naya, man, this is the best roast yam I ever have. Glad I wake you up this morning."

So we eat.

The food has been excellent, we have seen the view from Spur Tree, and father is finally ready to set out on his quest.

"You drive in the front with Everton. Open the back there, Everton, let Angela put her things in the van." I wish someone would ask my opinion on these things. I am not saying I would have refused, but he could have at least asked me if I could give her a ride. Nothing much, just a simple, *Everton, can she come with us?* But suddenly, whether I like it or not, my car has an extra passenger. Suddenly there is a woman in the seat beside me.

She is curled sideways, so she is able look at him and then through the windscreen with just a swing of her head. This is a convenient position for her to sit in, for I am not sure what to say to her and this way she can engage in continuous conversation with my father.

I do not know where I am going and I certainly do not know where we are taking her.

"Is she part of the trip now?" This comes out into the car without my intending it to.

There is a short, uncomfortable silence as we slip down Spur Tree Hill into the deep indigo valley. I have insulted our guest. *But they could have at least asked me.*

"Turn left," he says at the bottom.

The countryside is dry, and my father points this out. That takes care of the silence.

Everything down here contradicts the view from the jerk pit on the hill. The land is dry along the road, and the grass is like a dirty gray carpet. The greenery is in trees that fan out on both sides farther back toward the hill and to the homes that sprinkle the countryside. There is a fierce sense of independence to the place, for every house we pass is on a large plot of land, and every plot adjoins another large area with vegetation and a crop of some kind.

Father and Angela are discussing bush fires.

"Things not so bad now," she says to him. "Sometimes down at Ballards Valley the fields burn without anybody lighting them."

"Bush fires are common down here," he responds. "That is the only thing with St. Elizabeth. It gets too dry sometimes. Pretty, beautiful people, but not much rain."

"I can imagine how a place like this would burn easily," I try to join the conversation.

"One time I saw two cows fight over water, right down here," my father says.

Angela giggles. I shake my head. Sometimes when he tells a story it is hard to know if he is telling the truth or simply trying to lighten the mood.

"Right up by Junction," he says. "Right up there— cow kill its mother over little water in the pass."

"Is that where we are going, Junction?" I ask as I stop to let a line of goats cross the road.

"I am going to Ballards Valley. That is on the other side from where you going."

And where is that again? So now I am the only one who does not know where we are going. I hold my tongue. "Okay."

By the time we get to Ballards Valley, I have thawed a bit. I learn that Angela has not been home for three years and has come because she had gotten word that her mother is not well. She is anxious because she is not sure what reception awaits her. She had left for a three-month hospitality course at the HEART Academy in Runaway Bay and had not returned nor sent a message since then.

But now she is back. And the closer we get the quieter she becomes, the sadder her countenance, and the more she pulls at the false hair that hangs down her face.

I cannot help but wonder what secrets she holds behind that sad face and what fears she seeks to calm by tugging at the ends of her hair. But though I am part of the conversation, I remain a passenger in it. My father seems to understand her and they have obviously established something that makes him know what not to ask her.

Father disembarks with her and offers to help with her bags. "Let me walk with you."

But she takes them from him and tells him it's all right.

He walks with her all the same and pats her arm as he leaves her at the gate. I feel now that I should have tried harder to at least forge a closer bond. She sat beside me for over two hours, and as we part, the only person she says goodbye to is my father.

"She is a nice child," he says as he reenters the car.

"It seems so," I respond.

"A nice child, just want somebody to take care of her."

Ballards Valley is in a place where the land seems to want to hurry from the hill to the sea and one does not notice how steep the hill is until one is trying to get back out. I would not like to be caught on this road when it rains. "This road turn valley and all the water from Junction and the south side use this road like river." My father smiles at my concern.

We crest the hill and I stop the car at the foot of a barren rise of land. I ease the stick to park, put my feet on the dashboard, and push my seat back a bit.

Father smiles. "The place nice, don't it? That is the spirit—you must relax more."

"The place dry, Daddy! Place dry. I am not relaxing. I am stopping so you can tell me the plan. I have done everything you told me to. I gave up my week. And now I think you need to tell me the plan. Where are we going? What are we doing at this spot, right now? What is the next move . . . and so on and so forth."

His features soften a bit as he looks at me, then through the windscreen down the valley from which we have come. "The old man trying your patience, don't it?"

"That is an understatement."

"All right then, we have to go to Alligator Pond."

"Where is that?"

"'Bout half an hour down the road."

"And that is where she is, Daddy, Alligator Pond? So this stop was on the way?"

"Yes, that is why I gave her a ride. It is on the way. And she is a nice child."

"I don't have a problem with giving her a ride. I just need to know. I need information. You know how easy it would have been if you had just told me?"

"You're cantankerous, you know that?"

"So that is where this woman is, Alligator Pond?"

"Yes, I will meet her there and then we can go home. I will meet her at her cousin's home."

"So today I meet this woman."

"No, you meet her tomorrow."

"So we are going to Alligator Pond now."

"No, man. I want to show you something first."

"But what about Alligator Pond?"

"Yes, we going there, but I have something to show you first. I have a surprise for you."

"A surprise for me? Daddy, how you must have a surprise for me when you did not even know I would be here this moment, today? How you must have surprise, what you take me for?"

"Come, man, drive the car. Turn this way. I have something to show you, a big surprise."

EIGHT

We stop at the edge of the sloping road. There is little shelter from the sun here. The trees are farther in and the little access road turns quickly from bare red dirt to large clumps of sharp limestone rocks. As I step outside, a dry wind wraps the heat around my face and pushes it under my clothing. In five paces I am sweating like a racing dog.

The land slopes with the road and ahead the limestone rises to where dry trees lie, broken and shattered, along the hillside. The tall trees with leaves that are still standing are few and far between. Off to our left there is a flatland of dry grass and an old field.

Father has begun to make his way up the large part of the hill to my right. I run after him and by the time I catch up I am panting.

"Where you going, old man?"

"Just over that hill."

I hate that he is breathing so well, while my words gasp for air. "Is pure bush!" I yell.

But he ignores me and is walking enthusiastically. I have no choice but to follow him.

It is a hard climb, for the rugged surface is covered by dry fallen trees. So to get one's balance, one has to grab a short stubby cactus or fall into a thicket of prickle. He pauses ahead to wait for me, looking back with a broad smile on his face. Puffing and wheezing, I try to catch my breath. A small pain jags through me.

"Don't stop. Come, man, don't bother stop."

So I straighten from the rock on which I am leaning and go to meet him at the top where the trees and the land seem to bend away.

He reaches for me. "Give me you hand."

I ignore him and make my way. He grabs my arm and pulls me to him anyway.

"Look at this!" He smiles and waves his hand in front of him.

The land has fallen away to become a massive plateau that stretches for about a mile or two before it grades into another mountain range. It is a series of pastures and tracks of flat empty land with corn-colored grass that fades to white under the glare of the sun. I cannot see much of it for the grass is high where we stand. I walk to a clump of mango trees a bit up the rise and lean into the low crotch of one to rest. I look back to where we have come from to find a view to the sea as beautiful as the one we saw at Spur Tree.

"Twenty-five acres."

"How you know that?"

"It is mine. It is yours."

"Yes, Father, that is a good one. I believe you."

I lean back into the tree. The wind is hot, but the grass cools it before it gets to me. I must contemplate the fact that as my father is getting on in years, his mind may go and come.

He walks away from me up a small rise and stands the way Jesus must have stood when He addressed the multitude and begins to chant. I have lost a week of my vacation, I am a mile up a hill in the hot sun, and my father is having a nervous breakdown.

"Daddy," I call softly to him, "what happen to you, what you singing?"

But he does not seem crazed. His eyes are focused, he looks happy and free. He is bursting with the pride of a father at Christmas time. On his face is the Santa smile that holds a secret that will blow the mind of a simple, unsuspecting child. But I am not a simple unsuspecting child, he is not a Santa Claus, I can see no gifts, and this is not his land.

". . . manumise enfranchise and from every tie of slavery or servitude set free a certain negro woman named Bethesda to hold the same manumission liberty and enfranchisement so thereby granted onto the said Bethesda and her future issue and increase—"

"What is all this!"

But he rambles on: "And then is such case I give onto Bethesda all that parcel of land, all that settlement or pen commonly known as Dorril Pen or Guava Nook containing . . ." He smiles at me. "You understand that?"

"Daddy," I place my arm around him, "come out of the sun."

"I am fitter than you." He smiles again. "There is a story to this place that you must know."

"Come, Father, come. You might get sunstroke."

"I have been coming here all the time and I never got sunstroke. But what you think?"

"Think of what . . . the land?" I pause to find the right thing to tell him, to calm him so he does not get angry. "Well, it . . ." I turn toward the view of the coast, then I smile back at him. "But it . . ." I turn toward the grassy range that extends farther than I had thought now that I have joined him on the little mound. But before I can finish, we notice, halfway to the hill, a large clearing of more than an acre rimmed by large trees where a quadrangle had been deliberately cleared, settled, and farmed.

His face darkens with curiosity. "I wonder who that is." He tramps off and disappears on a path through the high grass. I trot to catch up with him, and as I do, we burst through the grass into a large tomato field.

"Who could this be?"

"The owner, perhaps," I quip. "The whole place is farmed up."

We stop, and he surveys the rows and rows of tomato plants. Neat furrows in the red earth show careful cultivation, each root covered with grass and each plant strong and waist high.

"Come!" He makes his way through the heart of the tomatoes.

I am thirty paces into the field before I realize that the tomatoes have given way to marijuana.

"Daddy, stop, is a marijuana field."

"So I see." He slows for me to catch up. "I wonder who planting ganja up here."

"Daddy, come, let us turn back. Come now!"

"Why?"

"Because we are standing in the middle of a ganja field on someone's property in the middle of nowhere in St. Elizabeth."

"But is my land."

"Is it your ganja field, Daddy?"

"What kind of damn stupid question that? Is my land!"

"Well, it might be your land, old man, but is somebody else's property and I suggest we leave. As a matter of fact, come. Now!"

"But it is your land. I wanted to show you today. It is your surprise."

"Trust me, Daddy, I am very surprised. Come!"

An engine roars. A jeep is speeding down the hillside, bouncing furiously as it plunges through the high grass toward us.

"Somebody coming!"

Behind us, two men emerge from beyond the mango tree in which I rested, cutting off our way back down the side of the hill to the car. One has a cutlass and the other has a big gun over his shoulder.

"They have guns!" I pull him down and reach for my cell phone. "I must call the police. What is the name of this place?" I ask him as I flip it open. "Where are we?" But there is no service on the cell phone. "Daddy!" I scream at him as he begins to tremble slightly. "Daddy, you really know this land?"

"Yes."

"Then, how do we get off it? How we get away?"

"The river, down that way."

"River! You have river in St. Elizabeth?"

I stand to look around. The jeep has stopped. The men have alighted and are making their way across the field toward us. One of them has a gun too. Behind us the other two are getting much closer. The one with the gun waves it at us.

"Hey!" he shouts. "Hey, hold on there!"

I duck, and we begin to walk quickly toward the southeastern corner of the field.

Someone fires, and the sound is loud in my ears. "Run Daddy, run!" I do not have to tell him twice.

We will be killed here on the hill. No one will know about it. No one saw us come. The killers will steal my van and burn it or hide it. We will die up here, no one will find us. Dead at thirty-seven and I never even had a chance to see Venus Williams play tennis.

There is a thud of heavy feet and the harsh rustling of dry grass. I can hear their voices. Another bullet rings out. My father stumbles ahead.

"Father, you shot?"

"No, I'm tired." He is fit but not for running.

"We need to get out of the field," I pant after him as I catch up.

"Yes, I know."

I hold his hand and pull him. "You can run a little more?"

"If I have to, I have to."

"You have to."

He is going to die of exhaustion. He is sixty-seven years old—he will surely have a heart attack.

"Turn this way," he points.

"Where it go?"

"Out!"

I follow the direction of his finger. But there is no path here, no neat furrow in which to run. The land rises. The crop turns to tomato. A few paces more and we are on a bank of dry grass. The grass is high and brown and holds the heat of the day. As we plunge into it, sharp blades cut into our skin. I can hardly breathe. But I cannot stop. I hold onto him and drag him along through the hot, dense grass till I feel my head glance off the trunk of a large mango tree.

We pause here.

I turn on my knees and look beyond the grass to the center of the field. From where we are, I can see all things below and away toward the large hills. The five men are convening near the southeastern end of the field. They are not sure where we are, but their eyes scan everywhere and do not stray much from our general direction.

"You know where we are?" I ask him. For I have completely lost my bearings. He glances around and whispers that he is not so sure. But it looks like we are close to the river. He points down the hill. "Way over there, looks like Alligator Pond River."

Alligator Pond River! A river that leads to an alligator pond!

"Alligator Pond River?"

"Yeah." There is a sparkle in his eyes. He winks at me. "You think it is a river filled with alligators? It's just the name of the river and the town. From down there the whole mountain range looks like an alligator. That's why they call it that." He amazes me. His face is scratched and dirty, his hair is ragged upon his head, men are chasing us with guns, and he has time to wink at me.

"That's it?"

"It looks so. That's the way we have to go. But I not so sure how far from the river we are."

"Well, we're going to find out," I tell him. For even as we whisper, the large red-skinned one who seems to be the leader has hoisted over his big gun to one who had none and sent three of them in our general direction, while he and another return through the field.

"Find them!"

The three fan out and head for us.

If we are careful, we can slip away into the dense grass and be lost in the bush where it slopes away after a few meters or so. So we crawl together into the dry, hot waving grass. It smells like dust, its blades are sharp against my face. Ants and bugs cover my clothes. They bite and crawl. The sun and the heat fill me with fatigue. But we dare not stand to run upright or look back.

I am weary, I am tired. I am going to die.

A week ago all I could think of were the long legs of the most graceful tennis player in the world. Today I am about to die in the dusty hills of St. Elizabeth, playing Indiana Jones with my father.

How quickly things change.

"This way," he says, veering to the left. "Come . . . and watch your step."

The grass is thinning, and I am a bit unsteady because the ground is sloping downward, and off to my right the trees are a bit denser and the shadow is thick among them. I head for their coolness.

"Stay with me." I hear the short whisper, but he is heading down, away from the coolness of the long trees.

He is getting his second wind and is now racing ahead, low and fast like a rabbit. Through the thinning bush, I see a trailhead to the right. I yell at him. "Stop! No, Daddy, it's this way. Come!"

He stops quickly and calls back to me, but I am already dashing eagerly through the grass. Suddenly the ground drops away from in front of me and I am plunging down a jagged bushy hillside.

I hear my father scream my name. The shout is like a gunshot in the afternoon. Maybe there is a gunshot too, but it does not matter for the ground before me has disappeared and I have catapulted over the steep sloping edge. My face buries into the hot red dirt, my body summersaults, slamming me flat on my back, and I am sliding through the bush like a Rastaman on a bobsled.

I feel the razor-like grate of every inch of every ridge of this jagged limestone mountainside. I knock into the trunk of every tree. I am grazed and scratched by the whip and snarl of every angry twig. I am going so fast I cannot hold on to anything. I dig dirt with my fingers. I even try to grab the jagged limestone. I hit a large tree. I hug it quickly, but it is prickly and I cannot hold on. I snap my hand away from the sharp thorns and I am heading down again to God knows where. Then directly ahead of me a large clump of grass appears and I slam, crotch-first, into it, my legs splayed on both sides, my face burying into its dry hot blades.

I am numb with pain, but a clump of hot, dusty, bug-infested grass has never felt so good. I hug into it like a child burrowing into the folds of his mother's dress. I close my eyes momentarily, to calm myself and try to fight an uncontrollable urge to sob. What in heaven's name am I doing here in this place on the side of a hill, lying in this grass?

What the hell am I doing here, how did my day turn to this?

So I rise now—or make to rise—and as I do, I realize that this is just the beginning of my problems. For whereas I am able to gain purchase against a hard surface with my left foot, my right foot, from the heel forward, seems to be suspended in air. I part the grass from my face with a tentative hand and see with gut-wrenching terror that the clump of grass holding me is the last piece of vegetation or tree on the hillside.

I am sitting on the edge of a cliff. All I see beyond the grass is empty space. And I cannot tell how far it drops. Now I am sure I will die today.

Somewhere up above I hear my father call my name again.

I hope he shouts loud enough for them to hear so they may catch him and skin him alive for getting me into this. I hope he never survives this after I am dead.

But I cannot curse my father now. I must think. I must move. I look around me.

Though steep, it is the kind of hillside that a man could make his way up or down if he walks slowly and cautiously enough, if he picks his spots and grips the shrubbery or even the craggy limestone carefully. It is near the end, where I now sit, that the danger is, for this spot is void of all vegetation, and except for loose dirt and gravel, the rock is as close to smooth as limestone can get. Had it not been for the clump of grass, I would have shot off into the air like goods from a chute. For about six to ten feet behind me, the rock has little to hold on to and is too steep to crawl on. But if I can launch myself from the grass, I may catch one of the trees above me and haul myself to a more vegetated space. From there it would be just a matter of picking my way carefully up the hill.

But first I must cross this barren space.

My only chance is to backpedal till I am able to place my foot at the root of the grass that now holds my crotch. Then perhaps I may stretch my full length up the slope to a tree behind me and pull myself to safety.

My Bally loafers are the color of dirt.

I move my foot gingerly and begin to inch up the incline on my backside. My shoes are not designed to climb loose-graveled mountainsides. So it is my bottom that holds the ground as I edge my way backward up the hill.

I am almost there. I bend my legs to place them in the center of the clump of grass. First one, then the other, then I straighten them gently. I stretch my arms to their full length but I don't feel the tree behind me. I must spin around to lie on my belly. I close my eyes, test the root of the grass, cross my legs, and spin around. The root feels firm and good. Just one leg is grounded there, but I am flat on my belly and my body's friction is holding me down. I place the other leg carefully down, glancing back to make sure my feet are on either side of the clump's center.

Now I turn my attention to the mountainside and the tree above me. It is half an arm's length from my reaching fingers. I measure and lunge gently, missing and sliding slowly down onto the grass root again. That was a trial attempt. To get there I must lunge higher and harder. I measure my feet against the grass root, bend my legs, and check again. If I miss, I must return to the exact spot on the grass root; hitting it wide on the return could be disastrous. I practice one last time, measuring the distance to the tree, coil my full weight and force into the tension of my bending legs, and then lunge forward toward the tree.

I am halfway forward when I feel the grass root split beneath my right foot.

Suddenly, I am slipping and sliding through the

middle of the clump of grass, and before my desperate fingers can grab something, I have been shot from the cliff into the middle of empty space, dropping like a stone, screaming like a man on fire, my hands flaying frantically, grabbing onto air to finally discover in the most painful way where the river is.

The water is like concrete. I feel every bone in my body shatter as I hit. My teeth snap against my tongue, almost halving it. Pain shoots like sharp needles through every inch of my body and all my senses explode. Everything is blank for a minute, then I begin to fight and struggle against the waters, thrusting and kicking as if against a thousand devils; screaming in terror with visions of alligators slipping through the murky depths to eat me. I'm fighting with desperation, but I am unable to control my functions or prevent myself from sinking.

But the river is not too deep. I touch a muddy bottom almost immediately. I easily make surface and look round me. I am in green water, in a riverbed twice as wide as the water in it. I swim toward the dry section and drag myself onto the gravel there. As soon as I touch land, I stretch out, so exhausted I can hardly move my legs. My palms burn, half my shirt is missing, my pants have no backside left, and one of my legs doesn't seem to be moving. Exhausted, I close my eyes and pray to God that Alligator Pond really is just the name of the town and nothing more.

"Everton!"

"Yes, I will take a drink."

"Everton!"

The sun bears down viciously. The sand I lie on is as hot as coals. The air is dry around me and to open my eyes is to feel the heat drag across my eyeballs, taking every bit of lubrication with it.

"Everton!"

I finally open my eyes against the glare of the afternoon. I glance around and do not see my father, then turn onto my aching side to peer across the river from where I have come. Then I see him making his way down the hillside like a country goat.

Somehow he has found a decent path a few yards to the left of where I fell. And he is moving very quickly and expertly down.

The foot of the hill is a few feet from the edge of the river. As he gets there, he tiptoes to the edge and calls, "Everton!"

I wave at him.

"Come!" he beckons. "Come."

There is no way I will move. *You come.* I wave at him. *You cross the water, you feel the hot sun too. Everything is me. You feel some of the pain too. All of this is carried in the wave.*

"Come!" he shouts as loudly as a whisper may rise. Then he points his hand above his head. I realize what he is saying at the same time that I see the bush move and hear a gunshot reverberate. He does not have to call again. I dive into the water and do not surface until I feel the embankment on the other side.

"You all right?" There is an excited worry in his voice. "Come." He pulls me from the water. "We have to move. They can't see us here and so they can't follow us."

Without a word, I jog and limp beside him, half-dead, half-crawling, sheltered by the mountain, following the river for about fifteen minutes. Here the river leaves the mountain and tracks through the sloping, flattening land while the mountain and the hills curve westward and back on themselves.

"If we keep following the river, we will find the beach just down there so," he says to me. "But let us rest little."

"Rest a little?" I pant.

"I don't think they are coming after us anymore. It look like they just wanted to frighten us."

I limp to the clearing at the root of a large mango tree in the middle of the tall grass. I sit so its trunk shades me from the sun, stretch my body on the ground, groan, and close my eyes.

NINE

all your father now, no.
My breath is hot in my nostrils, tears of anger burn my eyes as I run, and blood drips down my face where a stone has hit my head.

Call your father now, no.

There are three boys after me.

One, I could beat easily. Two, I could take a chance and stand and fight. But three is too much for me. They have my knapsack. I had to discard it when the ugly one grabbed it some minutes ago, twisting my neck as he pulled at it to try and stop me. But I swiveled hard and left it in his hand. Dirt splatters from a wall in front of me as another rock is thrown at my head. I run and zig-zag through the narrow lane where the cracked, broken sidewalk is just as wide as the dirt track it shadows for a road.

Call your father now, no.

"Touch me," I had said, "lay one finger on me or any of my friends, and I will call my father to lock you up and make them run you family off the dirty old hut you live in. My father is in charge of all cane fields from here to Clarendon. Touch me—no, open your mouth—and I will call my father and you and all your ugly family will turn beggars."

A shove had gone with that too. A little boy in torn

khaki was at the end of that shove too, standing there with his friend, trying to hustle money from us, John and me. Saying how he liked my shoes. Young snarling dirty boys who hardly passed through the school gate except to get their names noted on the register once or twice a week as their minds tell them. Sullen boys, dirty boys with downturned eyes, hating school as much as school hated them. Maybe because they smelled so much . . . too poor to change their clothes or bathe anywhere except the irrigation canal that fed the cane fields till their skins were as chalky and scaly as fish left to die in the sun. Always there, standing at the gate, intimidating anyone they could, fondling the girls, threatening those they thought were soft.

But I would not be soft. I stood up to them

"You never had to insult them so, we could just walk them out," John said.

"I never insult them—I just tell them the truth."

"But we could o' just walk them out. Leave them alone. Them will kill you, those people have gun."

"Cho, they don't want me to call my father."

Now they chase me down a lane that leads to a place I don't know. *And where is John now? Disappeared the moment he saw them. Wasn't he the one who got me into this? Wasn't he the one I defended when I took them on? Wasn't he the one who I offered to follow home though it was miles out of my way because he was scared to pass alone through the area where the dirty ugly boys live? Now he is gone and I am alone far away from my home and even farther away from the safety of the school crowd where I took them on.*

There is no shelter here in Portmore, just the sun beating down on this concrete place with its intermittent tracks of dirt. I am dashing from one strange lane to another. I don't know where I am going and I am running out of breath.

Call your father now, no.

I wish I could call him; I wish he would come. Drive his big car, park it at the end of the ally down which my tired legs now make me falter, open his arms to my charge while lifting his larger-than-life self to its full height, raising his hand like Moses pushing back a storm . . . like the great defender I boast him to be. *Touch him, no; touch my big son; just touch one hair on his head, if you think you're bad.*

But I am alone. I have no father to come.

Call your father now, no.

I run hard. I am tired. The open fences, dirty houses, are all part of one hot, hazy blur around me.

I cannot go much farther.

A large light post looms. It is a crossroad with an alleyway to my left and right. I brace myself and swing right. The feet behind me are closer and seem multiplied in my ears. I swerve around the corner, and before me are houses on every side. Then there is a cul-de-sac with a narrow lane feeding off to its left-most corner. I swing toward the lane; it is the only escape from this box that traps me. But standing there is a snarling boy with a knife in his hands. I have been herded into a dead end.

I pull up quickly, but lose my footing and fall, skating in the dust on the seat of my pants till my backside burns from the grating gravel.

Call your father now, no.

Anytime you need me, he had said, *just call. Just call, man, and I will come.* I now realize just how deceptive a promise that had been, for how could I call him? How do I know where he is at any time of day, and even if I did, by what means would I call him? How stupid I was to believe that I could call . . . and even more stupid I have been to think that he would come.

Call your father.

Call me when you ready! Though he knows I have no way to do so. *I will come when you want.* Though he knows he will never come, will never be there when I want. Nor will he be there when I return home after I have been beaten to death.

Big son, my big son.

Maybe after this, when I am dead, he will come. Maybe then he will find me whom he has neglected. Big son! Yes, big son in the dust now, faced down by a knife and two cowards. Maybe when I am dead, maybe then. Someone else will call and then he will have no choice but to come. Someone will call and tell him, *Your big son dead, man* . . . Then he will come. Then he will know . . . that I wanted him, that I called and he did not come.

"Call your father now, no." Big, ugly, bulky kid, whose name I do not know, on the right edge of the circle of three that converges on me.

"Your father not coming now? So I live in a shack, I live in a cane field . . . so your father goin' chase me out like a dog? Your father is a bad man? You call him? I don' see him. Call him now, no."

He has spoken my thoughts into the hot day. He should not have done that. My hatred for my father is my own. So I choose him. I choose him now, that boy of sixteen years or so, two years older than me, a head and a half taller, big and broad like a mature footballer, with a knife in his hand as long as my arm and a mocking snarl on his face—I choose him this day to die with.

I am at his throat, from crouching in the dust, through the air so fast it is as if the earth has tilted to meet his slamming back. There is no strategy to the attack, no form to the madness. I am an animal broken loose, teeth bared, biting, sinking into dirty flesh till blood runs down my face. Head butting, stiff arms tightening around an ugly thick neck, knees pumping, kicking, legs flaying. Angry animal gurgling and savage grunts coming from me. It is an expulsion of something deep and deadly inside for I shall give everything here in this dirty place, in this hot dusty road. I shall vomit everything here and now, for I shall not return from this place this day. I shall not return to be anything he wants; not to ambition and good grades; not to school and empty stands when I compete. I shall not return to a lonely home and a mother who tells me to turn the cheek all the time, nor to the empty spaces of my room and the echoes of empty promises and a voice so strong, a smile so sweet, and face so godly and strong. I shall not return from this place. I shall kill him now. I shall die right here with him, with this ugly, thick, smelly person. I shall kill him now and die right here in the hot dust of a strange and ugly street. I shall die for him; I shall die with him . . . I with this empty space that I see is my father.

Call your father now. Leave me alone, police people. I do not want to know I almost killed him.

Call your father now. Leave me alone, hospital people. Leave the knife right there buried in my shoulder.

Call your father now. Leave me alone, mother people. I do not know, I cannot tell what is wrong with me.

Call your father now. Leave me alone, father people. Let

the scowl drop from your face, for I called and you did not come. I wanted you and you were not there. You are never there when I need you! Leave me alone, Father . . . for when I call, when I need you . . . you do not come.

Call your father now, no. No, I will not call him. I have no voice to call. I am alone and I am empty . . . I have no one to call . . . I have no father to call . . . I have no one . . . I am alone . . . Let me die alone . . . I have no one . . . I have no father.

Call your father, call your father, call your father . . . father . . . father . . . father!

TEN

I must have fallen asleep. For I open my eyes to a cooler place, and my father is seated beside me by the trunk of the tree. He seems quiet, contemplative. His little brown book of poetry is in his left hand resting on his leg. It is late afternoon; I can tell by the position of the sun and by the color of the grass on the hillside.

I wonder what time it is exactly and lift my wrist to check. It is empty. I jump to my feet. A pain shoots through my left leg. I fall over. *Where is my watch? Where is my expensive Movado, my thousand-dollar-US birthday present? And my shoes, my two-hundred-dollar Bally loafers, where are they? What are these crusted dirty torn things on my feet? Where is half my shirt? Why does my palm hurt so? Why does my ass feel so cold, why are my underpants exposed? Where is the seat of my pants? Where is my wallet?*

"You all right?"

I do not answer because I am not sure how to react to him, to this man I call my father. And I must wonder at that now, this father thing. Is this man the father I have loved all my life? Waited some evenings on the streets just to see his car whiz by and tell my friends, "See my father there, is a Toyota Crown that him driving." Or for those days when I would come home from school to see him stealing out of my mother's bedroom, so he could pat my head and ask how I was doing.

But now I have him with me and he is not what I want for a father. This weird mischievous old man trying to drag me through his old-man fantasies. He will have me lose everything, including, possibly, my life, because I am not sure those gunmen will allow us out of this godforsaken parish, now that we can identify their ganja field. I do not know this man.

"You lost your watch, no? It was a nice watch. I tell you, when I saw you drop over that hillside, I thought you were dead."

I do not know how to take these words. I do not know how to read that look on his face. So I do not respond to him.

"Never frightened so in all my life. Never run so fast yet. You all right though?" He rises and brushes the red dirt from his pants. His hair is a mess of bush and dirt and weed, his face and hands are scratched, his clothes torn, but that seems not to affect the elegance in him as he joins me.

"Which way?" I still do not have a notion of how to approach more than a few syllables of conversation with him. I am much too close to a boil.

He nods his head southward. "If we follow the river, we can catch the beach about a mile or so down there so. Then we should find somebody on the beach or a cottage or a small hotel or something."

I turn to join the river's path. He is beside me.

"As soon as we reach down, we'll get some people and the police so we can come right back and look on the land."

"Daddy, forget the land."

"You can't forget it. Is my land, is your land."

"Daddy," I pause to look at him, "you don't own any land, and even if you did, you don't own it now. Bad men with guns own it. Ganjaman land now, Daddy."

"Well, they'll have to kill me first. It is your birthright. It is your birthright!"

"Daddy!" I stop. "Daddy, if I hear *land* one more time, I am going to explode! Jesus, old man. When you goin' come to reality, eeh?"

"You would almost die for nothing?"

I stop again and hold his shoulders. "Daddy, I don't want the land, okay? I don't want it. Give it to Holly, okay? You know what I want, Father? I want to go home. I want to take you home to your wife. I want you to be all right. I want to go home, lay in my Jacuzzi, in some warm water. Soak, Daddy, soak for a while, then jump on a plane and go watch Venus Williams play tennis. You understand? I say it now: I want to watch Venus Williams in the US Open. I have been saving my vacation for it and agreed to give you one of those weeks so I could work with you, spend some time with you. But now I want to go home. Now I want to take you home. So come." I move off again. "Come, Daddy, let us go home."

"You need to know the story of the land. If you knew the story of the land, you wouldn't talk like that." He is a dripping pipe on a night when all I want is to fall asleep. I am tired of him. I am tired of this talk of land. I am tired of this day. I wish the week would start over.

"Why, Daddy, why?"

"Why what?"

"Why me? Tell me, why me? You have three children, why me? You are at home and you want company, they call me. You sick, they call me. You need help with law-yer, they call me. Why me? How is it that all of a sudden I am so important? Tell me something, Daddy: where were you? Answer just one question: why didn't you come to my graduation? Can you answer that?"

He hesitates.

"Right, you can't answer because you were never there. I was never important. I am the bastard, the one outside. And who get everything, who live in big house and have car-drive to school every day? Me? No, Daddy— Holly, Meagan, they get everything. Sometimes I feel that the only way my name is Dorril is that someone threw it on me, not because it is your name. How come I name Dorril when I am always outside? Now every-thing you want, you call me. Where are they? Why they not going through bush with you, losing everything they save money to buy, have gunman shoot after them, get-ting land on the wrong side of some damn river? Why me, today, this day, why? When you were in you prime, I never saw you. I suffered every day and you never even knew. Now you losing you mind, you call me. Now I am the one who must die on some hill like some damn In-diana Jones movie. Why me? Why me? I don't want any land. I want my watch, I buy that myself. I want my van, I buy that myself. I want my life, I make that myself. So if you coming, come. But I don't want to hear anything about any land. I don't want any land."

I have hit him hard. He shudders into himself and tries to find his footing like a man struggling in a high wind, then he fades away and is silent.

I begin to feel horrible. But I tell myself that he needs a dose of reality. And I have been chosen to give him that. It is my lot to suffer. Sometimes one is just destined for a job.

He does not meet my gaze when I look at him.

"Come, Father, come."

He turns away from me, but I do not follow.

I am weary now. I can hardly walk from the pain and bruises throughout my body, I am tired of the quarrel and the games and moods. He needs his moment and that is fine. But night is almost upon us and we are lost on a hillside.

"Come, Daddy, I want to go home."

He does not respond, but I don't care anymore. I strike out along the river to where he said I could veer to the beach. After a while I turn to see that with a limp I had not noticed, he is walking slowly after me.

ELEVEN

It is perhaps the ninetieth minute of our silence. Every inch of my body hurts with a different pain. Ahead and to the right I spot the lights of the motel the fisherman down the beach told us we would have seen perhaps an hour ago—the distance of country people is usually twice as long as they tell you. It is a large compound with a long driveway that leads to what amounts to a two-story apartment complex curving around a pool. A sign says, *Memories By the Sea*.

We must look a picture to the man standing behind the counter of the bar. I tell him good evening and ask for the receptionist.

"What happen to onoo?"

"What happened to us? We are not doing so well. Could I see the receptionist?"

"Where onoo coming from?"

Where are we coming from? I can't see how that could be important to him. "Are you the receptionist?"

"This is the bar," he says. "Is the bar this. What happen to onoo?"

"May we book a room?"

"Yes, is the bar this, what you want? Where onoo coming from?"

There is a sound from inside. He turns, pushes his head through a half-open door. "Just two man walk in look like them beggars from Kingston. Like them homeless people."

I am too tired to get angry. I feel like Tina Turner in that movie, walking battered to the front desk of a hotel to book a room on the strength of her name alone. *What's Love Got to Do with It*. Ah, some titles are so appropriate.

"The thing is, my good sir . . ." Father takes over. "The thing is, we were chased by gunmen off a property we went to look at up the road."

Thank you, Daddy for not saying "chased off my land." Thank you, God, he has sobered, and he is quieter, more dignified. He does not look at me, but that will come as time wears on, when we get back to Hampshire he will be back around.

"So we have been running from over near the river mouth all evening." He sits on the barstool as if about to order a drink.

"We lost our van and everything," I slip in.

"Yes." My father ignores me. "So we are tired."

The man turns to the inside room again. "Them say gunman chase them round river." Then he turns to us: "Where?"

"The land above the river—round near the river mouth."

"With a big ganja field," I bellow even as Father seems to sigh. "A big ganja field and men with guns. You have a phone there?" I remember my van. "We need to call the police."

"Where you say?" The man drags his finger through the hair on his face. He is about forty-five, short and red. His eyes are old and quiet and his smile is polite. But he seems more interested in the story than our well-being and I am getting impatient.

"Can we get a room? Can we get a tub of hot water to soak in? We have been walking for over three hours."

"Hot water is in the room."

"Can we have a room?" I almost shout.

I am the only flustered person. Father sits as easy as a mango on a tree and speaks casually. "You don't know the land way round near the river on the north side, about three hours down the road from here and about an hour from Ballards Valley?"

"Yes, but I don't know where up there you say you see a farm. And what you doing, you alone up there? Onoo come from town." His head disappears inside for a moment. Then out with his head again to address us. "Is my father." He nods toward the curtain. "Him say is up by Dorril."

"What? What did you say?" My jaw drops. .

"Up by Dorril. All the land on that side you talking 'bout owned by some people name Dorril."

As he speaks, I feel the emotions contort my face. I do not know how to react or how to look at my father as he sits there dignified, ignoring me, leaving me to wallow in my embarrassment. The curtain parts, the man behind the counter shifts and a much older one emerges. He makes to speak and then his eye catches my father. He pauses and squints like a man trying to see past the glare of the sun.

"Wait, Dorril? Nigel Dorril, boy, you still alive!"

"You!" my father yells, pointing his finger like a gun. "I know you."

"Damn right!"

"Green! Green from Bull Savannah? You look like Green."

"Yes, is me, Eustace Green. Must be ages, man, Dorril. But stop. Is you they shoot after? Man shoot after you on you own land? Is him name Dorril." He turns to his son and points at my father. "Is Dorril this. Is my son this, you know, Nigel. Is my boy this. You remember him? Him was small."

"Yes," says my father. "Well, this is my son too." He nods at me. "First time down this way in ages."

"But Dorril, you turn old man, man."

"And you have not aged." My father laughs.

"What a thing, eeh?" Eustace's face has broken out into a thousand wrinkles. "What a thing? You know who I see yesterday? Ezekiel Brown. You remember Brown, man? Him was the first one get license to drive water truck, but couldn't read. Own the piece o' desert near Treasure Beach. Him son them farm it now. You remember?"

"Ezekiel, couldn't play a domino." My father laughs again. "I thought him was in England."

"Right. Him come back now, returning resident, they call them. Might even come here tonight."

"You don't have any whites there?"

White rum! Half a day in the sun, chased through a ganja field, walked how many miles, tired, and the first thing my father orders is rum, overproof white rum.

And you know something? I don't care, I will let him. For I am on the outside of something I do not grasp. And he is on the upswing of something not even he understands. I am too tired even to be embarrassed. I take the key offered by Tom, the son.

"Restaurant lock, but we can rustle up something," Tom says. "Bring some salt to put in the hot water for you foot." He fans his hand at the two old men and the bottle of rum. "Them all right."

So I take the key and follow his directions. Once in the room, I set the water to hot and leave it running so the bath may fill.

The bed is firm. *Up by Dorril.* I have never in my whole life known anyone who owned so much land it was named after them . . . I try to imagine him there at the bar. I shake my head. I do not want to think of him, do not care about him now. If and when tomorrow comes, I will take it from there. But one thing I tell myself: no matter what he says, what he does, how he behaves, there is no way I will apologize to my father.

TWELVE

Someone is beating down the door. That must be the son with the salt for my feet. I have forgotten the pipe is running. I must get up and turn it off before the tub overflows. But my body is heavy; I do not have the strength to raise myself. The knock continues.

"Yes! Come!" I yell.

Tom pushes the door and enters. "What happen, you want some lunch? You father say if you want some lunch."

"Lunch!"

"Is eleven o'clock, you know. You sleep through the night and the whole morning."

"Sir," I tell him slowly, "to tell you the truth, I cannot move."

He laughs. "But you father frisky, boy. Oh . . ." He catches himself and drops the bag he has been holding. "You van come. So I just bring up you bag for you."

"The van is here? The police came? Why didn't you call me?"

He laughs again. "You don' see you can' get up. No man, no police involved. The van parked downstairs."

I drop back onto the bed and close my eyes. I don't care about anything anymore.

It is about two o'clock when I finally make my way toward the bar/reception area. I am still weary and sore, but my stomach has become a dry cavernous place; it echoes when I yawn.

I discover that my ordeal has not damaged me beyond a few scratches and a large uncomfortable bruise where the seat of my pants tore away. My right palm is also stiff. But I will live. Now I am happy my father insisted on buying some shorts and slippers, though I still hate the sneakers.

Everybody is my friend. Tom the bartender/receptionist looks up at me and asks what I would like to drink. I tell him orange juice, and he seems disappointed. "Make a see if I find some."

"You have any food? I could eat a cow."

"The restaurant closed, but we can find something," he mumbles.

"You don't have anything at all to eat?"

"The restaurant not open, but we will rustle up something."

"Rustle up? How long will that take?"

"'Bout half an hour."

I figure that would be an hour or so in real time. "What about fruits? Can I have fruits?"

"You mean like some banana or so? Oh, melon, man. You want melon? This is melon country."

He asks where I would like to sit and I choose a table outside, off the edge of the pool where it seems to be most private. As I make my way to it, I see my van parked near the side of the building. I approach it but the door is locked, so I just peer inside. Everything seems to be intact. I do not understand its sudden appearance, but I expect that Father will have the answers for me when I see him. For now I just want to sit in a quiet place.

There seem to be few guests at the hotel. Few cars are in the driveway, and there is no one in the pool, though the water sparkles invitingly. I can see why the guest-relations here are so abrupt. This must be one of those places where couples come for just a few hours at a time or no more than a night. It is built for maximum privacy, tucked away from the beach inside a small nest of trees. No wonder the restaurant is always closed; no one comes here to eat food.

I have been sitting for but a few minutes when the old man, Green, appears with a tray. He brings a large glass of orange juice and a tumbler of water. He puts this down then soon returns with some sugar cane and a large melon.

He places the melon on the table and with an expert hand slices it from end to end. He then swivels it and cuts it into large chunks. He is not a hotel chef; he is a man trying to work with me. I am too hungry to worry about that. I am grateful. I take a piece of melon, flick the seeds away with my fingers, and bite into it. It must have been planted with sugar in the seed. I am through the chunk before I realize that he has not moved but stands staring adoringly at me.

"So you are Dorril big son." He speaks slowly as he begins to shave the piece of cane with the long sharp knife. "You are Dorril big son. I see you one time when you was young. Dorril bring you down here, you was maybe four or five years old. Could play marble no bitch though."

"Thanks," I tell him.

"For what?" He sits in front of me and crosses his legs as he slices the skin from the cane. "Ah, Mass Everton," he says. "You favor him no bitch, you know."

"Yes."

"Yes, but that is how it is. You didn't know? The first pickney always like the father, the second always like the mother, the third is him own person."

"Have you seen my father?"

"Him gone walk, you know, 'bout an hour now. Say him gone stretch him legs."

"He is serious about his walk."

He nods. He has a patient smile and his hair is curly and brown, his eyes are dark, and his skin is close to the red of the land, but old and baked on him. Every movement he makes is with the patience and casual humility you find in good country people.

"Your father tell me you dive off the cliff from Dorril to the river," he says with a twinkle of very light brown eyes. I can see why he is my father's friend. They must have roamed this countryside breaking women's hearts from the hill to the sea.

"Is that what he said?"

"Yes! You brave for a town man, though. I tell you, Mass Everton, the last person who try that was a man they called Dove from Morton Flats. And him dived when the river was full. Him never make it back. Some say him drowned, but I tell you the truth, Mass Everton, I think him broke him neck."

I put the third piece of melon skin aside and reach for the orange juice. I wonder what stories my father has been telling about me or why he feels they need embellishing. The juice is freshly squeezed and good. "I don't know if I knew what was happening on that hill, you hear. I was just trying to get away from those damn people."

"Yes." He passes sticks of cane across to me.

I test a piece for softness. Its juice is warm and sweet against my tongue. He seems happy that I like it.

"So your father tell me that you taking him on a tour around the country. You know, there is nothing like a big son who love him father. My son love me, but him lazy. You soon see some woman come call him there now. I not saying him not a good boy, but these days young people not interested in taking care of them parents anymore. You are a good son . . . traveling around with your father, making him see him old friends them . . . boy." He sighs. "You know where I want to go? Montego Bay. Go there one time but not recent. I hear is pure tourism going on down there now. Even have . . ." He leans and whispers to me, "I hear they even have place down there where only naked people go. You not goin' stop there?"

"No, I don't think so."

"Oh, you have to be naked, I see." He chuckles. "Bet that would raise the dead."

"I bet it would." Where do these old men come from filled with mischief and secrets in their smiles? "So you have known my father a long time?"

"Long! Long, long time now. Can't even count the days. Help a lot o' people down here, especially with the land business. He is a good man."

He finishes with the cane and places the naked slices on my plate. I thank him and he stands to go. "You must come down and spend some time with us one week. Everybody goin' wan' meet you."

I tell him I will. I also try to thank him for the hospitality, but he fans my words aside. "Thanks for what?" His smile is a version of my father's.

And so he leaves me.

* * *

The orange juice is finished. Half the melon has disappeared. My stomach has settled—at least for the time being. I chew on the sugar cane and can't help wondering what stories my father has spread about me. And in wondering, my mind inevitably goes back to yesterday and the incidents that have brought us here. As I replay them my stomach begins to gradually ache again, this time not with hunger but with anxiety. *How did I get here to this place, to this peace and quiet?* Not the journey of it, for that I remember well, but how did I get *here*?

Yesterday, we encountered a large field of marijuana, we were chased and shot at by criminals, I almost lost my life. But today I am sitting here quietly, peacefully, with my vehicle returned, my new clothes intact, and my father gone on a peaceful walk.

How did it happen? Where are the police? How come I was not called? Are we now safe, here in this place?

Father must be tuned to my thoughts, for he joins me out of nowhere. "So you finally wake, son."

He has caught me in reverie so there is a beat before I respond and then my voice seems to have a dreamlike quality to it. "Yes, Mr. Dorril."

He sits, pulls another chair to the side, and stretches his feet into it. "I see the boys take care of you. I see you get fruit plate."

"How was your walk? You're not afraid? Didn't you get enough exercise yesterday."

"This walk is different."

He is as composed as a school teacher, but there is wariness in his eyes. He is not sure what side I woke up on this afternoon.

"You know you grandmother come from round here."

That has caught me off guard. "Really? Granny?"

"Yes, not right here, but round there so, up farther from the river. Our family has a long tradition round here."

I met my grandmother a few times, and each memory is like a tamarind ball in my mouth. When the other children would visit her or she would visit their home, I was never a part of it. But he took me to see her a few times, including once when they were having a birthday party for her at his house and she asked for me. Every time I saw her she would ask him why he did not bring me to see her more. She was a feisty old woman, with a deep sophistication and bleakness and sadness about her that I could not understand. But she liked me. And I loved visiting her and having her spoil me with sweets. But I never knew her . . . knew them. I do not know much of her or her story. Except that she lived in Kingston in a little place she refused to leave. But as she grew older, she moved to live with my father in Willodene, where she finally died.

"So grandmother was from here, and you are from here?"

"No, I was born in Kingston, as you know, but that is another story."

I laugh sarcastically at this and gesture to him, my hand almost imitating a table tennis stroke. "Stories, don't be afraid of telling me stories, Daddy. We have time. And you have plenty stories to tell."

"Well," he says, "if is story you want—"

"Daddy! Daddy, let us cut to the chase, man. What

are we doing here like this? You want explain to me what going on here?"

"How you mean?"

"You want explain this? How we get our clothes? How we get back the van? Why was no police involved? Why are you so happy? What is happening here, old man?"

"Oh, that . . ." He laughs. "That, I bet you couldn't tell me what happen! You wouldn't believe what happen."

"Indulge me."

He leans back into his chair. "You know, you need to have a little more faith."

"Faith?"

"Yes, faith. First, you have to believe it is my land. First, you have to believe it is *your* land. Then the story will make sense. You believe it is your land? You believe it is my land?"

I make my eyes burn into him. I stare at him so he can feel the fire in them.

"You remember Willy?" he finally asks.

"Willy?"

"Yesss . . . Willy. I use to bring you round here when you were a boy, you use to play marble with him. It was Willy up there. He is in charge of the land now. He thought we were trespassing."

Sometimes it feels like my father thinks I am either very stupid, still a child, or am so awed by him that he can tell me any stupid thing and I will believe him. "Faith?" I nod at him. "Just like that! Faith, the evidence of things not seen, right? You take me up on a hill and tell me it is yours. Okay, let's say it's yours. And don't raise your eyebrows at me. I was shot at yesterday. I dropped off a cliff. I almost died. And you brush it off as: *It was Willy.*"

"He didn't know it was us."

"I don't care. You don't see what I see. He shot at us. I lost my things, I almost died."

"But your things come back."

I lift my hand to show him my Movado is still missing.

"Everton," he says to me, "why you working up yourself like this. It's just a misunderstanding, why you working up yourself like this?"

"Because you are insulting my intelligence, man. Just level with me, just for once. What is happening here?"

"But I'm trying to tell you and you not listening."

"That it's Willy! That it's nothing to worry about. Come on, Daddy."

"See."

"Is your ganja field, Daddy? Daddy, is it your marijuana up there?"

He sighs at me.

"But I have to ask. I have to ask because I cannot make sense out of this stupid conversation."

"Shut up and listen. Jesus Christ," he snaps. "What is wrong with you? I did not know he was there. His mother is in charge of the land. I have not seen him in how many years. His mother takes care of the land for me. It is laying there; twenty-five acres, nothing is on it. So he is doing little farming on it? Who is goin' to go up there to check? His mother is taking care of it for me, but she is too old now. He is her oldest son. What is hard to see in that?"

"But he is growing ganja up there."

"So what?"

"So what?!"

"Yes, so what?"

"Is ganja, Daddy. These men are criminals. We should be calling the police. They shot at us. They almost killed us."

"Use to have a little man up the road name Joe Blades," he says. "They called him that because he could swing a machete so smooth and easy. He owned a piece of land way over there near Junction. His children own it now. Blades used to do farm work in the United States . . . did several years of it. Used to have a funny story 'bout Joe. Every time Joe went to America to farm work and come back, his wife was either pregnant or had a new baby.

"Now you know how people are. Of course, the first story that spread was that those could not be Joe's children. *Joe getting jacket; Joe getting bun.* Did anybody check if the wife's pregnancy was in good time, meaning did anybody time Joe's departure with the arrival of his children? Of course not. Who interested in truth when a good story is better. *Joe getting bun, man,* they said. *Joe getting jacket.* So one day a good neighbor couldn't take it any longer, and decided to have a talk with Joe on the matter.

"So he said to Joe: *Joe, how you explain that every time for the last three years you go to farm work, when you come back you have a new baby? Is mail? You mail it?*

"Joe said, *Well, when I am at home, I take care of my business. When I gone, God take care of His.*

"So he said to Joe, *What you mean by that?*

"Joe repeat: *I say, when I am here, I take care of my business.*

When I am not here, God take care of His business . . . That is why all my children look like me.

"Neighbor says: *Yes, Joe, that is true, but remember it is you brother living beside your yard. Even* his *children look like you.*

"Joe scratched his head and opened his eyes in terror. *You think him notice?! How him find out?*"

Father slaps his feet and laughs loudly at his joke. "*You think him notice? How him find out?*" He wipes tears from his eyes.

"And I am supposed to laugh at that?" I try to restrain the smile dripping from my lips.

"You don't get the joke?"

"Joe is a fool."

"No. Joe is a happy man. Joe knows he cannot control what happens when he is not around, so when he is around he makes damn good use of the time and then . . . leave the rest to God. "*You think him notice. How him find out?* That Joe was something else . . . boy, something else.""

"And the moral of the story is that I should . . . what?"

"I don't know, Everton, but why kill yourself over something that you goin' leave unattended for another long time? May as well you just enjoy the moment, make use of the time . . . and have a whole heap o' faith."

"Really? Now?"

He reaches for my water glass, empties it, and refills it from the tumbler. "Tell you what." He smiles as he takes a drink. "You deal with it."

"Pardon me?"

"It is your land, you deal with it. You call the police and you tell Willy to take his ganja off the hill."

"My land? Now it is my land?"

"I told you that before they started shooting. So don't be afraid. It is your land, you tell him. You call the police."

"You want me deal with it, Daddy?"

"Yes."

"You want me take care of it? Because I don't want that to ruin your relationships around here. I will do the right thing. I will call the police, and if I catch that Willy, I'll chase him off that hillside, let him find out what it feels like to drop seventy feet."

Father grins smugly at me. "And you don't have to wait too long. See him coming through the gate there."

THIRTEEN

He is the color of the dry grass when the sun sets on it, and his eyes are the gray of a sleepy cat. I do have an inch on him, but his charm is easy, his smile quick and guarded, and his nature and mannerisms magnanimous. He wears jeans, red farming boots, and a Perry Ellis shirt rolled to the elbow. I could beat him in a fight, but I wouldn't introduce my girlfriend to him.

"Dads." He hugs my father and shakes his hand. "Dads, Father Dorril." He turns to me and his eyes light up "Everton, long, long, long time. You still play marble? Boy, you could play marble, no bitch."

"So I hear," is all I can say.

"So, everything all right?" He nods at me. "Everything okay, you get back you stuff and things?"

"Yes. Thanks." I can't believe I just thanked him.

"Boy," he speaks as he sits, "what a thing happen yesterday, eeh, man? What a thing. Father Dorril, Everton, when you coming you must make us know, man."

"But your mother knows," my father says to him. "She knows I am coming."

"She knows?!"

I am asking the same thing myself, but I am past being surprised by surprises. My father has developed quite a knack for them.

"Well, you know Mamma." Willy hardly skips a beat. "She's so secretive, especially these days. You know she gone to Montego Bay? Didn't even tell me where she gone."

If my father were white, his face would have turned rose pink—it burns with the guilt of something.

"Somebody else tell me that she coming back tomorrow," Willy continues. "And now I hear I must tell you she not coming till tomorrow. So, that is how secretive she is."

"When you say she coming?" Father is trying too hard to be casual.

"Tomorrow evening."

"What exactly did the message say?"

"Tell Mr. Dorril that they won't come till tomorrow evening."

"Them or she?"

"Them or she, I don't even remember. It matter though?"

"And Everton was planning to leave this evening." He glances at me, though there is relief in his eyes. The hypocrite has even managed to look sad. But I know him better, and I will take him up on the issue of our departure soon. But now I must deal with this man in front of me.

"Well, she says to tell you that she will see you tomorrow," he is telling my father. "But everything is everything and everything all right."

Everything is everything and everything all right. Just like that. A man almost kills you, has an acre of weed on your land, then sits with you at a table over fruits and tells you everything is everything and everything is all right. This is a different world, a different class of people, and my father fits in so easily it scares me.

"So what happen, Everton?" He turns to me. "You remember them days we use to play marble? You could play marble, boy. You remember?"

"I don't remember." My voice is not quite ice, but it is getting there.

He looks from me to my father and even though Daddy's face is not as hard as mine, there is disapproval there, and I know he is with me.

Willy feels the need for explanation and offers a sober look. "Father Dorril, I must tell you." He has lost the looseness and his language becomes formal, his English perfect. He is very, very good. "It is unfortunate, you know. A real unfortunate thing happened here yesterday. I am hoping we can deal with it and put it behind us. I mean, you put me in charge to take care of the place and this is what you come and find. But I am sorry. And I will deal with it. You just tell me how you want me to deal with it."

"Your mother know what you doing up there?" Father asks him.

His eyes never waver. "You want to see me dead? Our business doesn't have to include Mamma."

"Our business!" I am amazed. "*Our* business. I don't own a ganja farm!"

"Father Dorril, what you want me to do? Just tell me."

"It is not my land." Father nods at me, "It is Everton's land now."

Willy turns to me and smiles without skipping a beat. "Everton, so you are the new governor man. I am working for you now. Mother passed on the caretaking to me, and Daddy D. pass on the land to you. It is like a generation thing."

I doubt that Willy will ever work for anyone, least of all me.

"Let me tell you the truth." I almost believe the sincerity in his eyes. "Sometimes it is better to plant a little weed than to be lazy. It gives the boys around here something to do. Better that than go Kingston go carry a gun. At least down here a man can buy a half an acre from it and build a little house."

"Well, grow carrots, grow thyme like everybody else," I tell him.

"Well, we do that too, you know, but the drought and so. So what you want me to do?"

"Burn it. Burn everything and turn over the gunmen to the police."

He laughs lightly. "Everton, you can't burn anything on the hillside this time o' year, man. Bush fire would burn down half the countryside. Plus, the men just got carried away. They weren't trying to shoot you—they just got carried away."

"We could have died. I almost broke my neck! My father is almost seventy years old."

"But we didn't know you was going jump, man. Nobody never dive off that hill yet."

"I never dived," I almost scream.

"All right, Everton, I am sorry. Tell you what I will do. I will get rid of it. You see like how you come now. You see like how I know now that you against the weed thing. I would never plant another seed up there. Now that I know, now that we talk face to face, it is new thing now."

As he speaks, it gradually dawns on me that my father is right. What am I doing? Willy probably knows

every policeman from here to Black River. He knows
that I will be leaving tomorrow and he knows I may not
be back here for years to come. Who am I fooling, why
would he cut down his weed for me? Who knows how
many other fields he may have around, probably planting each new crop in a different place. And I am sitting
here thinking that I can change that, that I can have the
better of this man in a situation in which he is the mas-
ter. I am beginning to lose the energy for the encounter.
The conversation is starting to feel like a waste of time.

So we sit here in the warm afternoon in this place
called Memories By the Sea and he talks of how sorry he
is and how the next time we come we don't even have to
call. We can walk on any land up there and whoever is
there will have to answer to us. And I from time to time
butt in, with my anger gradually replaced by boredom.
And the conversation lightens and moves and he begins
to laugh and tell stories and jokes he has heard from his
mother about my father. And every now and then I must
fend off a comment on how well I played marbles. And
Father sits there, all pleased, looking at us as if he is
looking at two sons together having a mature conversation for the first time. And I wouldn't be surprised if one
of the secrets down here is that Willy is his son too.

So the afternoon wears on and the talk continues till
the little old man appears and interrupts us to say that
the fish has not come and the food will be another half
an hour—and to ask if I would like more fruits.

This gives Willy an immediate excuse to be gra-
cious. He looks with surprise at me and asks how come
I haven't eaten lunch yet. So I tell him I woke late. He
smiles and tells me he understands. "So that is all you

eat for lunch?" He motions to the half-eaten fruits on the table.

"I was waiting for the chef to rustle up something."

"Chef!" He laughs and beckons to the old man. "See what the man them calling you. *Chef*. You need to change you ways, old man."

"Is Tom him talking."

"Tom can cook? Is my brother this, you know. This is Mr. Dorril. This is my brother. You can't *rustle up* food for my brother. What you rustling up? What you cooking?"

"Well, I was thinking 'bout some fried fish and thing, but we send gone get some fish."

"Tell you what, don't worry too much about that. Don't bother with that. Let me just take them to Little Ochi and go eat some fish. Don't worry 'bout it, I will take care of it."

"All right." The old man smiles. "All right, Willy. No problem."

"And you can organize to send the stuff down to the cottage. I will send Razor or Breds for them."

"What is that about?" I ask as the old man walks away.

"You can't eat this food, man. Come we go Little Ochi. When last you go Little Ochi, Mr. Dorril?"

"Couldn't tell," Father says with a smile.

"And what is this about a cottage and moving our things?"

"Well, we have a cottage on the beach. Why you want to stay here when you have a cottage?"

"My cottage?"

"Not so. It is my cottage, but my cottage is your cottage. See the key here, you don't have to give it back.

When you ready, just come, just give me call and come. It is your cottage."

"But don't we need to shower . . . change our clothes?"

"For what? You in the country. This is the south coast. You are a tourist. You ever see tourist bathe?" Then he laughs as I draw up to my full height. "Jesus, man, Eva, I'm joking, just joking, man. By the way . . ." He reaches into his breast pocket. "Is your Movado this?"

Tears almost come as I reach for my watch.

So I am sitting here in a boat with a thatched roof on stilts in the middle of a large yard by the sea. Three women are standing in front of us with six platters of fish and lobster.

"What you want?" Willy asks. "What kind o' fish: parrot or grunt or butter fish or snapper? You want lobster?"

I cannot make up my mind.

"Just mix up and do little of everything." He smiles at the waitress. "Fry some and steam some with some bammy—both steamed and fried bammy and so." He sends her away. "First you come down here, Everton?"

"Yes."

"Well, they say that if you miss you wife one day, this is where she is with her lover."

"Well, I am from Kingston."

"Exactly. This is where all the bosses from Kingston bring their secretaries—three hour out of Kingston and back by nightfall. Eat fish, good conversation, some ocean breeze . . ."

"And a few hours at Memories By the Sea," I add.

"I didn't say that. You hear me say that, Daddy Dorril?"

"You never say that," my father replies.

"Onoo come a good day," Willy says. "A good day."

"How so?"

"Tonight is the Great Bay Carnival. We could go on down there. It runs from ten in the morning all through the night. The day part is mainly for the children, it is not much. It is the night that goin' be nice. Music, dance, beauty contest, deejay contest, all kind o' things. I help put it on every year with some other farmers round the place. You guys should come. As a matter of fact . . ." he checks his watch, "don't even have to go to the cottage. We can just leave here and go down there."

"I would need to rest first," I tell him.

"I am not tired," my father asserts.

"Boy, Daddy Dorril, you frisky, ehh, man?"

Frisky indeed!

I wonder how long my father intends to stay down here. I had planned on returning to Kingston tonight. Now I'll be here at least until tomorrow. A yawn forces itself from me, a sign of both hunger and fatigue. As soon as I eat, I intend to sleep wherever I can find a place to put my head.

FOURTEEN

Someone is calling my name and banging on the door. I pull the large pillow over my head to shut it out. But the shouting continues and with the banging it feels like a strange ugly symphony echoing down a dark valley to my ear. Then the sounds pause as if the caller is catching his breath and I feel that I must rise quickly to prevent them from starting again and increasing the throbbing in my head. I stumble through the unfamiliar room, drag my hand across the wall till I find a switch. It only lights the bathroom but it is enough to make my way to the living room where a dim light is on. As I get to the door the banging starts again.

"What is it?" I shout. "Who is it?"

"Mass Everton, you father call you. Say you must make haste and come."

"My father?" *What time is it? Does he ever sleep?* "Tell him I soon come," I call back. I have no intention of leaving this cabin tonight. "What time is it?"

"'Bout eight o'clock. Him say the beauty contest soon start and that you must come."

"Beauty contest? What beauty contest that?"

"The beauty contest up at the carnival. You have to come before it start. Him say the judges must be in place before it start."

"Judge? What judge? What does that have to do with me?"

"You are one of the judges."

I do not believe what I am hearing. But it does not matter. There is no way I am leaving this cabin. I refuse to be manipulated.

"Yes, all right, tell him I soon come!" I yell, and head straight back into the large soft bed.

This seems to be one of those places that you do not know how hot it is until you wake up and try to go back to sleep again. I toss around for ten minutes and cannot sleep.

I am forced from the bed. By the light of the bathroom, I am able to find other switches that bring soft lights on from two small lamps, one at the bedside and another on a small table over by a large love seat.

I am actually noticing the room for the first time. It is cozy, with large drapes covering one wall and green patterns of birds and trees and all kinds and shapes. The bed is on a large straw mat that protrudes on all sides. I sit on the edge of it wondering what time it really is. My watch is on a large dresser that covers the wall in front of me; it lies carelessly near an ashtray made of seashells and a neatly folded towel.

It is eight thirty. I clean the watch against my pants and reach for the cell phone that is also lying there. I am halfway from the room before I realize that my wallet is missing. It is not in the shorts I'm wearing—they have no pockets. *When was the last time I saw my wallet?* Was it there this morning when I woke sick and tired from the evening before? I must have had it before we went onto the hill, but I do not recall it after the fall, after the river.

I suddenly feel anxious.

My bag is at the side of the love seat. I begin to dig for the old pants I was wearing—the ones that lost their seat on the slide down the hillside. I find them. The backside is missing, but the pockets seem intact. I empty the contents on the floor and it is the last thing that falls out. The leather is stiff in my hand. All the cards are there, the money is there, some bills still soft and moist. I pull them gingerly from the wallet, but that is not what I am looking for. Somehow I am trembling as I slowly unzip the inner pocket. My movements are as delicate as a surgeon's. I open the pocket wide even before I attempt to reach inside for the old folded paper there.

My list is soft and moist. I lay it gently on the dresser and look at it for a while. Then I try to unfold it, but the old creases seem to have collapsed, and there is little to hinge the folds as I peel them away. The old ink has been so smudged that the words I scratched so many years ago have soaked into the facing page. Nothing is clear as I peel the layers back, only parts of words, edges of phrases, smudges of the numbers that listed my feelings. I am peeling, I am trembling, and my heart is sinking. Everything is unraveling softly in my hands and nothing is whole, nothing is legible, except the very center of it. I try to read, but . . . try to make sense of it, try to recall; I see a *Why do you*. I see the makings of I, or is it S? But there is no straight line. The old paper, having journeyed for nearly twenty-five years, from a lonely room, through college, through university, through a million hesitations and stops and starts—it is now mush in my hands . . . and the only thing really legible is a strange ragged line at the edge of the central fold. *You . . . You . . .* I peel it back gently. There is a *love you* beside the line. And on the other side the beginning of the sentence: *How do you* . . . My list has died.

I clutch the last of it, the half-complete scrap with the question interrupted by the smudges and diluted ink. I stumble from the room and find a beer in the over-stocked fridge and make my way through sliding doors to the veranda.

I do not know how I feel. I really am not sure. On one hand, there is a panic in me, a sense that time has disappeared; a feeling that everything has gone and that I have wasted my opportunities, that I am running out of time and if I do not find the guts to corner my father then these questions will disappear from me, unanswered forever. Relief, too, is what I may be feeling, like a load has been lifted from my heart. I find a chair and sit and look out into the night with the scrap of paper in my hand and the beer untouched on the ground beside me.

Twenty-five years. Now this.

How do you . . . love you.

This could be either of two questions, perhaps a part of a third. *How do you . . . love you.* There is so much that could be placed in the middle to make sense of the two ends. And that is the thing: Why does it feel so when I know all the questions by heart. Why this sense of loss, this numbness, this sadness, this quietness, when I know all those questions as if I had written them yesterday, though I had modified and changed them over the years. Why do I feel so, why does this question feel so fractured when even as I look at it I know exactly where it fell on the list and exactly what it said and exactly what I had felt when I wrote it twenty-five years ago?

And why is this the part that is left? Why is this the one that remains on the scrap of paper? *How do you . . . love you.*

Why this one, this night?

My mother used to tell me I needed to learn to let things go.

"If you don't, you won't have many friends," she had said after I'd beaten my friend to a pulp under the ficus tree at primary school. "Sometimes you have to let things go."

Maybe it is time to let these memories go, these unanswered questions. This dead list.

How do you . . . love you.

Let it go.

Audrey accuses me of that too, in many ways—of holding on to things too long. She does not tell me all the time, but I see it in her eyes when we quarrel, when she tries to reach me, stares at me too intensely straight out of a passionate moment and sometimes even in the heart of those most intimate times. I know she feels that if I would let go of our past we would be further along in our relationship by now.

I wonder what she is doing now. Where she is, what is on her mind? She must have called me a dozen times by now. There were three missed calls from her on the phone by the time we were eating breakfast on the hillside in Mandeville. But I did not feel I could call her back. And now down here there is no signal on the phone, so I cannot call her if I wanted, and she will not get through no matter how she tries.

She is the only woman I have ever thought of marrying.

She would enjoy a night like this. Quite on the edge of nowhere with the light of the moon skipping across the waters and the old town blinking lights along the bay as if the stars have dropped to ground level. She has a body for the beach and the love for it too. Father thinks she is a bit too slim, but he likes her mind. And she liked his stories too. The few times we went out together, he would have her in stitches by the time we got back home.

The only woman I have ever thought of marrying.

I met her modeling bikinis at a client-appreciation Christmas party—a model with dreams of managing a large hotel and eventually owning one. She already had her first degree then and was looking for a place to study hospitality management. It took her two years to secure a scholarship in England and during that time our relationship blossomed.

When her scholarship was finalized, we sat across from each other at that little restaurant at Devon House, and she told me that if I asked her to, she would not go and we could start our family. I told her no, that she should go, study, see some of the world. When she returned there would be time enough.

I didn't see her again for two years though we wrote each other and spoke regularly on the phone. And then last summer she returned home.

I can still sense her now, that night on the beach at Sandals, Ocho Rios, as her moans of passion turned in an instant to quiet sobs and hot tears burning against my skin—because I paused, in the middle of lovemaking, to ask where she had learned to move like that.

No man wants to hear that his woman has given herself to someone else. No matter how long she has been away, no matter how cold and lonely the English winters she had been forced to experience by herself—no man wants to know that.

I knew it might have been partly my fault—it was the winter I should have visited, but had postponed the trip because of work. She had been lonely, she said, loneliness made worse by the disappointment of me not coming . . . so she had succumbed to advances she had resisted for over a year. But still it was hard for me to accept that someone had had such access to that which I held dearest and closest to my heart.

Now she is back. Now she tells me I only love myself.

And I am not sure what to do or how to see her or how to be with her all the time; though I feel we have come to some understanding, I also sense that deep inside she has been made to feel that somehow she is now unworthy of me.

You don't love me. You only love yourself.

How do you . . . love you.

Let it go. Deal with it or let it go.

That is the thing. Not just to let it go.

That is what I am being told tonight. That is what my list is telling me. It is time to deal with it, whatever it is, and move on.

How do you . . . love you.

But not today. Not tonight. When we get to Kingston tomorrow, I will sit him down and I will let him know. Then I will sit with my woman and I will do what must be done.

But not tonight.

Tonight I will get up. I will shake these feelings that

have me here. I will walk across that beach and see what the noise and the carnival is all about.

How do you . . . love you

Jesus.

FIFTEEN

Twenty minutes later I am showered, dressed, and making my way up the beach toward the noise of the carnival. It is like one big dance. The music is blaring from all around, there is a bonfire near one side close to the water. The smell of weed is mixed with that of food, perfumes, and party. Stalls dot the large beach. Food of every kind and gambling tables—a big party in full swing. People mill around, play games, lie on the beach, and dance, wrapped around each other.

In one corner there is a makeshift stage. I walk over there to find my father and Willy sitting at a long table. Daddy has his reading glasses at the tip of his nose and is looking quite official with a sheaf of paper in front of him. Willy is leaning across the desk and gesturing to some other people as they work feverishly to organize about a dozen scantily clad young women into a corner where a curtain creates a backstage area. I shake my head in wonder. I just cannot keep up with him. A day in St. Elizabeth and he has copped the job of the party.

His pace will grind me into the dust. He is like a hound dog.

I swear he has a way of smelling me because he turns the instant I arrive, his face lights up, and he beckons me over, pointing at a seat beside him.

I pat him on his back. "You don't sleep, old man?"

He smiles broadly, winks at me, and jabs Willy. "Willy, see the man just come. Take your seat, judge." He slaps at me.

"What, man on spot?" Willy turns to me. "You ready to do some judging?" He waves his magnanimous hands toward the girls getting ready to parade their skin.

"I don't know, I'm not sure. This is old man work." I nod at the drug cultivator. "You and Daddy can manage, man." I am definitely not feeling the vibes for judging this one.

"No, we need three judges," Father insists.

"I soon come," I tell them as I gaze across the yard. "I'm going to get a drink; hold the fort for me till I come."

A woman has caught my eye. She is just beyond those gathering for the beauty contest and leaning easily against a stall of some sort. I catch her stare across the space, double-check to be sure I have not read her wrong, and now make my way over. I am not in the mood, but one look at the makeshift stage and the scrawny contenders with Father and Willy, licking their lips, is enough to make me want to return to the cottage. I may as well talk to someone who stands so beautifully against the stall in the night.

I am a foot from her before I realize she is Angela from Ballards Valley. Too close to change course or turn away, I halt in front of her and say, "Hi."

Her hello is soft against the night, and there is a kind of relief in her voice as if she too is bored and hoping to see a familiar face.

Something has changed about her. The troubled nervous look is not there now. There is a womanliness and an experience and a calm. There is a mystery too and an intimidating sensuality.

"What are you doing here?" I ask.

She smiles. "Is carnival. I should be asking what *you* are doing here."

"I see."

"So?"

"Pardon me?"

"What are *you* doing here?"

That is what I mean. She was not so bold yesterday. No smile played on her lips, no mischievous inquiry was in her eyes.

"It's carnival," I tell her.

"I thought you and your father were back in Kingston by now."

"Well, we've had a setback. And as you see, Father has to judge a beauty contest."

"So I hear."

"What have you heard?"

"Is true that you dive off Dorril Hill into the river? You know is only one person ever do that and him never live?"

I am not sure if she is laughing at me or if she is amused by my open mouth and startled eyes. "Where you hear that?"

She whips the tail of her braids from her shoulder so they run neatly down the small of her back. "Everybody talking 'bout it."

"Everybody? What they saying?"

"They too out of order, though," she says seriously. "That is what they do. They go round the place and plant ganja on people land. They just move from land to land all over the place and plant weed. Somebody tell me that last week police locked up about three o' them from my district. They too out of order."

Now I feel stupid for having thought Willy might have known all the policemen in the area. Maybe I could have locked up the vagabond, permission or not. The memories are coming back, and I feel cheated that I had not insisted on calling the police. Instead I am on the beach at carnival, living in his cabin, and here now to judge a beauty contest with him and my father. All of a sudden I feel small and stupid.

"How you get so serious?"

"Nothing," I tell her. "Would you like to get something to drink?"

She looks over my shoulder toward the makeshift stage. I follow her eyes to see that the beauty contest is about to start. "Oh, I see, you want to watch the beauty contest."

"No sir!" she exclaims. "You not one of the judges? It looks like they ready for you now."

And it is true; they are motioning in my direction. I see my father whisper to a man and send him toward me. But the anger at feeling like a fool has swollen in me, and there is no way I will be made a further one by sitting on the stage with Willy, as if nothing has happened.

So I tell her I do not feel like judging a beauty contest tonight.

She gives me a searching look. "You sure? I don't want to get into any problem with your father."

"No, they will find someone else. Come, come before that man gets over here."

She straightens from the counter, and we walk away from the messenger hustling through the crowd.

The night is nice and warm. Here and there the speakers tremble with the music. With every step we take across the beach, men glance at her. She notices but does not seem to care. I am trying to work her out even as I order a beer from the man inside the bamboo stall. "Ting," she greets my inquiry. The man digs for a moment into the drum of ice and water and bottles of every kind. He produces our drinks.

She takes the Ting from me and murmurs how bad it is that this is a big, big carnival and one can't even get a mixed drink. I figure she is trying to impress me, so I let it slide and motion across the compound to the stage where some other man is taking a seat as the third judge beside my father.

I wonder what she is all about. I wonder what troubles her now, what troubled her then. But I am finding it hard to bridge the gap because she does not give me much to hold. Sometimes I see women like her, in bars and in clubs and other places, and I do not know what to say to them, for they speak another language, as if they come from another world. She is not my type, the kind for good conversation. Not my kind of body either, too aggressive in the hips, too much swirl, too much force to her walk, too saucy, too sexy.

"What you looking on?" She raises her eyebrows as if she has caught me at something. "Come, we walk little, the place boring." She scowls into the night. "Tired o' them old boys, them looking on me like they never see woman yet."

"But you look good."

"But you don' see how some o' them look hungry."
She laughs breezily.

We are just beyond the bonfire now and most of the
crowd is behind us. Here the groups are smaller, the
smell of weed stronger, and the water is just ahead of us
down the gentle sloping black sand.

"You like the beach?" I ask her.

She shrugs and looks up haughtily at me. It seems
the mood is getting to her, for there are lovers here too,
couples strewn everywhere. A moment is being thrust
upon me that I did not anticipate.

"What kinda work you do?" she asks.

"Why?"

She shrugs. "What kinda work? You look like them
manager."

"I am. I'm into marketing."

"Marketing, and you look so serious?" It is not the
answer I am expecting, but it is a mistake that people
usually make, confusing marketing with public relations.

"Well, marketing is a serious thing, but why you say
I'm serious?" I try to lighten my voice.

"You know, I never see you laugh yet. You just serious. You come like them whiskey man."

"Whiskey man?"

"Yes, you can tell a man by what kinda drink him
drink. You know, a whiskey man—mature and kinda
boring, English always proper, whiskey man who like
long conversation. *On the rocks or neat?* You know, a whiskey man." She smothers the smile playing on her lips by
placing the tip of the bottle there.

"Oh, so I am an old man."

"Not old, just a whiskey man."

"What kind of work you do?" I make to redirect the discomfort.

"Me? Guess."

"I must guess?"

"Yes, what you think?"

"A bartender?" She could be a poker player the way the smugness covers her face, as if she has lured me into a trap and I have walked right into it.

"Why, because I call you a whiskey man?"

"No, I wasn't trying to insult you or anything, I was just saying, I mean . . ."

There is a moment of silence. She finishes the drink and drops the bottle right there on the ground. I watch our footsteps as the sand closes over them. It could be a picture for an ad of one of those hotels. A beer bottle, lying on the beach with two sets of footprints moving away from it . . . with sexy lettering that says: FOOT-PRINTS. I wonder if there is a hotel called Footprints on the coast. Now that is an idea to sell.

"I study it in school, yes."

"What?"

"Bartending, I study it in school, yes."

I smile to myself. "Where?"

"At the HEART School, it was part of my course. I was very good. I mix any drink—it's like I did have a way with mixing drinks . . ." Her voice trails off, and the sadness is creeping in. And it tells me that I must now be careful in my tone. But I cannot find an appropriate thing to say just now. So we walk silently along the beach for a while. My beer too is finished. I hold the bottle for a few minutes hoping to find a bin, and then I shrug and drop it in a footprint as I make it.

"Your father really love you though," she says, as if we had been having a conversation all along and she is responding to something I just said.

I am tempted to tell her that what passes between my father and me is not her business. But I guess my mood is changing a bit, and I do not want to be accused of being a *whiskey man* again.

"My father never love me. Him say me feisty. But I not feisty. I never liked how him treated my mother. So I tell him. Some man just think a woman is something to use."

Usually, walking down a beach on a night like this with a woman, my hand would already be around her waist, and I would be steering the conversation in a particular direction. But this woman does not provide a manner in which to shift the focus of the discussion. It is very difficult to tell what she is thinking at any one moment, or to gauge her emotions. This is not the type of woman I am accustomed to.

Suddenly we are alone.

There is no sound from the party we just left. No one is walking on either side of us. I know the cottage is about fifteen minutes in the direction we are heading, but here there is no one but us, and nothing but the water breaking on some distant reef to spend itself foaming on the black sand beach.

"We are alone." I should not have said it, I know. But with this woman it is hard to know what to say or how to say it.

"You want sit down little?"

"If you want," I tell her.

"All right." She waits and waves me down as if to indicate that there is some arrangement to the sitting. So I just drop right there in the middle of the beach.

She pushes my knee. "Fix yourself."

So I let it fall and give her space so she may sit between my legs and rest her head upon my stomach. She is soft against me, but I am not sure if I should hold her, or how to if I do. Should I caress her hair, or play my hand against her skin? Should I press my palm against her hard flat stomach and sweep it up the plane of her torso to her breasts or stroke down to the curve of her and play with the elasticity of her stretch jeans? Instead, I press my elbow into the sand to steady myself and place my other hand upon my own knee.

"You know you don't set good," she says. "You lean back too much, you elbow soon start hurt you." She eases up. "Sit forward little."

I reposition and sit so that my legs are spread but not fully down and my back isn't quite erect. This is more comfortable.

"All right, come," I tell her. As she makes to sit, she holds my hand to steady herself. Now she is deep into me, I would call it a hug or something like that, and I find that she has not let go of my left hand and my right has found a place across her waist. Her skin is like the silk of the apple blossom. I am quickly aroused with the ache of my teenage days. It bores into her back.

There are several reasons why I should ease away from this moment. Reasons about her and reasons of earlier about my woman, about love, about decisions I must make and things I must do. I should act, grab hold of this erection forcing against her, pull away from the firm sensuous back, untangle myself. But I feel lost now, at sea by the turmoil she is causing, unable to handle all the emotions inside of me.

I lean against her and she receives me. I let my lips roam the back of her neck. As she tilts her neck toward the kiss, I know her eyes are closed, and I feel her head move in a sensuous arc as she responds. I press my lips to her ear and I whisper, "I want to make love to you."

"Make love?" she whispers back huskily. "Make love . . . I don't make love. I fuck."

My erection wilts. I do not know now what to do. But she doesn't move except to rub her head back and forth against mine and pat my knee as if to comfort me.

SIXTEEN

Father reaches down into the soil where the grass is dry. He drags a handful and rubs it between his fingers so I may see it turn to dust in his hands.

"Ah, the land, this land, this is the be-all and end-all of everything. It is this land that started it, this land that finished it, this land. You see this, this is the challenge. This! To make the crop grow on this—that is the challenge, the same way T.P. Lecky made a cow to survive our climate and be totally Jamaican. I wanted to make a way to grow crop on this land."

"And how is that?"

"This," he says. "This grass is the most important thing. You put the grass to cover the crop, to trap and hold the moisture. As the crop grows, the same grass deteriorates and becomes fertilizer . . . and you cover the root with more. Till rain comes . . . if it does, but even if it does not . . . the grass is hope."

It is a hot afternoon. Hot and dry. And the shadows of the thin leaves of the mango tree do not extend far beyond its root. But they shift in a hesitant breeze to play on my father as he sits and speaks. There is a dreamlike quality to his speech now, and there is lowness to it as if he is going back to days long before me when he was but a youth whose head was filled with dreams . . . and his path a sad one.

There is love in his voice; there are sixty-seven years of dreams in there. And emerging is a father I have never seen.

"But why this land?"

"Because it is mine."

"But you could have bought land anywhere in the country."

"Because it is mine, because it is yours. This is our land—given from generations, through manumission, from slavery. Your great-great-grandmother was the first woman to own land of this size here. This land cost her her life and many other things. This land has struggle, this land has history."

"Yes? This land?"

"This land. You see all of that side? The river use to run through it from where you are right up here. But when your great-great-grandmother got the land they diverted the river to dry her out. Poor woman never knew anything. But now we know. Now I know how to fix it."

"I don't understand. Where is all of this coming from, old man?"

"All right, you see this tree I am sitting under right now? One of your ancestors was hanged right here in this tree. Use to have a man called Vassel—all this land from the mountain here right back to the sea was called Vassel Pen. Cruel old man, that Vassel, came from England during slavery to work as overseer on a large plantation in Savanna-la-Mar. Was a poor white man who never know much about farming, buy the land because he felt he could make Alligator Pond into a thriving port, and plus of course in those days everybody wanted to own land and slaves and get *Esquire* on their name. The river ran right there where you standing and all this hillside was green with peppers and small crops and even rice used to be planted up here.

"Wasn't a wealthy man but him had about twenty slaves or so, cattle too. It is all there in the archives in Spanish Town in his will, what and what he left to who and who. Never brought a woman with him come down here from England. Loved black women gone to bed. So he was one of those who never married, had about ten or so woman slaves and treated them just like his own personal harem. And the head of that harem was your great-great-grandmother, Carla. Lived like man and wife with her for years, and when he died he willed it to her right here. Maybe out of conscience or what. Or maybe this was the piece she asked for—we will never know. But he willed to her the same piece of land where him hanged her husband after him beat him for two days in the sun and made half a dozen slaves defecate in his mouth. Right here, killed your great-great-grandfather, right here, hanged him like dead meat on this very tree, then willed it to your great-great-grandmother, first woman slave in these parts ever to own any kind of land.

"And one year later, they chopped away the river from one mile up the road so that the new path was half a mile beneath her land. *Dry her out*, they said, *dry her out*.

"And I always told myself that this place, this land, was a place that could grow things. Even without the river. Now we know how."

"How long since you come to this land?" I ask him gently.

"Ten years," he says longingly. "Maybe ten years, and before that maybe another ten years more."

"So long?"

He does not answer but stands and walks away from me. He looks out as if trying hard to find something in the distance. His eyes linger for a while in the direction of the ganja field that Willy had so expertly skirted as he brought us back here. And it is an odd place, a sort of craggy lump of limestone rocks surrounded by clusters of mango and lignum vitae trees. It would be an oasis if there were water, and now that he has mentioned that the river ran here once, I can understand that it may have been a waterfall of sorts. And where we sit in the shadow of the small hill is almost a lap of the old fall, and the trees are green here though the grass at our feet is dried to dust. It is a good place to be, to sit, if you like that kind of thing.

I ease down on the smooth side of a jagged hunk of limestone and watch him as he stands a yard or so away from me. "If you love it, why you took so long to come back? Why you never did anything about it?"

"It is a long story," he tells me. "Sometimes things get in the way. Sometimes you wait and time passes like so. And you realize you sitting down in the same place. But there was a time I use to come here every week. Every weekend I would be down here. And the land hasn't changed much, just the places round it. You see how many houses round the place—schools, small villages? When we use to come here, it wasn't like that, we use to walk through the same trail and come up here and have picnics, same place there where you are sitting down."

"We?"

"Yes, me and Hope. We use to come up here."

"Hope, that is the woman you have come to see after all these years?"

He nods, then sits across from me at the root of the tree. We are facing each other, man to man.

"Left Kingston, come down here, walked through bush to come up here. Why?" I ask.

He looks at me now with an air of superiority. "It's because you never love a woman yet. You need to open yourself to more adventures, more excitement."

"Me?"

"You climbed the mountain last night?"

"What, what mountain?"

He laughs. "My big son, I bet you never climb it."

"Climb what mountain! Are you asking me what I think you are asking me, old man? You think I would tell you? That is not your business."

"That is a serious girl. That is one experience I bet you would never forget. You would never want that model again."

My laugh is a light one. "Well, maybe I am not as sharp as you. But let me ask you something, Father. Let me ask you something now: do you plan to climb the mountain tonight?"

"Well . . ." He picks a blade of grass that has survived the sun. "Nobody say you have to be as good as me."

"You not answering the question."

He is still silent.

"How much women you use to have, Daddy, in those days when you traveled the country as, what you call it, field officer for the Ministry of Agriculture? How many women you use to have in those days? Women in every parish or something like that?"

"It wasn't field officer, I was an extension officer. And it wasn't how many woman you have, the thing is to get the woman you want. There is a difference."

"Really."

"Well, you see, I grew handsome. When I was your age, I was too good looking for my own good. Women never told me no. If I asked a woman 'the question' and she said no, it was perhaps because she never heard me properly. That is how I moved in those days." We have never talked like this before and now he is telling me things that I would blush to tell my son—if I ever have one. He pats my shoulder. "Now, if you weren't so proud, I would give you a few tips. But you are going make a whole heap of mistakes."

"Don't you see the kind of women I talk to?"

"Cho." He turns from me and looks down the land toward the river and his features darken.

"You loved her, don't it? You really loved Hope."

"Boy," he says, "love is not the only word." His face is softening now. And he is not looking at me. He is speaking almost to himself. "You see, when you love a woman, it is as if she is not made of flesh and blood. She doesn't have skin—silk, velvet, food, but not skin. Everything different: as if she is not human . . . not flesh. Even her sweat is sweet when you smell it and there is no scent to her. And her voice . . . don't even talk 'bout that . . . especially when she whisper to you. When you love a woman, you would move hell or high water to get to her . . . be with her. And you never ask yourself the question, you know, never wonder why, in the moment, you making a fool of yourself, risking your life, risking everything that brought you to that moment. Like a devil is in you and you must get to her, be with her or do what she wants . . . when you love a woman.

"And you know the worst thing about it? You don't know when it goin' happen; whether it is the first time you see her or the second time, whether it is her picture on the television or her back walking down the street or her figure in a bathing suit on the beach, you can never tell, when you love a woman. Not flesh and blood, something else, but not flesh and blood."

I could tell him that all memories are like that; we all remember things in the same way, not as they truly were, but magnified. But he would have an answer for that and I do not wish to dilute what he sees as love, right now.

"May I ask you something, old man?"

"You can ask, I not sure I'll answer."

"How does she fit in? What about Una? Where does she fit? I mean, who was first, who was second? Where do I fit? My mother, how does she fit? What is the sequence?"

"Sequence? This is not a story or a novel, son, there is no sequence to things like this. Is life. Things roll into one another, things mixed up and confusing. Everything does not have explanation. And time is not enough to just lay it before you with the kind of logic you may expect."

"But everything seemed to have happened around the same time. And you must imagine I would want to understand the logic. So what is the problem here? Why bring me here, show me this land, and now say there is no logic? You know me, I want explanations, Daddy."

So he eases back as if to meet the evening as it comes and looks across the hills toward the sea, where the multicolored clouds are strewn across the skies as if by the hand of a careless painter.

"You know, I don't even remember who win the Miss Jamaica that night. But I remember every detail of the dress Hope was wearing—a yellow all-in-one, taffeta mini with the hem one inch above where ladies like to wear it then, but not so far up you would say that she was loose, you understand . . . a yellow taffeta dress, so tight on her that not even ants could pass between it and her skin.

"The crowning was at the Pegasus and it was the biggest event of the year. I went to the bar to order drinks and left with the most beautiful woman in the room on my hands. She was standing there, leaning casually against the counter, bored, and every man at that bar wanted to say something but did not have the nerve."

I am not sure he understands that I do not want these details. But he is like a man about to cleanse himself. We are not ready for this kind of sharing. It is not normal for fathers to give these kinds of details that are falling so easily from his lips.

But he continues with a dreamy smile: "As I touch the bar, the man that stood between us moved, as if by cue. So I ordered my drinks and then turned to her and said something silly—I don't know where it come from, *Take the ribbon from your hair*. And she looked at me and never skipped a beat: *Shake it loose and let it fall*.

"You see, the thing is she never had a ribbon in her hair. It was just something silly for her to respond to, so

I could work my way into the conversation. And her hair had that . . . you know, fluffed-out and half-wild look, as if someone just take the ribbon from it and she just shaking it loose. Ninety-nine out of a hundred women would have said the obvious, *I have no ribbon in my hair*, but she said, *Shake it loose and let it fall*, as if to say, *I can match you*. And just then, the bartender gave her one of the two drinks I ordered, as if I had ordered it for her, but I had not. But once she took it, I just pretended it was hers in the first place. And every time I remember that, I still believe it was just destiny.

"So she told me thanks and she drank the drink and ask me why I stopped there, if I had forgotten my line, *Ain't it sad to be alone*.

"*That is your line*, I told her. *My line is*, Help me make it through the night. Sometimes you have to be original." Father smiles at me.

"I am waiting to hear if you ever began to be, old man."

He ignores me. "She had come from Montego Bay just to volunteer for the festival and independence celebrations. In those days, that is how it was: the festival and Miss Jamaica pageant and these things were much closer to the people and volunteers would come from all over the island just to help coordinate and organize the events. So I asked her why she never entered the contest and she smiled and told me that only white people win the Miss Jamaica beauty contest.

"So I raised my glass and tell her, *White flat batty women, without shape. You wouldn't qualify. And if you had been on the stage, I wouldn't have had the guts to invite you for a walk.*

"And she said, *Come, I am tired of this anyway.*

"And you see how it is now. I have wondered about that all my life. Why did I go with her? You see, I was never really inviting her. I just made a statement—it just came out—the right words for what she felt at the time. She took it for an invitation, said yes, and I had to go. I just swallowed the drink and walked out with her. And that was the beginning of that."

"Or the end of that." I stare him square.

"What you mean?"

"Who was the other drink for, the one she took? That was the end of that, wasn't it?"

"Oh, well, that is not important right now." He is sheepish and for the first time does not meet my eye.

"So who did you walk out on? Your friends? No, don't tell me, another woman, wasn't it? You went to the contest with one woman, met another woman, and walked out on her."

"Well, it's not like that and that's not important right now. Just let me finish the story."

"Father, how can you just brush people aside like that?"

"It was the woman."

"Same thing Adam said. Oh, I forgot, she wasn't flesh and blood and the other one was. So what happened to that other person?"

He goes silent for a while. "Everton," he finally says, "sometimes life just push you in a certain direction and you just have to go, follow your heart, take a chance."

"I hear you. But thirty-five years later you are chasing after her. What went wrong, you went to another bar, met another woman? Why you coming now to search for her? Wasn't she your heart's desire? Or she turned flesh and blood?"

"She never changed. She never did."

"So, why, what happened? Why are you not with her now, Daddy?"

"Ambition . . . and show off." It is a whisper on the hot afternoon.

"Yes?"

"Airs too." A sad, low sigh.

"Airs, she had airs?"

"She had none. I was full of it."

"I see, a young, cocky civil servant, who grew handsome. She wasn't good enough for you."

"Let me tell you a story about her."

I grow still to let him speak.

"About a year after we met, the people of West Prospect made a resolution to have water tanks placed at strategic locations along the road from the river to their district. So there was a meeting and the resolution was made. As the extension officer, I took the resolution to Kingston and lodged it with the agricultural office."

"Resolution?"

"Yes. Those were formal days. There would be a meeting and the farmers would get up and say something like: *Be it known that on this day so and so, the people of West Prospect have resolved that three tanks should be placed at so and so place and near so and so road adjoining West Prospect and Boagaville and a road should be cut for movement of traffic, people, and livestock,* et cetera."

"Really?"

"Yes. And I would take it back signed and everything to the Jamaican Agricultural Society for them to action. So after about six months, no news was forthcoming and the farmers demanded to see the minister.

So I invited him. To everybody's surprise and probably because it was politically expedient, the minister agreed to see them.

"So anyway, I picked her up for our usual weekend down here and since the meeting was the Friday night, I took her along with me. She was a woman who loved agriculture and we had many great ideas for developing this land and the whole countryside. She knew most of my ideas including the fact that I wanted to run for parish representative.

"Everybody was at the meeting—the head of the Agricultural Society and all the senior farmers of the area. And I had a special pride of place as the man credited for having arranged the meeting when the parish representative had tried for years and had been unable to do it.

"So the argument about the tanks began and the minister started explaining how things take time and that he never heard about the situation or he would have fixed it right away. And that he never knew things were so bad. Anyway, the long and short of it is that by the time my president and the minister finish with the people, every farmer there was convinced that they had done their best and could not do any more.

"But not Hope, she raised her hand and said she had a question. So the minister ask her, *Yes?*

"*Mr. Minister, how long have you been in charge of this constituency?*

"So he said, *Since independence.*

"*And it is just now that you know that the people want tanks?*

"By the time he could answer, she laid into him, man. She really gave it to him. *You are a hypocrite*, she said. *If it wasn't election time, you wouldn't be here and that liar beside you is no different. I know for a fact that the resolutions went to his office directly and he has done nothing about it. All politicians are hypocrites.* And the whole time she was speaking, I was trying to tell her to stop. But she gave them such a tracing that day that when she finished even the farmers she defended distanced themselves—everybody including me. Not even I defended her."

"Well, disrespect is difficult to defend."

"No, but you don't understand: everything she said were my words. Everything was what we discussed. She was saying the things I told her, things I wanted to say."

"Yes, but good judgment is good judgment. You don't get anywhere by embarrassing the minister and the head of the Agricultural Society."

"But they needed to be. Those resolutions would circulate in that office for three years. When I was there, I don't remember a file ever being retired. And the Ministry of Works was just down the road. Can you imagine a file in an office that takes three years to get to another office half a block around the corner? They deserved it."

"So what's the problem?"

"I was a fool. I was a coward. Ah, this land, this Jamaica hope."

He stands and braces himself against the tree as if the storytelling has weakened him. He looks across the land and whispers it again, "Jamaica hope."

"What is that?"

"You don't see it? This was our dream. We planned to develop this land, the whole south coast, into the bread basket of Jamaica."

"It is the bread basket."

"But it is not half that it could be. Look at all of this . . . still forest."

"It is above the river."

"That's it. That was the challenge. That is what we wanted to do with our lives then. The challenge we had."

"Daddy, I am sure whatever choices you made were the correct ones. Why are you killing yourself over this thing?"

"I let her down."

"*You* let her down?"

"Yes."

"How come?"

"I wanted to be a civil servant so bad. I wanted the job. You see, they wanted a new parish representative to challenge for the head of the JAS. I was the man they wanted because I had the land down here, I had the name, I was an extension officer who got things done, and I had the education. The only way they felt we could fix this place was if we were in charge of something in Kingston. I was to be the challenger. That was the only way I could have fulfilled the dream, our dream."

"So?"

"A man who wants a certain office must have a certain kind of woman. You understand? After that speech she made . . . you know, it was going to be difficult. I had to make a choice."

"Oh, Daddy."

"You know, it is only in the evenings that it bothers me, this here memory of her. For we never usually got here before afternoon . . . never . . . no matter how early we started out. Only evening time, and she use to sit down right there and ask why we only make love in the afternoon. Sometimes it is like a burden on me, but I loved her. I loved her, you know."

"Yeah, not even flesh and blood."

"Never!"

He is crying. I find his side and wrap my arm around his shoulder as he wipes his eyes.

"Father, bringing up all this past is not good for you. Why you crying now, old man?"

"I want to see her again. I have to see her again. I want to look at her face again. I want to touch her one more time before I die."

"And when you see her, what then?"

"I want to tell her that I am sorry." Then he holds my hand. "Son . . ." He is more nervous than I have ever seen him; his fingers tremble on my flesh. "Son, when we see her this evening, you must give the old man some time." His eyes are watery and pleading. There is vulnerability in his face. He seems much older than yesterday. "If I want another day, I am going to beg you another day."

I will not resist him. My trip is ending. I will be back in Kingston very soon. I have only lost a week of leave. He can have all the time he needs.

"Old man, if you want another day, you have another day."

"And Everton?"

"Yes, old man."

"After this, after this trip, we have to talk. There are things I must tell you. Things I know you want to know."

I do not know the places he has been to. I do not know the things he has seen, and judging by his tears, I have never felt the love he has felt. But I stand here with him now, and he is like a child in my arms. I can only guess at the turmoil inside him. And I wonder what has brought us here. Why the land he sacrificed his love and woman for is still here after thirty-five years, untouched and undeveloped.

"We have time, old man, we have time."

Now my heart is full and my breast is swelling. I want to ask him if these things we will discuss are about my mother, about me, about the many days he was missing from my life. Is it finally time for my ten questions? But instead I pat his shoulder and turn from the tears in his eyes. I cannot ask much of him now. He is empty of stories for the evening.

Only tears now, only tears.

SEVENTEEN

The last time I saw my father cry was at my mother's funeral, at the casket, at the head of the line with Una by his side. I remember even through my grief looking on and wondering how strange it seemed that he was standing there with one woman at his side while mourning another.

Somehow he looked quite dignified and humbled to be standing there showing the level of his humanity. I was drawn to him even more after that because something of the moment forced me to question my conviction that he had never loved her.

Though she loved him till she died.

She never married. And sometimes I would tease her about it. How she lived a life in the shadow of this man who did not care for her, as if waiting for him to return to the point wherever it was that they separated; waiting to begin again, to be young again, and to have him ask her to marry him.

And even those days and nights when I was sure that I heard him sneaking in and out of the house, it seems she was content to live with just a piece of him, or maybe she felt that no other man was good enough, or maybe the sweet nobility in her was too proud to betray her heart. Or maybe she was afraid to ever love or trust again.

She did not talk about him much, but sometimes at

my prodding or when she was in a certain mood, she would sigh and tell me not to ask her anymore why they never married. Or say sadly that "is only one woman you father ever love." And all my life I thought that woman was Una.

But now I know differently.

My mother told me they met while she was a young church girl working alongside the chief of the Agricultural Society, and he was a young and brash field officer with dreams of running the whole thing someday. "Him was very ambitious," she would say, "very ambitious."

Now having for the first time gotten a good glimpse at his life, I am not sure what ambition has brought. I had only seen it before through the eyes of an infatuated child. But now I am forced to see it objectively and I am not sure I am able to get the sum of it.

Sixty-seven years old, retired some months ago with a pension and a few acres in Hampshire. Over forty years in the civil service, a brash young man with ambitions of leading it all, yet forty years later he is retired, having moved no further than assistant section head.

Why? How come, in a world and a time of independence, when the country yearned and craved for young men like my father, when lesser men had become ministers and ambassadors, has my father not achieved more? Is the answer to all this somehow wrapped up inside this quest on which he has taken me?

And my mother, where does she fit into all this? I hear of this woman Hope, and I have a small sense of how Una came about. But what about my mother? How did she fit in, where did she fit in? Why did he not love my mother?

Does my father love me?

"Him love you," she always said when I insisted he did not.

"Then why him don't make me live with him in him big house?" I would ask.

She would turn the question back at me: "This house not big enough for you?"

I always felt she deserved more.

And even on her deathbed, she still wished the best for him, for near her last breath she whispered that I should love my father. That he was a good man and one day he might need me.

And oh, I have dreamed of that day, when I, the stone that the builder refused, would become the head corner stone. But I have grown beyond that now. I moved out on my own and wanted less and less the responsibility of anything but my own life and career. And in any event, he always seemed so strong, so large and competent, that I had always believed I would probably need his help long before he would ever need mine.

My mother was not an educated woman, having barely completed primary school. But she could cook. Her gift was to feed people. She was trained by her mother to keep house and take care of a man. That is all she knew to do: cook and keep house. And if the Lord provides a man, take care of him with heart and her life.

She made a living by both. Working as a helper and cooking for families in Jacks Hill. Then when she joined the church, she started cooking at conventions and special occasions till the word spread and she was able to stay home and fulfill cooking contracts from her own little kitchen. Later she got a contract to run the kitchen at the steel factory in Spanish Town. From that she bought the house in which we lived and which she had rented for years. Later the same contract sent me through school.

Between steady work and the church, she found contentment that few others I knew ever achieved. But no matter how she tried, no matter what she said, I knew there were places in her heart so parched that nothing else could ever grow. And no matter what she told me, I knew that those were the places where my father resided.

I wondered at times at the fairness of it; that while she had remained so scarred, he had healed so well to be always laughing, happy and on top of the world.

And though the doctor said it was diabetes, no one can convince me that she did not die of a broken heart.

The night she died, I tore his picture from her wall and shredded and burnt it to yellow-gray ashes. And then I searched through her things for everything of his that she had and I made an altar of them and set fire to that too. For I hated that she should have died so; that she should have loved so much that it killed her.

And though the anger burned in me so much that at times when he visited, I could not meet his eyes, I have never felt that I could hurt him back the way I think he deserved. Because she worked so hard to make me love him. "He is your father."

I have grown past that now . . . past those sudden feelings that sometimes overtook me.

And now I wonder if this is what she was talking about when she said he might need me one day. But I do not think so. I do not think she would have dreamed that he would want me to follow him on this crazy journey.

Nor do I think that she would have imagined that he could break down over the memory of another woman.

So now he has promised that we will talk. And God knows I have questions. I will make a new list of questions as long as this journey on which he has taken me, and I hope he is ready to answer them.

I draw the Pathfinder up to the gate of the cabin. It is the end of a silent ride back. As he disembarks I see he is not as bright as he was when he invited me back to see the land again this afternoon. But his spirits lift as we round the corner to the back door, and we see there on the veranda, looking out onto the pool, a little old lady sitting as if half asleep. As we come into view she opens her eyes and raises herself. She is close to the red of the bauxite earth and her skin is as clean and smooth as if she were just turning forty, but her eyes tell me that she has seen enough to fill many more years than that.

She gives a loud yelp, jumps into my father's arms, and scolds him for the fact that she has been waiting on him for two hours.

EIGHTEEN

Father does not seem too happy as he walks down the beach toward me. He walks alone and his head is slightly bowed. A passing stranger would probably believe he is sunk in wise contemplation, but I know him better than that. He is deeply troubled. I could have warned him that feelings do not rejoin themselves after thirty-five years; I could have told him it would not be as it was before; that the days of joy would not immediately return and that she would not appear from the past and suddenly make him happy—but it is good he has discovered it for himself.

I watch him as he turns through the small gate into the yard and give him some time before I step from the water to comfort him and ask where down the beach he has left his thirty-five-year itch.

"I see you went swimming," he says as I join him on the veranda.

"Yes."

"The water is nice, isn't it? You know, they say the black sand keeps the water warmer than the white sand of the north coast, something about the sand absorbing light rather than reflecting it."

I nod at that. It sounds sensible, but then most often my father does sound sensible . . . except when he is chasing thirty-five-year-old crushes.

"So what happen to your girlfriend?"

He passes me the towel I had left on the chair and smiles sheepishly. "That is what I have to talk to you about."

"What?" I sit on the edge of the veranda with him.

"She didn't come." He speaks quickly, sharply.

"What?!"

"She is not coming till next week or so. And she is not coming down here. We have to go to Montego Bay."

"And who was that?" My hand is shaking as I point down the beach.

"Oh, that was Tara, that was Willy's mother."

"Why didn't you tell me?"

"You walked away."

"I was giving you time with her. I have to go to work. I have a job, Daddy, I am not going to Montego Bay. I am not staying down here."

"I know, I know." He tries to calm me. "Listen, no. Listen, I know."

"You know? I don't think so. Daddy, I don't think you understand at all."

"No, I know. That is what I am telling you. You can go on now. You can leave me here. I will be okay. I know you have to work and you have lost one week of your leave already. This is what I want to tell you. Go on, I will stay here. I am fine; Tara said I could ask Willy to take me."

Ah, there is a trick in this somewhere. I pause to absorb this thing, to come to terms with the wiles of this devious old man.

"You mean to tell me, Daddy, that all this time you had me believe that this was the woman, Hope, while you were out there hatching a plan to stay here without me and I am just waiting here like a fool?"

"No one is hatching any plan. Why are you always making a mountain out of a mole hill, Everton? No one made you believe anything. You saw what you wanted to see, you heard what you wanted to hear. You're too busy."

"I am too busy?"

"Yes, your mind is always working. It's not good for you."

"I am not leaving you down here."

"You're starting with that again!" He pauses at that, stands, and begins to make his way toward the door of the cottage. "When you get to my age, you learn to ignore statements like that."

I am trying to recall the man who was in tears an hour ago, who had broken down at the memory of the failures in his life. But clearly that had been a moment of weakness. The father before me is composed and seemingly bored. And for some reason I feel on the defensive. "I need an explanation, Daddy."

"Everton . . ." He pauses and looks at me. "Everton, what must I explain to you? I don't have anything to explain. I have told you everything. You don't see this is something I have to do. It's as simple as that. This is something I have to do. You have to go to work. I have to go to Montego Bay. I am tired, Everton. The old man tired, son."

With that he slips quietly through the door and leaves it to bang softly as it closes. I am left trying to form a response to him, but half the words are stuck in my throat, the rest are feelings, unformed, deep in my gut, wherever feelings lie before they are made into expressions. I can do nothing but shake my head as anger starts to boil within me. There is something wrong with this man. There is something wrong with my father. As God lives, there is something wrong with him. Either that, or there is something drastically wrong with me.

NINETEEN

I t is early Sunday afternoon; I have deliberately slept in. I would have left last night, but the beautiful Tara came by to invite us to dinner and out of courtesy I accepted. Over the meal she asked us to church this morning, but though Father accepted, I declined. Knowing that church would begin close to twelve o'clock, I deliberately slept in so I would not have to face my father. And by the time he returns I will be gone. I do not understand these feelings I have, or the depth of the anger that burns in me.

We barely spoke through the dinner, but that was a group affair with Tara, her husband, and Willy. There were so many stories to tell, and then there was the memory of my marble-playing prowess, that I do not believe anyone would have picked up the growing void between me and my father. But had they been in the Pathfinder on the ride back, they would have been appalled at the thick ugly silence between us.

I know when I am beaten. I know when there is nothing to say on a subject. And I accept now that there is nothing I can do to prevent him from staying. And duty and responsibility ensure that I must leave. He is retired, he has had a wonderful career, while I am still starting mine and cannot afford to lose my opportunities, only to be chasing them forty years later with tears in my eyes and fantasies in my head. I have to leave, I must go home. I have to be at work tomorrow.

I pack the final pieces of clothing in the duffel bag we bought together, the brown Polo shirt he liked, the jeans I insisted on, and the T-shirt I bought as insurance against the style he was forcing on me. Thirty-seven years. Most kids fight with their father over fashion and clothing in their teenage years. My time comes at thirty-seven. Thirty-seven years old and my first full week with my father alone—and now this, this silence, this void.

The church is not a big one as churches go. It is white with a high roof and is pushed back into the yard so there is much space in the front for cars to park and children to mill around. It has a white picket fence with a low wooden gate that is wide open. I wonder what he is doing in there. Maybe trying to coerce God into some adventure or other, maybe trying to work his way into heaven through the back door. He was never a religious man. But he has gone to church because Tara invited him. And it seems to me a very hard thing to say no to Tara.

I park the van a little way ahead on the soft shoulder of the road and walk back to satisfy my curiosity. I am not sure why I am doing this. I had resolved not to see him today, but I guess that just a glimpse of him in church through the window at the side could not be harmful to me or my resolutions.

I walk with unsure steps, with a sense of guilt I do not understand. The ground under my feet is red and hard. It contrasts starkly against the bright white of the fence and the blue and white of the church. There is an old smell in the air, as if the space of the churchyard is ancient and preserved. A few children chase each other irreverently around the yard.

Inside is full the way only churches can be, with people on every inch of pew until someone else comes and fits where no space seemed to have been before. I stand at the window and survey the crowd as they sing. The pastor may have just finished preaching for his Bible is still in his hand as he sings and beckons to the crowd. And the song is not as lively as those that start services. But what do I know, I have not been to a church in years. Plus, this is the country and who knows how they do things down here.

It takes me awhile to locate him. And it is only as they sit that I do. He is in the middle of the left half of the church on my side and I see him by his hair: white and silky and needing a bit of barbering, distinct, even though there are older people on all sides of him. Beside him in a big white hat is Tara and beside her, turning almost instinctively to meet my eyes, is Angela from Ballards Valley. I could fall with surprise at her presence there and more so at the fact that I am sure she recognizes me through the louvers. She does not react, though I am sure she recognizes me.

But there is little time to react for my father is standing. He straightens the borrowed jacket he is wearing, excuses his way by the knees of the brethren and sistren, and makes his way reverently toward the altar. The walk is not the proud upward gait I am used to. It lacks the upright proud strides and squared shoulders. His posture is angled a few inches forward of erect, his movement is closer to a shuffle than a stride, and the aura around him is one of humility, so that as he gets to the altar, his kneeling and bowing of head seems as natural as if the walk had prepared him for it and that place where he now kneels is where he has been heading all his life.

There is a sense of privacy and independence about him as he kneels. He seems at a place now where no one needs to interrupt his conversation, a place where he has all he needs. My worries about him are unimportant. For no one matters to him now; I do not matter; he does not need me or anyone. I am useless to him and all this fussing and headache I have been having about leaving him seems ridiculous in the moment before me.

I do not know why I feel hurt and dejected, but I do. I do not know why this loneliness is washing over me—or this sadness—but it does. I have nothing to do here. I turn from the window as the pastor places his hand on my father's head and make my way through the gate toward my Pathfinder.

TWENTY

Halfway to the car I hear her call my name. The day is uncomfortable already. The place is bare, without trees. It is close to midday and there is a haze to the sky. She calls my name again. And I do not have to turn to know it is Angela, but I do, and even as I spin around I can feel the sun lean against me as if it has taken a liking to my face. I wish to be in the cabin of my van, with the air-conditioning on high and its nose pointing toward Kingston.

She is in a black dress that wraps her body like a second skin, not that it is tight but it just works its way along her contours and every curve, every sink is highlighted. Her hair is up in a bun, and the curls at the top are like a small pom-pom those cheerleaders use. You see that it is false and the sheen of it is almost plastic, but it makes no difference to the way she appears. As a matter of fact, on her, with that body, with that smile, with that walk, it complements a sort of country vivaciousness, so that everything looks stylish and right.

"What happen?" she says as she stops.

"Pardon me?" I feel a need to be formal with her.

"Me think you gone."

"No, I am just leaving."

"You father said you couldn't come church because you have to leave early."

Something occurs to me that has been on the edge of my consciousness since the other day. "Are you related to my father?" I ask—because I do not trust him nor do I trust the fact that she keeps popping up at the oddest of places. "Are you perhaps my sister?"

"What?"

She is everywhere, unexplained, in the most unexpected places, just like the rest of this trip, so I am not ashamed to lay it out there. Even after the other night on the beach. "Are you my sister, my father's child? Is this some kind of game everyone is playing?"

"What! What you mean?" Her voice rings with incredulity and sincere bewilderment.

"Never mind," I tell her.

"What happen to you, how you look like that?"

"How do I look?"

"You know, vexed. Angry."

She is right up to me now. Her scent is like the sweet part of the earth that sits on the air when a short rain has kicked up the dust and is gone. There is this muskiness that she exudes like a pungent aphrodisiac. I must get away from her.

"What are you doing here? Don't you live way around so?" I point with my nose.

"Come church," she asserts.

"From so far?"

"How church must far? And is here I baptized."

"You are baptized?"

"Yes," she tells me. "You not baptized? Everybody baptized."

I am silent at that.

"You not baptized?" She looks earnestly at me. "Everybody baptized and backslide even one time in them life."

I am never prepared for this woman or the things she says. And I feel one of those moments coming on when she will render me completely speechless and inadequate.

"So what are you up to?" I need to get out of the burning sun. But I must have sounded quite aggressive for she retreats a bit as if I have put a small dent in her mood.

"I was goin' ask you fi a ride, but it's all right."

I want to ask her how she got here in the first place. And what she would have done if I had not stopped to look at my father. But I do not. I tell her that it would be no problem; her home is on the way.

"You sure?" She stares at me.

"Yes."

"Okay, let me get mi bag."

By the time she returns the air-conditioning is on full blast and the tinted windows have shut the sun outside. She is now in a better mood than I have seen her, although sadness still lurks beneath her surface like a suspicion. But her mood is lighter and she seems more open to conversation. Though sadly this has come at a time when I am not.

"You driving too fast," she says to me, words that remind me of my father.

I ignore her.

"You don't see the road winding and goin' uphill?"

"I know what I am doing."

"Yes, but the road have a lot of trucks. You know the road?"

This is not a good day to have a woman nag me, especially one who for some reason is now finding her voice. Especially one who is sounding uncannily like my father, on that fateful night on that road, an eternity ago it seems, when this stupid *Sanford and Son* thing began.

"You driving too fast," again in my ear.

"This is not fast." I glance at her. "This is my normal speed. You worry too much."

"Yes, but you don't know country people and how they drive."

I turn to answer her, and as I do she screams, "Look out!'"

I swing around to see an old farm truck swaying around the corner ahead, on my side of the road. The truck's body is wide and low and fitted to a lorry like a table too wide for its base. As he swerves to avoid me, the back, filled with melons, rocks and dips, and for some reason he swings again toward me. I slam the brakes and turn hard to my left, close to the bushes that line the side of the road. But the lurching truck is still coming at me, almost sideways now. I turn my van into the bushes and hear them lap against the side of the cabin. My left front wheel hits a rock and lifts high as if to capsize us toward the road. I fight desperately to gain control of the vehicle as it pushes through the bush, momentarily on three wheels. We slam down hard onto the asphalt, late enough to miss the swinging tail of the lorry as it careens down the hill. But we are in the middle of the road and the steering wheel is suddenly stiff and my vehicle is dragging to one side.

I regain control and find my side of the road just as a

car comes speeding down the hill. Breathless and scared out of my wits, I bring the van to a halt in a clearing up ahead.

"You puncture," she says dryly across the seat.

It takes all I have to hold back the expletives at the back of my teeth and disembark to see for myself.

Before my foot touches the ground, I feel sweat running down my back. When I bend to look at the tire, my shirt is sticking against my skin. The tire has a hole at the side apparently sliced by the large stone we hit down the road. Not only is it flat, it obviously cannot be repaired. I curse loudly. For now I will have to drive to Kingston without a spare.

I check my watch. It is close to one thirty. I do not want the night to catch me on the road.

As I remove the tools from the back of the vehicle, I notice that Angela has stepped out and is standing by the punctured wheel. I drop the tools on the ground near her. She stands inspecting the tire with a look on her face as if she knows something about these things.

"Excuse me," I begin to fit the jack under the wheel. She steps aside and I can feel her eyes on me as I get to work.

"You nah kotch the wheel?" she asks

"What?" I look up at her.

"You nah kotch the wheel—put a stone behind it? You want the van roll down the hill?" Even as she speaks she walks into the bush and returns with an average-sized rock. She moves past me and places it behind the left rear wheel to kotch it. I watch her, bemused as she shakes her head at the rock and walks back into the bush.

As I grudgingly concede that she has noticed what I overlooked, she shouts from the bush that she has found a better rock but cannot manage to lift it. I join her. She is standing beside a large rock that is partially embedded in the red dirt. It is shaped ideally to block the wheel. I kick it loose, lift it, and force it hard against the other rear tire.

"Thank you," I tell her, finding it hard now to give her the silent treatment my anger had wanted me to.

"You are welcome," she says. I am sure I can detect some feistiness in her tone.

The vehicle secure, I begin to work in earnest, spinning the awkward handle of the jack to raise it.

"Why you don't take off your shirt?" She is stooping now in front of me. Her hand is on the tire and her eyes are staring knowingly into mine, as if to say she understands me more than I think—like she knows why I am angry and why I am making a fool of myself. "You don't see you sweating?"

But I am stubborn and I continue to turn the awkward handle.

"And why you don't take the spare tire off the back before you start jack up the wheel so that you have it beside you when you ready? And why you don't loosen the lugs on the tire before you start jack up the van?"

She is a very sexy woman. She is stooping, and her already short dress has slid farther up her legs. The sheer stockings leave little of the color of her skin for me to imagine. Her legs are smooth, they are like the insides of naseberry. I admire their shape and smoothness and I know that the way she is stooping, if I flick my eyelids, I can trace her legs to where they join the rest of her. It is hot, I am miserable, I am sweating, and I have suddenly gained an erection.

"Take off you shirt, nuh. You don't see how you sweating?"

Now it isn't pride that prevents me. I am embarrassed to stand and show the bulge in my pants.

"I am fine," I tell her.

"Well, suit yourself. But you not doing it right. Anyway, let me stop bother you. Next thing you go insult me." With that she stands and moves away to the front of the vehicle.

She is right and I know it. Not just about the shirt, but about the loosening of the lugs and the removing of the tire from the back. She was right about the rocks to kotch the vehicle and the speed at which I drove up the road. She has been right about everything and if I had not been busy being angry, things would probably not have gotten to this.

In one way I am happy that she has walked away because it gives me a chance to stand and fix myself in my jeans before I remove my shirt. It takes me a few minutes to take the tire from the back, but all the time I do not hear her, I do not see her. I place it on the ground near the front of the vehicle and she is not there looking over the wheel. I move to loosen the lugs on the wheel and see her shoes. She is sitting on the bumper at the far side of the vehicle and her legs are stretched out in front of her. I do not know what to say to her. I do not know how to approach. So I loosen the nuts, lay the wheel on the ground, and continue silently to jack the vehicle up.

There is a new silence, one I do not control. One I do not want. But I work on. The van is high enough. I stand to remove the punctured wheel and she is leaning against the front of the van now looking at me with a hint of satisfaction on her face. Not smugness, not an I-tell-you-so satisfaction—just a simple satisfied look with a bit of approval in it.

I pause before removing the tire and meet her stare across the space. Our eyes lock for a moment and the silence between us changes immediately. If we never speak another word, this silence would not be an uncomfortable place to be.

"Where did you learn so much about cars?" I break the silence.

She removes herself from the front of the Pathfinder and comes toward me to stand near the wheel as I pull it from the axle. I sense she is leaning on the fender as she speaks. "My stepfather was a mechanic."

"Yes?"

"So I learn. But him was always sad. I don't know who can run mechanic shop in that part of St. Elizabeth. Mus' be donkey him was goin' fix."

I chuckle at that. "Well, you learned something."

She hisses her teeth. "Not enough vehicles in this part of St. Elizabeth to support a mechanic shop."

"Well, you should tell him."

"Him stupid like what. Mamma have farmer boyfriend now. She much happier. At least him give her food."

The tire change complete, she holds the door for me as I throw the useless tire inside and slam it shut.

"You have to wash off yourself," she says as she

heads for the passenger side. "You can't put on your shirt so."

"And some food, I need some food," I tell her. "I am starving to death." Strange, I have just lost a tire yet my anger is evaporating.

TWENTY-ONE

oday Little Ochi is teeming with people. There is
mix of Kingstonians, tourists, and some with the
excited look of returning residents. Ten minutes
in the bathroom at the restaurant and I am now as fresh
as I can expect and I have on a clean Polo shirt from my
bag.

As we enter the large yard, we are met by a man as
straight as a cane stalk in a black and white uniform.
He points us to a hut like a boat near the sea. We climb
the short stairs into it, and I, with my best imitation of
Willy's air, tell him to bring us some fish to choose from.

Before I can settle or the man can leave the booth,
Angela rises and stares at me. "So you not goin' choose
you fish?"

"No." I sit back. "Let him bring them. The sun too
hot."

"Well, I not goin' make him choose any stale fish for
me! You ever hear anybody come to Little Ochi and don't
choose their fish?"

I almost tell her that Willy does, but I do not trust
how that will make me look, so I stand reluctantly.

We walk into the main building toward the back
where there is a bank of large freezers thrown open. The
assistant gestures toward them. I point to a large snapper for myself and then ask her which she wants.

"I don't want none a those," she quips, and gives him a haughty but sweet smile. "Where the fresh one them?"

"All a them fresh." He smiles back.

"Today fish," she tells him, and moves off around the back to where women are busy scaling. She stops at another freezer, looks inside, and points to a fish almost identical in size to the one I had chosen, almost identical in every way. "How about that one?"

He smiles and picks it up.

"And the one beside it!"

So he collects the two fish, each about twice the length of my palm and as thick as my hands when I cup them into prayer.

I order mine steamed and she wants hers fried.

"So what's the difference?" I am trying my best not to sound agitated as our guide leaves with the fish. "You must try not to insult these people, you know. I never insult people before they cook my food."

"You don't see the difference?" She calls out and asks the man to stop. "Look at the eyes. You see how they clear, like glass, like ice water in a glass, like you can see through them? All right, now look at the one you was going to buy. You see how the eyes start getting white, like the eyeballs them start get white and cloudy? Okay, well, the whiter the eyes the staler they are. And you see that one?" She points to a fish near the corner. "You see how most o' that one eyes white like milk? Well, that one soon start to spoil. When they keep the deep freeze open like this, the fish can't keep a hundred percent fresh so one and two get old. Them won' sell them to you spoil but I don't like when them stale."

I keep my mouth shut.

At the spacious and ample bar, she orders a lime squash and tells the bartender she does not want it too sweet and that she prefers it with two cherries. He laughs and tells her that if she does not like it when the waiter brings it, she should just send it back and tell him how it tastes.

There is a kind of charm about her as she moves and makes her demands. Her voice is always strong and firm, her manner direct and a little saucy, and sometimes as she speaks I am tempted to raise a cautionary hand. But her delivery causes no offense; it draws smiles, sometimes even laughter . . . a kind of respect.

We sit to wait. The day continues to grow hotter, but we are right on the beach and there is a wind blowing across the place. As I look around I can see a space filled with activity: people milling around, some strolling along the beach, others, like us, sitting in booths waiting for their food.

Tourists, Kingstonians, fishermen, and common folk mixing into one melee of color and activity. Off to my left, a bit down the coast, I see a small boat being beached. A few people move toward it as two fishermen disembark while it settles in the sand.

"The whole process is here." I smile at her.

"What you mean?"

"From the fish in the water to the fish on your plate, you can see the whole process. You see the man catch it. You see the people buy it, you see it being scaled, and then cooked, then eaten . . . the whole process."

"And you did want to buy stale fish."

I smile at that. "Well, that's why you're here, to make sure I don't. And thanks."

"You are welcome," she says with playful sarcasm.

"And thanks about down the road," I tell her too. "Helping with the car. Some women . . ." I think of Audrey. "Some women would just sit in the car and wait. Thanks."

"Eeem," she says, staring at me squarely. This time she really is pleased, so her reaction is less open, less buoyant. As if a shyness is creeping in, or a blush, and she needs to control herself.

Three old men walk toward our booth in straw hats. They pause below us, between our booth and another, a bit off from the traffic and closer to where the people take a break from the sun. They find a large coconut tree. Two have banjos and the other has a small drum.

They are old; average age maybe between sixty-five and seventy. They seem a remnant of some mento band from the Harry Belafonte days when sweet mellow ballads with stories of love and obeah could bring a crown to life. They seem spent, wizened—as if by congregating around the tree they are spared the force of the wind long enough to be able to stand and strum a few tunes.

The lead singer is thin as a toothpick, tall as I am but so stooped that he seems five inches shorter. The melody they squeeze from the old banjos is mellow and old but some around seem to enjoy it. I don't—they look as ridiculous as those people in straw hats the minister of tourism has singing "Welcome to Jamaica" at the airports. I turn my eyes from them.

"Why you don't love you father?"

The question takes me by surprise and I am not sure how to answer. I mean, I know how to answer it. I can either be firm, and put her in her place, or make a conversation of it because after this lunch, I am sure I will not see her again.

But since the day has been improving and I do not wish to be as boorish as I was in the van, I decide to engage her. "How can you ask that? He is my father."

"No, you don't love him, you know. Him love you but you don't love him."

I am thirty-seven years old and she cannot be more than twenty-two or -three. I do not think this is a conversation I would want to pursue with someone like this. But she has a maturity beyond her years, an oldness in the way she looks at me, and a certainty in her analysis and observations.

"You're not easy. How can you just say that? You don't know me and you don't know my father."

"I know though. I can tell."

"You can?"

"Is the work that I do. A man can come up to me and I just know him so. Just know certain things right away. I can know if him lonely, if him happy, if him wicked or show-off. I just know."

"And you know I don't love my father?"

"I can see it in your eyes. Everything is in your eyes. Is not that you don't have love for him, you know. You just don't love him."

"And how," I ask with a hint of sarcasm, "do you differentiate between those?"

"How you mean! You have love for him, you just don't love him. Is like food: the fact that somebody hungry don't mean they don't have food. They probably have the food and just don't feel to eat it. You never hear people go on hunger strike yet?"

I laugh aloud. "That is pretty good." Our drinks come so she does not respond. She eyes the waiter easily as he places the lime squash before her. She checks with a lazy sip but the waiter is not fooled by it. He waits even as I drink my beer. She takes another sip, cocks her eye in a sort of absentminded approval. The man smiles and leaves.

"Me . . ." She looks slightly away to the beach. "Me, I don't like my father. I hate him like poison."

"Why?"

She hisses her teeth. "Have too much woman. If it wasn't for him my mother wouldn't have to take up with that dirty old mechanic. Wouldn't have so much pickney. But she all right now and is a good thing him gone too."

And that is the thing about her. In five seconds, she has clearly stated how she feels about her father and why. Just like that. No beating around the bush. Just open and straight. She would not make a good executive. Yet in everything she does she makes me feel inadequate about myself.

"Him never love nobody but himself. Not even me."

"When you say *gone* what do you mean?"

"Gone. Just gone, you know. Him find another woman and just gone."

"And you don't know where he is?"

"Know, yes, know more than that too."

"So you see him then."

"Me?" She hisses through her teeth again. "The day I was leaving to go HEART, my mother told me to stop by him house and get some money. Instead I stop by him workplace—first time me ever go out to that big old bauxite factory. Lean on the gate and red up mi clothes. Me ask him for some money, him look on me and give me two thousand dollars. So I ask him if that is all. You know what him tell me say?"

"What?"

"That me is a woman and I will survive."

"And you did."

"I did have to survive, yes. But the day him visit *my* workplace him nearly get a heart attack. Him tell me to survive, but him couldn't take it when I turn up to serve him."

She seems to be entering a place of reflection, so I allow the quietness to stand with us. Then she turns to me with the lime squash almost halfway down the glass and the straw in her hands working one of the cherries to the brim. "But your father, now, I like him. Him nice. Him just cool."

"Yes," I nod at her, but do not finish the line as I think it, *women like my father*. "But he is troublesome sometimes and mischievous."

"But him love you though. You can see it every time him look on you."

"You think so?" I sigh a laugh into the space.

"So why you don' love him?"

I laugh slowly. "You think I have chosen not to love my father?"

"Yes. Why?"

"What kind of work do you do?"

"I can read you like a book, you know?" She looks at me with those wise old eyes.

"No, I am going to answer your question. I just want

to know where you learn to be so wise and sure about everything. Is it the bartending?"

"So now the next thing you goin' tell me is that this is not a bar and you not some lonely man who need somebody to confess to. I can read you like a book," she says again, and turns away from me with the same air with which she walked away from me half an hour ago when I patronized her at my punctured vehicle. Only now she is not as dismissive. Just easily letting go of something she feels is not worth pursuing. Just a sort of backing away from me, not to kill the mood, but to leave me to my space and my privacy, while she watches the three old men of the makeshift mento band trying to bring life to a memory that is perhaps only in their own heads.

I wish the food would come, but as far as I look, there is no sign of our attendant. So I join Angela's line of vision to watch the trio sitting on the stools.

"It's not that I don't love him," I finally say. For my beer is finished, and there is nothing to do, so words are filling the space between us. "It is not that I don't love him. I love my father. It's just that he gives me too much trouble sometimes."

"So you say." She speaks lazily as if she is through with the conversation or bored by it.

"You don't believe me?"

"If you love him, how come you leaving him down here?"

"He wants to stay."

"So if you have a baby and him want do something that is not good for him, you goin' let him do it?"

"You tell my father that. You call him a baby, and let him hear. My father is fitter than me, he is no child."

"*Once a man twice a child*—you ever hear that?"

"Well, he hasn't reached his second childhood yet. You know why my father is down here?" I look at her and I don't know why I am telling her all this, but it is so easy to do. I do not allow her to answer. "He is here because he is trying to find a woman that he has been in love with for thirty-five years. Left his wife, run away from home to find a woman who is married and he has not seen for thirty-five years. And drags me with him, with all kinds of trickery. I left my work for a week now and I have an important job. And every day the story changes and he adds another day, and then he has another story. Till now I have been here a week and he wants me to do another week. If I am not careful, I would be down here a month with him."

"So what wrong with that?"

"What!" She is such a strange woman. How can a rational person ask a question like that? "How you mean if something wrong with that? I am an executive. People pay me a lot of money to take care of their very important business. I can't just walk off like that. How can you ask me a question like that?"

She turns back to me so that we are facing each other once again. A slow sober intelligence fills her face. She has things to say and she feels that I have given her space to say them. So I pause to hear what she has to say. First she says nothing, just stares at me for a while, then she finally speaks.

"Make me ask you something. What better? To spend time with your father who love you or to go America to watch Venus Williams play tennis, which one better?"

"He told you that?!"

"Which one better?" she insists.

"That's a very technical question to answer. It's not as easy as that. There's timing here. I have to go to work."

"All right, let me ask you something else. Suppose no woman exist. Suppose your father don't come to look for any woman. Suppose him just want to see the country one more time and want to see it with him favorite son. Suppose him proud and don't know how to really tell you. Suppose him dying. Suppose this is him last trip. Which one better, eh? Which one better?"

What manner of woman is this? What kind of woman has God put in my life this day to ask me questions that shut me up and fill me with guilt and feelings of inadequacy? What kind of work does she do to make her so old for her twenty-two or -three?

"The fry fish is my own and I want another lime squash." The food is here and she has taken charge for I am now staring open-mouthed at the three old men working the tunes from their tired instruments, and my world is suddenly not the same. My focus is gone. I do not see anything except old men working to make sense of old dreams in their heads. And I see my father alone somewhere on a beach reaching out to me for help and I'm not giving it to him but allowing him to search in places where he would never have searched before.

And I remember a conclusion I had come to my last Sunday at his house in Hampshire. A date that now seems an eternity separated by adventures and exploits I could not have imagined then. He had been helping me up the hill from the wine cellar and I had said to myself, *My father is lonely. My father needs me.* And in all the adventures and exploits I have forgotten that. And it has taken a young woman I do not know—do not care about or understand—to remind me of that. *Suppose him dying. Suppose this is him last trip.* Jesus Christ.

"You not eating?"

"Yes," I tell her. "Yes. But I would know if he is dying."

She smiles. I do not remember ever seeing her do that. It is a powerful thing that smile, huge and sexy. A squaring of her lips, a baring of her teeth that reminds me that she is not as old as she speaks.

"I would know if he was dying."

And the smile holds. "How you look so frightened?"

"I do?"

"Yes. I never want to frighten you. I just tell you because I see it already. The steam fish good, don't it?"

I taste the food and it is good. I expected it to be, as it is the same steam fish I had the last time. I slip two okras into my mouth and slurp them down. The flesh of the fish eases onto the fork without much prodding and, yes, it is succulent and the seasoning fills my senses as I eat.

"What do you mean you see it already?"

She grows quiet and the smile disappears. Now she is paying more attention to her food than it demands. She has regained her old features and the smile has gone as quickly as the sun at the threat of the May rains.

But I will not let it go. The moment had led her to overreach and I will not allow her to scamper back inside. I must know what she is hiding. What is it that keeps that sadness and the flicker of shame so close to the surface, that holds that smile perpetually in check in the same way she suggests that I hold the love for my father in check, like a hunger strike. What is her hunger strike?

"What do you mean you see it already?" My voice is softer.

Now she lifts her face to look tentatively, bravely at me. "You know . . . where I work. I see it there, already."

"And where is that, where you work? What did you see?"

"Nothing, just one old man. Never good-looking like you father or anything like that but him was nice. And him come in and nobody wanted to touch him, to look after him. So I do it. I take care of him. And it was something like that, you know. An old man who was just searching for somebody to just listen and understand— if only for a short time."

"So that is it?"

"That is what?"

"What kinda work do you do? You not a waitress or bartender, are you?"

"No, but I have the training."

She drops the fork and takes the drink from the waiter. She ignores him and he leaves quickly, handing me my beer as he goes. I wait for her to drink and I place my beer near my plate. She knows I will not touch my food till she answers.

"I work in a massage parlor," she says.

"Oh . . ." I hiss my teeth, pick up my fork, and place another chunk of steamed fish into my mouth. I had been worried she would say something worse than that.

"So you are a masseuse. What could be so bad about that?"

"I am not a masseuse. I don't work at that kind of parlor. I am a *massager*."

"Masseuse."

"No. *Massager*! You never hear 'bout *sensuous* massage yet? You play with men. They come in and you play with them. You massage them, you know, the whole way."

"The whole way?"

"Lord! You play with them. You feel they up till them come. How you so hard to understand?"

All of a sudden the steamed fish is raw and uncooked and smells like unwashed stale flesh, left unclean in a hot damp place for much too long.

"So this man come in," she says. And now I want to shut her up, but I see that she is almost in tears. No, she *is* in tears—not much, just a small one in the corner of her eyes. And there is a determination in her face, as if she must say this thing. As if to say it is a sacrifice she has decided on, and I must make her go through with it, no matter what.

"So this man come in, and him old and nobody wouldn't tend to him. So I take him. And when we go in the room, him never so bad, him clean and so and him firm still, you know. You wouldn't even know him age, for you know short people don't show age. And him tell me say him wife dead fifteen years and that the doctor told him that him time is near. So him say that in five years a woman never touch him. Him never see a woman naked. Just a little old man, you know, that is how him say it. Little and neat, talk nice and decent. Just want see a woman naked one more time. So I take him and take care of him.

"That's how I know that old people stay like that sometimes. Sometimes them have a final journey to make and they need somebody to help them with it, you know, like the song that your father always singing, you know? *Help me make it through the night*."

"What do you mean *take care of him*?"

She looks up at me and there are full tears now. There is a dignity too, and strength—a determination, as if to say, *Fuck you and your high horse*.

But I ignore it. "So you massaged him, you helped?"

"You think it easy, you think is something I like? You know how much cock you have to play with for one day, how much dirty, stinking cock I have to play with? But old people need help. And him never see a woman naked in five years, and me believe him. So I help him."

"You slept with him?"

"I help him."

"You slept with him?"

"Why men always ask question that they can't take the answer, eeh? Why onoo always ask question and onoo know onoo can't deal with the answer?"

"You slept with him!"

"What I should do? Him was dying, him needed me, and him give a big tip."

I cannot eat this food. I cannot look at her anymore. I wish I could cry. I wish I could know what to do. I was not constructed for moments like this.

"Don't it?" she is saying. "Don't it?" Somehow she is still talking to me.

"What?" I whisper.

"Don't it?"

"What!"

"You goin' hate me now, don't it? You goin' scorn me now, don't it?"

TWENTY-TWO

There is a half-filled bottle of my father's pimento wine on the table in the small veranda of the cottage. Beside it is a glass with a finger of wine in it and close to that is a half-smoked spliff. I always figured my father was drinking his pimento wine when he knew he would not be seeing me, but I didn't know he was smoking weed. But what should I expect? I have left him here to be chaperoned by a man who owns a marijuana field on the St. Elizabeth hillside. Father has found his freedom at last. Maybe this is what he has been searching for, a simple life where he can smoke his weed, drink his pimento wine, and die in peace.

My instinct tells me he is not here. But I check the cottage anyway. The rooms are empty and the beds are made. He may have gone to play dominoes or have dinner with his friends. He may have just gone for a walk. Whatever the case, I have no option but to wait on him.

"Sometimes people have to wait long on your father," my mother once told me. I do not remember what it was that led her to say this. But I was sure that he would always come when he promised. Till he did not—and I would be waiting hours, then days, sometimes weeks before some word would come. And every time he promised, I would believe all over again. It seems I have always waited for my father. That was one thing about him I could always depend on.

"You are the lucky one," my mother said. And it was not something new between us. There came a time when I could anticipate when she would say it . . . *You are the lucky one.* Yet I could never understand what luck could be found in a child sitting and waiting on a father who did not come.

The only time I remember him coming the exact time he promised was when I was thirteen years old and I told him I wanted to be a Christian. My mother said he would be dead set against it. When I told him, he did not say much, only that first he wanted to meet with the pastor.

So we arranged a meeting at my home with the pastor, an evangelist, and my mother. Father was a world of friendliness and small talk. So light was the mood that I felt that my mother and I had worried over nothing.

As I remember, we were having a great conversation, talking about school, and my father was boasting about how well I was doing and how my writing had improved. I don't remember if he was even looking at me. Then out of nowhere he asked, "So why you want to be a Christian?"

"To serve the Lord and help my friends serve the Lord."

"Then do you want to be a Christian or serve God?" Before I could answer, he let loose a barrage of questions like bullets from a machine gun. "Do you know what a Muslim is? Do you know what a Hindu is? Do you know what a Catholic is? Why do you want to be a Pentecostal and not an Adventist? Why don't you want to be a Baptist?"

Then he turned to them and asked the very same questions in the very same order and of course they answered him with very patient, knowing, we-were-dying-for-you-to-test-us looks.

"Come now," he said to them with disbelief, "were you aware of all these differences before you were baptized?"

"Yes," they nodded confidently, with poise, waiting for his next question the way a batsman would wait patiently for a ball he had picked before the bowler lifted his hand.

"So why did you become a Pentecostal?"

This was my mother's favorite part, how they were waiting for the question, how they answered him for ten minutes, drawing from scriptures and stories and history. And how impressed and satisfied she was at how they had laid him straight. And how pleased I looked and how happy.

And how my father nodded in wonder as the scripture was expounded to him. Raising his eyebrows at times, widening his eyes. How patiently he sat, sipping his drink. And, when they had finished, how he nodded with the quietness of one who was truly amazed.

Then he lifted his glass, took a drink, crossed his legs, smiled shyly at them, and asked: "If you were aware of all of this before you made your choices, why would you want to deny my son the opportunity to become aware of them and then make up his own mind?"

Well, no, it was the silence that followed that was my mother's favorite part.

"Everton," he then said, "you are too young to make this decision for yourself. So God has given me to you to make them for you. I am more traveled, have read more books, have seen more things than all of these people here have seen. Take it from me, if you never listen to anything else I have to say, let this baptism thing wait. When you are fifteen, if you still want to get baptized, we will talk about it again."

"But suppose God comes before I am fifteen?" I asked.

"I will deal with him. I will take the blame. I will tell him is my fault. I stopped you. Just like Abraham, I will sacrifice myself. You don' worry about a thing." Then he turned to the respected pastor. "Please leave my child alone."

I hated him for six months. He was never there and when he came he crushed my dreams.

I never got baptized then, and I never quite got back to that place where I felt the conviction I had at twelve years old.

The whole episode became a sort of folklore in our house and sometimes it would come up out of the blue, and somewhere at the end or near the end, my mother would look at me and tell me how I am the lucky one. And I would never understand what she meant, for there was nothing about my existence that felt lucky. He was never around; I had to wait on him; I had to solve my own problems of youth and adolescence that boys needed fathers to guide them through.

I never felt lucky, for he and his other children lived in a nice house with a car in the garage: they were the lucky ones, they had him twenty-four hours a day.

But that was how she was, no matter what; when it came to my father, she always found a way to make some sort of an excuse for him. Like the day with the brethren, he had embarrassed her and still she found a way to admire the cleverness with which he had done it.

By the time he comes through the gate of the cottage, I am halfway into a third glass of his pimento wine. And the old dirt-crusted bottle is almost empty. It is a strong wine, and I usually don't drink more than a single glass.

He does not look any different to me as he opens the small gate from the beach. He does not look like a man who is about to die. He is shirtless and a long towel is strung over one shoulder. He has obviously been swimming for he is wearing shorts and, though he is dry, his skin is white from salt and his hair is unruly on his head. No, he does not look as if he is going to die. But he still could be, for anything is possible with this mischievous old man I call my father.

He steps past the pool, sees me, and wavers a bit in recognition.

I have planned on how I will approach him—the various topics are listed in my head like a management presentation. But as he opens his mouth to greet me, I shout at him, "Why you never loved my mother?"

I don't know where it came from. It was never a question on the list in my head. I have never contemplated it. But as he moves onto the veranda without answering, I stagger slightly to my feet. "Answer me right now, Daddy. Why you never loved my mother?"

"I loved your mother," he replied tiredly.

"You never loved her. It is because she was black, wasn't it? Is because she was black!"

"Una is black."

"But Una different, Una almost clear and she come from a different family."

"So now it's not a black thing?" He sits on the side of the veranda close to the door that leads inside. He picks up the bottle and checks to see what's left in it. He gives a sad smile. "Hmm."

"Why you never loved her?" I insist as if there is nothing left in my thought process.

"Do you have something to ask me, son?" he says softly, soberly. "Well, go ahead. I am sitting down and I am listening."

"I have asked you, and you have not answered."

"You sure that is what you want to ask?"

"It was she, wasn't it?" It comes to me as clear as a bell. "It was she, wasn't it, Father?"

"What now?"

"It was she, and it was me. It was she you left in that beauty contest to chase after this woman, wasn't it? She was pregnant with me, wasn't she? Remember, Daddy, I was born in October 1968. The beauty contest was August. She was seven months pregnant with me and you took her out to a beauty contest and left—went to buy her a drink and left her sitting there. You never remembered her for two days. It is she. It was me! Say I am lying, Daddy, tell me I am lying.

"And now you want me to leave my job and follow you all over Jamaica to find that same woman again. The woman who you used to destroy my mother, you using to destroy my career! She probably doesn't even exist now, probably died years ago, and you probably using her as an excuse like you use everybody else. To clear your conscience. Say is lie I'm telling, Daddy, say is lie I'm telling this evening."

"You know you drunk!"

"Do not patronize me, old man! I have asked you a question. And I deserve an answer."

"You asked several questions and you haven't given me a chance to answer any."

"Well, answer me now."

"I do not have to explain anything to you." He makes to rise.

But I am close to him and my anger is real. "Do not move until you answer me."

"And what you goin' do? Punch me out? Lay me down?" He waves me away and stands anyway. "I walk miles of life already, so what you goin' do now, big son? I walk miles already and every inch of those days have some part that I don't like—that I wish never went the way it went. Every life has regrets. But one thing I never regret is your mother. You think you know the story, but you don't know."

"I know." I am beginning to tremble. "For I lived with her all my life and I see her wait her life for you. You think I don't know that day after day and night after night you sneaked in and out of her bedroom? You know how many nights I lay in my bed and wish you would stay, that I would wake up the next day and see your car parked there?"

"Everton . . ." There is exasperation in his voice, but guilt is shining through. "Everton, you know nothing."

"I know more than you think I do."

"Concepts, that is what you know. You don't know a thing. This is not some marketing thing with concepts that you young people talk about these days. Everything for you is some theory. Some concept that you sell, ideas that you can't touch that mean millions of dollars. This is man-and-woman story between your mother and me. Is not no damn concept in your head. That is not how life goes."

"I am efficient; I think logically, things must happen in a certain order."

"That thing you call precision and efficiency is anger and resentment."

"I know the difference."

"You know the difference. You so angry you can't see the good in anything. You suspect everything first and when the truth embarrasses you sometimes, you just shut up or move to another suspicion."

"It is my right to be angry."

"I see men get heart attack at a younger age than you."

"Tell me about my mother."

"It is not you damn business. Ask me, Everton, what you want to ask me. Tell me what you really want to say."

"I am asking you: why did you not love my mother?"

"This is a waste of time." He makes to leave.

"I am still talking to you."

"Stop using your mother as a damn excuse, boy." He shakes the empty bottle and almost slams it onto the table, but seems to make an effort to control himself. Then he casts it into the yard. It shatters on the concrete at the side of the pool. He is a stubborn old man who has no intention of answering me. And I am half-drunk, tired, and feeling as if I have just spent ten minutes spitting into the wind. So when he walks away into the cottage, I make no effort to stop him. Instead, I move over to sit on the wall and lay my legs along its length.

He only went to get a shirt and to find another bottle of his wine. He emerges now filling a clean glass as he comes. He stands against the column near my outstretched feet with both drink and bottle in his hand.

"As a child you was always like that, you know. Nobody never know what you was thinking. Not that you was a quiet child or anything. You could play marble no dickance though, boy."

"So I hear."

"And it is true, you could play marbles better than anybody. Holly couldn't match you and all you tried to teach him he wouldn't learn. He could beat the boys near the yard but when you came by you were the boss. I remember one weekend you came and won a whole Milo pan of marbles from him. He cried so much, you had to give them back before you left.

"But there was something about you though. Sometimes you would be just silent so and then you'd ask a question that floored everybody. Just out of the blue so. My mother used to call you Little Jesus. But Una, she knew you. Maybe that is why you two get along so well. She would say you are a sponge. You take in everything, *everything*, she used to say.

"And that was the thing. Since you were small I always talked to you like a big person. I took it for granted that you knew and understood everything because you were always like that. But Una told me that one day I would have to answer a lot of questions."

"Why didn't you come to my high school graduation?"

He pauses at that. Maybe I have thrown him again.

"I was with the minister," he finally says. "The minister needed my advice."

"Your son needed your presence."

"I do not remember why I did not make it to the one at the university though."

"You had to go to Meagan's high school graduation."

"That is what I told you? You never complained about anything. I do not even remember that."

"I remember because she had invited me to hers. And I had mine to do. And no one came to mine. Except Mother, that is. But that was okay, I had a girlfriend by then, and I had discovered ways to deal with disappointments that were more pleasurable."

He moves aside to put the bottle on the table. Then he spins and points across the yard with his filled glass. "I'm not good at catching things. I'm not good at seeing things. You see, when I use to come down here, a little old man name Bennett owned the whole of this beach side going straight across. He offered it to me one day for little and nothing; thirteen acres right along the seaside. I could have written him a check right there, that is how little he wanted for it . . . nothing. His family was moving to England and he couldn't find the fare. He never wanted the land anyway because you couldn't plant anything on it. So he practically gave it to me.

"You know what I told him? *I don't want it, can't even mulch on it*. Now this land is going for what, four million dollars an acre now—the whole thing is about what now, one, one point one million US dollars? Now I would be a millionaire. You still can't even mulch on it." He shakes his head.

"Mulch!"

"Yes. Because the land is so dry down here the farmers cut the grass and cover the roots of the plants. You remember, I show you the other day, the grass traps the moisture and when it rots it becomes fertilizer. This dry grass mulching is unique to St. Elizabeth."

"So you prefer to do things the hard way. That is what you are saying. You make wrong choices. The piece you kept is still not developed?"

"I know my failures, son."

"What does that mean?"

"Nothing. Who knows these things? Who knows what makes anybody grow, what makes anything a success? Sometimes you can just make a judgment. You don't have to be right all the time. Who knows what makes anything grow? Maybe if the damn land wasn't so dry, we would have enough water to grow everything."

"Thanks, Daddy," I shoot back. "I am rotting from the very thing that made me grow. That is what you are saying. What is it? Envy? I envied my brothers. Hate? I hated my life. I am a rotten, bitter person. That is what you are trying to say?"

"I am saying that anybody can make mistakes. But you never wanted for anything. You never ask for anything you never get."

"You were never around."

"That is what I'm telling you. You never look like you weren't all right."

"It is a parent's duty to know the difference. Mother knew. Una knew."

"I don't see everything the way everybody sees it. And you never use to say anything. You smiled, you laughed, you said, *What happen, old man?* You show more affection for me than anybody else. And you absorb and you absorb and you grow. And you never use to say anything."

"And now it is my fault."

"I never said that, but you never use to say anything."

"Trust me, Daddy, believe me, it would not have made difference. You would have had a smile and an answer for everything I tell you. You were always like that, fast and charming."

"But who's to tell?"

"Who's to tell indeed. Even now, I am talking and you are not listening. You want me to ask the questions you think I should ask."

"No, I want you to stop hiding your feelings and using your mother for an excuse. If you have something to tell me, just tell me." He swallows the wine in one gulp and sits on the seat to face me. Now we are both filled with liquor and bravery—staring at each other, square, honest, and fearful. And I do not know what to tell him.

"So now after all these years you finally have time for me, that is it? Now we are on a trip and you are trying to make up for lost time, luring me down here 'bout you going to look for woman, tricking me. You have time to listen now."

"You never use to say anything."

"What you wanted me to say? What you want me to tell you now?"

"Everton, if you hate your father, tell me." He does not give me space to avoid his stare, and I feel tears welling up inside me.

"I don't . . . I don't know, I don't know, I just don't

know if I love you. I don't know how to feel about you, Daddy, I don't know if I love you."

"Who knows about these things?" His voice is soft and hoarse as he reaches to fill our glasses with the biting pimento wine.

TWENTY-THREE

We sit in silence for a while. I have moved a bit to take the filled glass from him. It is not a bad or uncomfortable silence. It seems we have come some ways, as if we have climbed a slope and are resting till it's time to climb the next slope ahead. Tired men then, maybe, but also men who have come through a battle and have been drawn closer by the fury of it. After a while he reaches for his half-finished spliff, rolls its end tight, and lights it. I do not make any effort to stop him. Nothing in me wants to at this time.

I read somewhere that aging is like another country. As if on growing old we enter a brand-new territory, unexplored, a place where there are no words from those who have already gone ahead, for none has come back from that place. It is another place, another world that we step into across the great divide, and we are explorers there. We are new there, children again, discovering a place for which there is no map, a place that ends in our end. *Once a man, twice a child . . .* that is what Angela said.

"May I ask you a question?" I finally say.

"Yeah, what is it?"

"Are you dying? Are you dying, Daddy, and is this some last trip you want to do?"

"Why you ask a thing like that?"

"Just answer me. Is this a last trip, are you terminally ill?"

"Not that I know of, God not so merciful."

"You are sure?"

"I am sure."

"What do you want then, for there must be something that you need? Why come on this trip?"

"Old people need many things, young boy. Many things for which there isn't time enough."

"Yes, but why this place? Why the southeast? Why this trip? What do you want to do?"

"When Una said you would have questions, I don't think she imagined how many." He is looking like Caesar again. "This is the kind of land that grows on you. I use to come here or sit on the hill and just look out."

"So if you have a wish now, where would you like to go, what would you like to see?"

"I have seen everything already that there is to see."

"What would be the three top places you would like to see again?"

"You can't put numbers on things like that, Everton. You can't just pick things out of a hat like that. There are so many places. But you know what I would like to see. I have never been on the Appleton tour. I have never seen how they make rum. I always promised myself that before I died, I would go on the Appleton tour. You see, they never use to have it during my time."

"I bet you could show them a thing or two about brewing," I laugh.

"Ahh, see what I mean?" He drags the weed and the smoke surrounds me.

"Daddy . . ." I drop from my perch and turn to look at him. "Daddy, tell me one thing."

"What?"

"If I take you on this trip, if I take you to see your favorite places, would you come home? Would you leave and come home to your wife?"

"You want all kinda promises about all kinda things. Son, life is not a business deal. Suppose I never live to see another day. I couldn't come. Why you don't just take things a day at a time? I don't have any promises to give you 'bout two days down the road. Day by day is better, son."

"So let's do it then, Daddy. Let us see your country a bit. Would you come then?"

"What about you?"

"What about me?"

"Aren't you goin' see anything? You can't just go through life this fast—always planning ahead while the present just pass you. For instance, we are down here and all you thinking about is getting back to work and seeing some American woman play tennis."

"So what will it be?"

He seems disappointed at the answer, but I am getting tired. "Well, as you say, we will see. After three days, we will see."

Finally, some kind of commitment from him—if that is what I may call this response. But I am tired and my eyelids are heavy. "Ah, Daddy, you tire me out tonight. I am going to bed, I think you should too."

"No, you go in. You look like you drunk. I want to sit out here a little. I want to look out."

"You mean you want to smoke your weed."

"I want to look out. See the stars. See the place when the moon shines on it."

As I rise to leave him, I pat his shoulder and I can't help but ask the final question that lingers in my mind, has been lingering there all evening. "Tell me the truth, old man: it is a story, isn't it? This woman—this thirty-five-year love affair—it's a story, isn't it? I mean, I know she exists and so, but the story is a story . . . isn't it?"

"Yes," he shakes his head without looking at me, "a real story."

"Just a story, no true? Just something you make up so we could travel the coast together, right?"

"Does it matter?" He drains the last of the wine from the crusted bottle. "Does it matter what kinda story?"

And no, I guess it does not. I steady myself by tightening my grip on his shoulders. He is not as strong and firm and sinewy beneath the shirt as I remember. And as I leave and reach for the door with a tipsy hand, I can swear I hear him start to sing softly, the chorus of the old Kris Kristofferson song: "*I don't care who's right or wrong, I don't try to understand. Let the devil take tomorrow. Lord, tonight I need a friend . . .*"

So I close the door behind me with a quiet hand, but even as I do, the words I have heard him sing so many times seem to follow me to my room: "*Yesterday is dead and gone and tomorrow's out of sight. And it's sad to be alone. Help me make it through the night . . .*"

It is a hard thing when those you feel are as solid as rocks soften beneath your very touch. All of a sudden I must rescue the person I thought was Superman. Sixty-seven years old—three years from the three score and ten the Bible talks about. *Once a man, twice a child,* Angela had said. My father is entering his second childhood. He now has needs he himself does not even know how to fulfill. He now has fears, dreams, and contemplations I cannot fathom. He sees forms and visions and people in shadows that do not exist. But I, at least, I need to understand. *Help me make it through the night*. And now the fear in me is whether or not I can surmount these feelings that have been awakened tonight, and still be there for my father. But I will try, if that is what he wants. I will try as best as I can to be here for him.

TWENTY-FOUR

Rain has finally come to southern St. Elizabeth and for a while it seems the earth is too hard to absorb it. So it kicks the rain back up with the rust-colored dust and the walls and everything is splattered red, from the feet of the skittering stray dogs to the walls of buildings, the roots of trees, and the wheels and skirting of my Pathfinder.

Father says it will not last because the sky is not half as black as it should be if the showers are to be taken seriously. Therefore he has no intention of aborting his tour of the Appleton Estates. So after breakfast we pull out from the cottage to join the rain as it sweeps down the hill in the light breeze like the long straw skirt of a limbo dancer.

Now, I do not know everything, though there are those who will say I act as if I do. But I am a practical man and I believe that things must be logical and explainable. So forgive me if I do not know how to take this day as it unfolds.

For instance, I do not know why I turn toward Ballards Valley this morning as we head out, despite my father's mischievous smiles. And I cannot explain the feelings that come over me as she pushes her head through the window to ask what it is that makes us stop. Nor have I fully gotten a hang of how I feel when she finally skips from her house in tight jeans and a T-shirt that seems to have lost most of the bottom half. This strange sensation in my chest as she pauses, just to give me half a smile, before bounding into the outstretched arms of my father, is still a mystery to me.

I enjoy the ride through Malvern and its sweeping views of the hills. The air so fresh and cool it burns the throat at ten o'clock. Father insists I keep the windows open so I may feel the difference when we get to our next stop. I do and am impressed as we swoop from the crisp clear air of the hills of St. Elizabeth to the teaming sauna of the hottest town in Jamaica, Santa Cruz.

She makes a difference, though, in the van the moment she enters. Much like the change in a bachelor's apartment after a woman has moved in for a week, like the space had been missing something all along.

We buy snow cones in Santa Cruz, a treat I had not seen in years. I am fascinated by the little man standing over a block of ice grating his shear across it like a carpenter shaving wood. He snaps his shear open, stuffs the ice into a paper cup, bringing back thirty-year-old memories of ice cream mixed with syrup and sheared ice. Everything everywhere is sold in plastic bags and sanitized boxes these days; yet here in this hot musky town, a man still sells snow cones from shaved ice.

Father's stories seem more hilarious than they did before. There is a new ring to them, though I know he was never chased by a crocodile through the Black River in '75 because the scar he shows on his foot is one from that old accident he had when his car crashed in the cane field ages ago. But still I laugh as he tells his story. Angela and I listen attentively as he relates the history of the Appleton Estates, that it covers more than eleven thousand acres; and that it was the Caribbean planters who invented rum, which back then was called Kill Devil—the pure stuff is called John Crow Batty. That the same Ward who built the Ward Theatre in Kingston is the nephew who makes the rum: J. Wray & Nephew. I had never heard that before, but I do not question it. I find I am more patient with my father today.

We stop two miles or so in from Lacovia, and I watch in consternation as he haggles vociferously with a child no more than ten years old over a bucket of mangoes. At the price being suggested, we could take the bucket to Kingston and quadruple our investment. Yet on hearing the boy's offer my father jumps from the van, points to a neighboring pasture, and yells, "So much? Look at the tree, you never even had to climb it!"

And though I am on the child's side, I keep silent as he stands his ground and leans against the bucket like an old pro, while his friends gather to watch the barter. They have obviously done this before, and he hopes to be a hero by the time he has finished with my father. So he points to his friends and insists that they all need a cut of the money.

"Cut nothing!" my father yells and gestures to another bucket. "Whose bucket that? I will buy that one instead."

But they will not be divided and another calls out, "All of us bucket, sir."

A little old man sitting off to the side catches my eye and smiles.

"I am not giving you one dollar more than a hundred," Father counters, trying to intimidate the child. "What is your name?"

"Garfield, sir. And how you feel your pretty young daughter goin' think, sir?" The child motions at Angela. "Plus, take some for you grandchildren."

"You think I eat common mango at my yard?" Father reaches into his pocket to pay the child his $150 and have him throw the whole bucket into the back of my van.

My only concern is whether they have been washed. But he ignores me, rubs the head of the child, congratulates him on being a good businessman, then demands his brawta. The child, flushed with victory, beckons to another, who reaches into the bushes for a large mango that can hardly fit into his palm, and gives it to Angela with a smile. "The brawta is for you." So Father threatens him with a smile and comments on how old men never get anything.

We are off again toward the green hills of northern St. Elizabeth. *They* are *eating mangoes in the car. There is juice on the upholstery*. But I find I am not complaining. Neither about the mango juice nor the long stories my father is telling nor the noise they make when the mood shifts to singing country music and we discover that she loves the old Marty Robbins ballads I used to frown on. Soon I am eating a mango and singing along as well.

Maybe it is because it is his day. Maybe it is something else.

This side of St. Elizabeth is greener, and as we cruise along, I realize there is a hint of Hampshire here. For the pastures are big and wide, and the sugar cane finally appears, along with bamboos and gigantic mango trees. There are coconuts too, and large poinciana trees spread and dot the bushes with their flowers. Their arm-length pods litter the roadsides in places. The river is long and winding and bamboo lines its banks where the grass is lush and green. Father points to an occasional wild pink queen-of-flower flashing by. And everything sweeps back, back onto the massive range of Cockpit Country.

I catch her eyes in the rearview mirror as the two of them move through the Marty Robbins catalog and find the old favorite, *"Out in the West Texas town of El Paso, I fell in love with a Mexican girl."* And the magic in her eyes makes me join in at the end of the line when Robbins whirls the tune to a breathtaking high. Angela keeps her eyes there in the mirror till the song ends and winks at me when Father roars something about a big iron on his hips. This too is a song I like, about a marshal walking into town to get a famous outlaw with his big iron. But her wink, I am sure, is loaded with more than just the innocence of the lyrics, and I feel my insides churn. Then she turns mischievously and gives all her attention to my father.

And that is what I am talking about, for I am not sure of the feelings I am having when she stares at me, nor how I feel when she lavishes attention on my father.

So we come to Appleton. And she is a child rushing from the vehicle as it stops to find a water pipe near a massive rum bottle in the center of a perfect green lawn. The pipe is off to the side and we wash the mango juice from our hands and dry them on a large red towel my father pulls from his bag. He leans on the massive bottle and savors the scent of rotting and boiling cane being turned to rum.

"You can't wait, eh?" I ask him.

"Wait on what? Why wait? I am here."

So we take the cobblestoned walkway and enter a

building painted in orange, pink, and green. Here the reception area opens up to a sprawling bar. Father's face lights up. He heads straight for the bar and orders a sip of everything.

The bartender smiles and tells him he will have to pay for the tour first, and even then, all he will get is one complimentary rum punch made with a sampling of the rums made by Appleton.

"No sampling across the board?" Father shouts.

"After the tour," the bartender grins.

"Oh, so there is a *full* sampling."

"Yes, there is," says a portly, smiling guide who appears at our side. "There is a sampling of everything we make at the end of the tour."

Father immediately begins quizzing the guide, questioning his credentials as if he were interviewing him for a job. After a while, satisfied that the guide knows his business, Father drops in that he himself is a brewer of sorts. "Of wines, pimento wines . . . but of course," he winks, "the methods and formulae are top secret."

The guide winks back and they are at once old friends.

So it is his day.

The tour is long and filled with people of every sort, from college students working on their chemistry paper to tourists from Britain and North America, walking in the hot day with jugs of rum punch, half-naked and burnt from the sun. Fifteen minutes in and I am getting bored, but Father is like a pig in mud. He is ably assisting the guide in his tour, walking beside him, in front of him, or moving over to the side to expand a point to a group that may have strayed too near the periphery.

I am thinking more and more of the little tavern I saw off to the right of the perfect lawn at the front. It seems like a good place to wait on my father. I make my way through the throng to tell him where I'll be. He sees me coming and holds up his hand to make me pause, then puts an index finger across his lips as he nods toward the tour guide who is in the middle of some explanation.

"You mean someone steals the rum at night?" This from a bearded white man at the front.

"No," the tour guide replies, "we like to think the angels take it."

"The angels?"

"Yes, once we leave the rum to age," he points to the massive copper casks that store the liquor, "no matter how we fill it, when we get back years later, 10 or 15 percent is missing from the top."

"Really!"

"Yes. The angels take it. We call it the angels' share."

"The angels' share?"

"Yes!"

"It seems part of the natural process of evaporation and fermentation." The man insists on spoiling a good story.

"No, the angels take it!" Father shouts at him, rolls his eyes, shakes his head, and winks at me.

The crowd chuckles at the exchange.

I point toward the lawn away from the tour. *Tired*, I mouth at him. But he is still absorbed in the brewery talk around him. He is in a world of his own and nothing I do now will diminish the tour for him. He is happy, he is in his element.

* * *

So here I am, sitting in an old tavern that could have been a Henry Morgan drinking hole. Inside, all the furniture is made of the dark wooden casks in which the rum is aged. The tables are casks with rounded tops, and the chairs are casks with half the top cut away and the cover pushed down to make the seat.

As I sit, a large turkey, with its body a million glistening feathers, prances past to jump clumsily across a small pond where an old water wheel is turning.

It is Angela who has chased it. She stands there in the space where there could have been a wooden door, but there is none. Laughing gaily, she skips to plop into the dark barrel seat beside me. She sits on her down-turned palms and sprawls her feet so that the round of her legs is pronounced.

"Hey," she says. "Lord, you father can talk, eeh? Him know everything."

"That's my father, that's my old man."

"You tired?"

"Yes."

We talk a bit of things I do not expect. And the time passes and the wind is soft from off the fields. I ask her if she has told her mother about what she does for a living.

She blinks at me and asks why I am still thinking about that at a time like this.

And I do not want to tell her it was only conversation. She may feel I am taking her feelings lightly. So I tell her I had imagined it was what she is on her way to do.

That makes her pause for a while, then she asks what

good it would do. "And anyway, she probably senses it already."

"How is that?" I ask her.

"Well, I think she know I wasn't no waiter or hospitality worker. Plus I don't hide it. I just don't tell her everything. It matter though?"

And that is the question I keep asking myself: whether or not it matters what she is and what she does or did with her life. Or what it is that I would have expected her to do in the face of her circumstances—conditions that I can hardly imagine, however graphic her descriptions may be.

There is no music in the old tavern, there is no intimacy. It is an old dingy place and there is a film of dust on everything; yet somehow I get the feeling that we are closing in on each other. And I don't know how much I want this. Though my feelings tell me one thing, my mind tells me that she is a woman who needs more than I can promise her.

After a while we leave the dimness of the ancient tavern to stroll the grounds in a sort of easy silence. The beautiful lawns are dotted with relics of older times: metal pots in which the sugar was boiled a hundred years ago; old buses and trolleys that may have carried cane and people before I was born. Then, at the edge of the estate, where the immediate factory adjoins the vast spread of sugar land now spurting young green cane, we see the large coach of an old train now painted in the Appleton colors. We climb aboard and from there we can look out at the extent of the Appleton estate as it spreads eastward, taking up the whole Nassau Valley. It hogs the rain-shadowed expanse of the valley like an oversized child lying casually in the lap of the Mocho mountain range. All that is left for other habitation is only on the periphery.

It is here that she holds me.

I am leaning against the rail with her beside me. And as we lean out the window, I feel her body shift as it searches to find the space where I am angled from the side of the train. She slips in like a wedge and I ease back to let her come. Now she is firmly into me and reaches behind to wrap a hand around my neck. I am not sure what to do with my own hands. I have one on the windowsill but the other is loose at my side. She pulls it against her, finding the pocket of her jeans, and slips it in to rest, warm, against her legs.

As she settles into me, I grow hard against her. The harder I get the more she seems to press against me. Time passes, I am sure, though I cannot tell how much. Nor do I know how many words have passed between us because they are few and do not need to be many more. I wish she were naked or wore a skirt so I could extend my fantasies to their natural conclusion. For it all seems so natural that we should stand here locked together, looking out at the vast estates, and there is nothing about us now that could ever be out of place.

It is close to twilight when Father comes, drunk from testing rum, to tell us it is time to go.

She has been invited for dinner and I am not surprised. "Everton will take you home," is the extent of the invitation.

He is in the best mood that I can recall.

It seems the tour and the liquor have brought a new man to us. I have seen him mischievous and wild, but I have never really seen him like this. He is like a man in a new suit who suddenly remembers there is a proud way to stand.

No sooner are we back than he wants to go to the beach. He wants to take a short swim before we go to Tara for dinner. I am exhausted from the trip and I do not feel like the beach right now. But Angela is just as excited as he is. She says yes to everything he wishes. So I have to rummage through the cabin to find clothing for her. There are no shorts that will fit, but we find a large T-shirt. She changes into it, rolls her jeans past her knees, and walks away with him, carrying a folding chair that appears out of nowhere, to the black sand beach beyond the fence.

He takes her hand and pulls her to join him as he lies back on the chair. She sits and leans her head against the thigh of his outstretched leg. He pours from the crusted bottle of pimento wine and when the cups are filled he drops the bottle to the sand beside them. Before he drinks, he tips his glass and drops a bit of liquid on the sand. *The angels' share*, I think. My marketing mind freezes the picture of them sitting there framed by the wire fence with the open gate in the middle, a few wild weeds at the edge. It could be an ad for his pimento wine.

But there is also a strange tingling in me—hotness behind my eyes, a burning in my chest, and confusion in my head. It is not possible. I refuse to believe that what I feel is jealousy over a *massager* as she leans into the loose embrace of my sixty-seven-year-old father.

TWENTY-FIVE

There is a hammering at my door. It seems I will not have much sleep tonight. I do not want to get up; I burrow my head into the pillows in an effort to get back to the exact spot in my dreams where I lay down in a waterfall whose cascades are so soft they roll like balls of feathers against my skin . . . and my head is resting on the breast of an angel.

But the knock is incessant. I throw the pillow aside and am surprised to see that the light of morning is flooding the room. I must have slept like a lamb. But still I wish for more.

He is standing there, framed in the doorway, with a wicked grin on his face and his little book of poetry in his hand.

"Yes?" I ignore the buddy-buddy smirk. "You are dressed already?"

"It is daylight. You climbed the mountain last night, man. You need to be fit for these things."

"What time is it?"

"Does it matter? Come walk with me."

"Now?"

"You see any other time?" There is a hint of self-consciousness in his eyes.

"How all of a sudden you want me to walk with you? I never see anyone walk with you before."

"I want to tell you about your mother."

"I see."

I dress in a daze of sorts. For this has come straight out of nowhere and it throws me. But I find a pair of shorts from somewhere and all I need now is a T-shirt and there are many in the drawers. In less than two minutes I join him silently on the veranda.

"Why do you always walk with that book?" I ask him as we head for the beach.

"Poetry, son, poetry is the music of the soul."

"But why do you walk with it? How can you read while you walk? I never see you read while you walk."

"You've never seen me walk."

"I have seen you walk."

"Well if you ever see me read and walk, then that is when you see me walk."

"All right, old man, you are in a mood for parables today."

The sun is already on the sand, though the last of the morning breeze is still here, and some of the predawn gray lingers way over to the left where the sea curves away from the craggy hills in the distance.

As we stroll along the beach, the light is gold upon his head. He is silent for a while. I figure he is working out an entry into the topic. I wait. I walk with him and I wait. I will not help. He does not need me to. And eventually he starts speaking.

"You know how I meet your mother? In church. There were four sisters. They used to call them Johnson's four flowers. Four of them and all of them use to dress like beauty queens to go to church every Sunday. All the while in the back of my mind I always wanted a church girl. My father drilled that into my head till I must have seen it as a natural thing to be. *Get a church girl, boy—a nice country church girl. They are faithful, they can cook, and they don't ask too much questions. Aahh.*"

I let his memory and the morning work on him. For this story is not a light one, and it seems it is taking an effort from him.

"She was the second-oldest one. You see . . ." He pauses again. "You see, ahh, boy." Now he turns to me. "You know, last night I was sitting on the veranda looking out and I say to myself, *I must talk to Everton about this.* And I worked it out in my head what and what I would tell you. How we would walk the beach and by the time the walk is done, the story would be finished. But it not easy. You think it easy to tell you about your mother? A whole heap of it is feelings. Just feelings—and some of it is hard."

"Maybe you are trying to tell too much. I don't need to hear everything. Just a short version. Why you treated her like that? I don't think she ever understood why you never wanted her. I could see it in her. She never understood that."

"All right, you know why I married Una?" he tries again.

"That is obvious."

"No, it is not what you think. I married her because she did not need me."

"She never needed you."

"Yes. She never needed me. When a man wants to take chances in life, he wants to know that he can fail. And if you have a woman who depend on you for everything, then you can't fail, because you have nobody to support you if you fall. You understand?"

"My mother was not a burden. She was independent."

"But she was," he blurts. "Listen, Everton, you realize that your mother is the greatest cook in the family and she has the least education. The two youngest ones have education but can't cook at all. In those days parents used to make definite decisions about their children. They decided early who would go to school, who must clean house and take care of them, who must get good husband. That is what parents do. Your mother, from very early, was chosen to clean house and cook. She was never given the opportunity to go to school. Her parents chose the two youngest ones to go to school. They decided who they would spend money on."

"What are you saying?"

"I am saying that your mother represented a tradition that sees a man in only two lights: feed him and give him work to do. I am not that kind of man. I can take care of myself. I don't need a woman to do that. And that made her feel out of place."

"But you left her at the beauty contest. You deserted her. That is why she left you."

"Well . . ." He seems sad. "I did leave her and I am ashamed. But I am trying to tell you that we were never going to make it. She would have needed me too much and I could not have handled it."

"What kind of person leaves someone who needs them? Isn't that the time when you bind closer?"

"I saw what it did to my father. Every time he came home from work, my mother was just sitting there wanting money. And when his salary was not enough, half our needs had still not been met. So he spent half his time away from us. Because we needed him, he was our only source, and he knew he was not enough. We sucked every drop of blood from him and it was not enough. If only my mother had had a job, half a job, we would have been a better family. But she sat there and wanted more money, even when he had none. Forcing him to do stupid things to get money, to compromise himself. Borrow, worked several jobs, humiliate himself, while she sat there doing nothing but waiting for him to come home. I knew that sometimes he came home because he just couldn't do any better. He wanted to be musician, but his music died in him, he withered as a man, he could not venture after his dreams because we needed him too much. One person should not need another so, Everton.

"Some people feel that is what a man is for: bread-winner at all cost. I'm not made that way. Your mother was a bit like that. When she wanted money, she never cared what I did to get it or where I got it from. If I gave her the last cent, empty my wallet and show her, in ten minutes she would ask me for money again. It is just how she was. Her mother grew her and taught her how to take care of a man, not how to help him. That is how she made me feel at the time and it scared me to death."

"Then why didn't you tell her?"

"It is not easy to tell somebody something like that."

"So you take her to a beauty contest, leave with the first woman you find? You run away and leave her sitting there like a fool so she could get the message? *That*, Daddy, is an excuse? You know what you are sounding like, Daddy? A man who is looking for good things everywhere else but where he is for fear of something he himself does not even know or understand. That is how you sound."

"All right, Everton. Since you don't want to come off of that, since you think it so symbolic, let me explain this beauty contest thing. I did not leave her because I wanted to show her anything. I left because a woman blew my mind."

I remain silent.

"Right, a woman blew my mind and I am not ashamed of that. A man can live ten lifetimes and never experience that," he says into the sun. "And even now, when I think about it—every time I think about it I realize, I would do the same thing again. Not because it right, but because I know I would still not be able to control myself."

That brings the memory of my hardness pressed into the small of a back on an old train at Appleton. I try to blink the guilt from my eyes.

"Yes, I left her there, yes." He nods violently. "Yes, I leave her but I never went there expecting to do it. Is just how life went. I see the woman and the moment we start talk, is as if the world just change. It is as if everything different—as if the night started over, man. And people would think that we left and went to do something. We just talked, you know. We left Sombrero and just talked; we walked around the racecourse and we sat and we just talked. Talked and laughed till morning came. It was in her lap I dropped asleep and when she woke me and said she had to go home, it was morning like now. And it was then I realized I couldn't risk telling her that I had left a woman and come with her. I never wanted her to feel that I would probably do the same to her one day. So I walked her home, and she invited me for breakfast and I stayed. And I never left her house till eleven that morning, and if she had asked me to stay till night I wouldn't have left at all. And by that time, it never made sense going to look for your mother again. I wouldn't know what to tell her."

"But you leave that one too."

"I know, but it was for a different reason."

"Oh, I forgot, she was not your level. She would have held you back."

"You asked about your mother."

"You know what, Father?" I say to him. "You are right, I really don't care about your secrets anymore." I had wanted to hear so much, to pin him against a wall and demand that he give me some kind of restitution. But now it is bitter as cerasee in my mouth. I am not sure I want to hear more. What I really want to do is punch him flat on the ground. This vain, cruel person is not the father I adored. This is not the truth or honesty I wanted. But I asked for it and he has given it to me.

"You said you wanted to hear about your mother," he insists.

"All right, Father," I wrap his shoulder with my arm, "I get the picture now, all right. But you have hurt a few women in your life."

"I know."

"And you are hurting one now."

"I know, but I can't do better. This is something I must do. You understand that, don't you?"

"I understand that you can't run from one woman to another when one does not suit what you want at a particular time."

"I am not leaving Una."

"Tell her that."

"She will be all right. You don't worry about Una."

Then, after a while, after a short silence, as we watch the sun finally emerging, he reaches to press against my hand with his open palm. He may have sensed that I had started to drift.

"Your mother and I, we worked it out before she died. We were good friends."

"I can imagine." I am not sure I care how that sounds.

"But we did."

"But did you tell her why?"

"We worked it out."

"Well, I lived with her and I am not sure if she knew, till the day she died. And I don't think that matters now. Do you? All that is gone now, Daddy. All that is gone."

It is a hard thing to say, but I do not feel the need to pull any punches right now. He too has said some hard things, and even though I had asked for them to be said, the impact of his words is no less.

". . . So it is tomorrow then."

"What is happening tomorrow?" I am drawn back to him. His hands are in his pockets and he is looking out onto the sea. We are casually at ease. He has made some point I did not hear.

"In Montego Bay, we will meet tomorrow."

"Meet who in Montego Bay tomorrow?"

"Hope, she is coming. It looks like we had the flights mixed up."

Just when I think it is over, just when I think he is slowing to some level of sobriety, he jabs me like a relentless toothache. I am a cup that is filled to its brim, I am the bucket that is taken to the well once too often, I am the camel just before the feather breaks its back. If he were a child, I would lift him and shake sense into him, but he is a stubborn old man and all I can do is tremble with rage and face him with as much composure as I can muster.

"Why are you doing this to yourself, Daddy? She is gone. It is over, old man. She is not coming. You are sixty-seven years old but you acting like a schoolboy on a date. You are like me when I stood up at the Carib Theatre, waiting for the girl who told me to meet her there. You remember me standing there half an hour after the movie finished and she still nowhere in sight? What you tell me the evening when you passed by chance and saw me standing there? What did you tell me when you were giving me the ride home, you remember? You told me: *Everton, if she is half an hour late, she not coming again.* Daddy, if she is thirty-five years late, she not coming again."

He is not impressed. He stuffs his book into his pocket and turns toward the cottage. "You don't know a damn thing what you talking about. She will be there tomorrow. Are you coming or not?"

"Coming where?"

"For the breakfast—you weren't listening? We have to go back to the cottage now. I invited a few people over before we leave. Have a kind of breakfast and so. Say thanks for everything."

He constantly amazes me. These mood swings must be part of getting old. He speaks and moves so I have no chance to shape my feelings into a response.

"You go on ahead without me, old man, I need to be by myself awhile. You are right, maybe I should walk more . . . walk a bit and clear my head."

* * *

She is waiting for me right there on the edge of the morning where the sun slants from the beach to slice the veranda into two. Right there on the edge of it; sitting half in the light with her legs stretched out and hanging in the sun.

I do not feel surprised. I do not really know how I feel, and nothing about her is out of place.

Last night when I took her home to Ballards Valley she was so tired she slept the whole way. But how early must she have awakened to be here by this time?

"Hey."

"Wha' happen. You go walk."

"Yes."

I touch her hand. Her fingers are soft . . . warm against mine. And she rises as if I had pulled her to her feet, though the contact is as light as the sun against her skin. She follows me into the cabin.

There is a natural flow to things. I pause without knowing and she is as tight and soft against me as yesterday. She is a mix of delicious oils, fresh spring water, and a hint of cinnamon.

I sense the softness in her face, the tenderness in her look, but I do not see her eyes clearly, I do not know what they are telling me. But I know the moment before me as if I am already living there. The space beyond this instant is so clear and tenderly scripted, I can feel every sensation even before I enter it, I can see where we are going, and I can feel every emotion and every reaction to everything she does to me . . . there in that moment before me . . . every touch of her fingers, every boring of her naked breast into me, every grate, scrape, and drag of pubic hair; I feel the deepest, softest part of her wrap the hardest part of me. In that moment I am there already and every inch of my body is alive and even though we are now not touching, we are tied with energy as raw as a magnetic field.

The spaces close completely. She has merged into me, and I am pressed against a wall. Everything in me rises to meet the moment as it comes. I close my eyes as time converges. But the moment pushes back—trapping me against the thinnest edge of in-between. And something deep inside me hesitates, pauses, holds. And everything in me grows still and quiet, though I have not willed it to, as if a hurricane has just been envisioned, simulated, and has subsided. I pull her head softly against my neck as the moment slips away.

"We must go," I whisper, "we cannot be late for Father's party."

TWENTY-SIX

Leave it to my father to be in St. Elizabeth for less than a week and have enough people for a send-off breakfast. It is just after eight and already his friends have arrived. Angela has joined Tara in the kitchen. They are frying fish that came out of nowhere. Dumplings and other St. Elizabeth breakfast delights are being prepared simultaneously. The liquor is out early. Beer and Guinness are already cold. Rum and whiskey have already joined my father's pimento wine on the pool deck. Father is seated in his shorts with a leg in the pool while his friends laze around with him. There is a faint smell of weed about. A domino table is off to the right of the pool under a large mango tree, where Tom from Memories sits with another man lazily pushing the pieces around. A table with fruits sits in the middle of everything—cut melon, peeled oranges, ripe mangoes of every kind, sliced pineapples—just there for the taking, the munching, dog stoning, whatever one wants to do with fruits.

What is it about this man that people love so much?

Willy slaps my shoulder and motions to the domino table. "Come mek we mash up them boys." He smiles his magnanimous smile. He could be my father's son.

"I am not a domino player."

"You can match. Just match and I will do the rest, man."

I agree and fill a plate with pineapple and oranges on my way.

In five minutes we are two love down and Willy is in a rage, shouting at me across the table, "I not taking any six love, man! What kinda play is that, Everton, man?"

"I told you I can only match."

"But I never take you serious."

"Town man can't play domino. Which town man you ever see play domino good?" Tony is ecstatic.

"He can jump hill, but can he play?" the other laughs, and slams a domino onto the table.

"Jesus!" Willy wails. "A Jamaican man who can't play domino is like a Jamaican woman who can't dance. It just doesn't exist."

Three love down.

Willy shuffles the pieces, draws his hand, and winks at me. I wink back. As I gather my dominoes, I realize I am short. But there are no extra pieces on the table.

"I only have six," I announce. "Who have eight?"

"Your hand all right," Willy responds. "Stop the noise and play."

"But I only have six."

"Your hand all right, man."

Tom looks suspiciously at Willy and halts the game. "Let me see your hand," he demands. Sure enough, Willy has eight and I have six. We have to shuffle again and my partner's eyes blaze with feigned anger. "You can't play and you can't even thieve. I would ask you if you come from country, but people would laugh at me."

This is all in good fun and halfway through I find that I am winning.

And of course Willy is in heaven and is yelling at

me, "Slam down your domino harder than that, man!"
Then to Tony, "You think my partner stupid, he was
just testing—playing fool to catch wise."

And so we go on; some God is smiling at me, I have
won two games in a row. It seems the harder I slam the
dominoes down, the more I win and the more I enjoy
the game.

The food call comes and we converge on the pool area.

And what is there to say about it? Well, it is a feast of
fish and dumplings and roast yam and bananas. There is
freshly steamed cabbage and broccoli. It is an occasion
of warm friendship. We are all gathered around the pool
and the food is on the tables. We take what we want,
and we talk and we laugh.

Much is made of the fact that I am the only man who
jumped from the hillside and survived. And I have ceased
trying to tell them I had not intentionally jumped. I take
the applause and the comments and the compliments.
Much too is made of how I was an amazing marble player,
something I strangely still cannot remember. But I take
the compliments for that too.

"When you coming again?" they ask my father every
chance they get.

Mostly he looks at me or over at Tara with a knowing
smile. "When I come, I come. But I promise, it won't be
as long as it was the last time."

"Over ten years!" Mass Eustace or one of the others
shouts.

"It's too bad," another says, "that sometimes the
next time we see each other is at a funeral."

I do not know what they see in that to raise their
glasses to. But they do. This is a macabre crowd.

"I hear you like tennis," Tom's friend calls from across the table. "I hope you play it better than you play dominoes." The laughter for that one is long.

Wherever my father goes, my secrets disappear. "Like I play marbles," I tell him.

"Play or played?" He does not miss a tick. He has piled his plate with fish and moves to sit between Tom and his father.

"I played tennis while I was at Munro College. It's good game. Now I just watch it on TV. After high school there is nowhere to play. And Munro does not allow old boys to come and play. They should have tennis courts somewhere around here. I use to love playing that game."

"You ever watch the Williams sisters?" This is Willy. "Boy, I love to watch Serena play."

And then, surprisingly, an argument ensues as to who is the better of the two. The discussion is not just between the young men, Mass Eustace too has a say. He has time, I understand, to watch much tennis on TV, with the business they get. Moreover, I realize that most of them have satellite dishes or cable TV in their homes.

But tennis!

Suddenly it dawns on me that this year I will not be seeing Venus Williams play. I had begun to forget about it in these adventures with my father. Not only have I killed all my leave, I will no longer be able to afford the tickets. For I had booked a package deal that I should have paid for on the very day we were being chased around the hillside of south St. Elizabeth by drug cultivators. Now the price will be twice that.

But there is something about this day, this party, that makes me feel like it does not matter that I won't make it this year. Maybe next year I will. I look across the pool and watch him as he smiles and laughs with his friends and I can't help but feel good that I have been able to hang with him these few days.

"You all right?" Angela is at my side.

It is the first time we have spoken since earlier.

"I guess so."

"You eat?" She sits beside me on the low wall that separates the pool deck from the garden and crosses her legs.

"Of course I've eaten. And you?"

"When I cook, I don't eat. I would take a drink though."

"What?"

"You could bring my lime squash from the fridge?"

I rise quickly from the edge of the conversation and the laughing crowd and head to the kitchen and the large fridge. As I pass through the living room, I see my father's little poetry book lying on the center table. He must have been in a real hurry to leave it there. I pick it up. It has the weight of a small Bible and the leaves are almost as thin. For the first time I realize that it is custom-bound. The table of contents is divided by nationalities: British, American, and Caribbean. There is no title on the spine, just two words on the front—*Life Words*. Could it be that this is a book he has compiled and had bound just for himself? I must ask him about it.

I flip to the page in the Caribbean section where the silk marker is placed. The poet is a name strange to me:. *Martin Carter: "Poem of Shapes and Motion."* It is a long poem but one section seems more read than the rest.

I was never good at poetry, but this is not one of

those complex sonnets they forced on us in high school. This is straightforward enough. These are simple and beautiful words of concern and doubt—of a poet examining his limitations and possibilities as a man.

> I was wondering if the strange combustion of my days
> the tension of the world inside me
> the strength of my heart
> were enough

The words ring with a strange familiarity, and I cannot pull myself away as verse by verse the poet examines each element that makes him—from the strength of his heart, to the strife of his days, the nature of vague and distant decisions, and the haunting of unfulfilled dreams.

> . . . (will) the challenge of the space in my soul
> be filled by the shape I become.

And now it is not the poet I am hearing; the words I read are resonating something else, each verse, each line, each syllable, each uncertain question unveils to me the travails that haunt my father.

> I was wondering if I could find myself,
> all that I am in all I could be

The book almost falls from my trembling hand as I read the poem again. After the third read, I snap it shut and place it quietly on the table. I get it now, I get it now. In this one moment, I have completed my picture of my father.

Laughter erupts from the pool.

I find Angela's drink and bring it to her. But even as I sit, I realize that something has just changed in me. Angela senses this and looks at me strangely. "You all right?"

"Yes, for the first time now, I am sure I am all right."

"For the first time?"

"No, not so, I mean . . . but yes, I'm fine."

"You look different."

And I am, because I have a greater sense of what my father is about, I have a new angle on him. I know I should have seen it before, for God knows the signs were there: that evening at his house some weeks ago when a bottle of wine exploded and I saw his loneliness, his pleadings for me to come with him; his excessive sympathy for the old man at the mud lake and his anger and trembling at his death, *nobody care about old people*; his maverick behavior and tolerance for weed on his land and his gesticulating like a king when telling me the land is mine—all of these I should have picked up as signs of his searching.

The strength of my heart were enough . . . All that I am in all that I could be . . .

He has summed up all he is and the answer frightened him and sent him on a wild goose chase. And as I watch him smiling from face to face, making jokes and passing around his pimento wine, I realize that this is a man who is tying up loose ends. He is reaching backward into his life to make sure it is complete. That is why he wanted this trip and that is why he wants to meet this woman after thirty-five years.

Like those brewers at Appleton, having filled the

cask with rum and left it to age, returning twenty years later to find that the contents are short because of evaporation over time, Father has made a sum of his life and has found it less than full.

Will my father ever find those lost moments, will he ever be able to right all those wrongs, fill his life back with all those things that went with his aging? And what will he do when he discovers that, like aging rum, some of life is irretrievably gone? What will he do when he discovers that perhaps we will never be a hundred percent of what we can be . . . that some of our dreams and possibilities will evaporate—be taken by the angels—by the decisions and ravages of life . . . that maybe we all must give up that angels' share.

There is a roar. Everyone is laughing and looking at me. Glasses are being raised. Well, it must have to do with my jumping from the hill or my marble playing, so I salute and laugh with them. "A good son!" my father yells across the pool deck.

The beautiful Tara smiles and reaches across Angela to pat my leg. "Is a nice thing you doing taking round your father."

"Thank you," I tell her. "Thank you!" I shout across the space, and raise a bottle that is close to me. The cheer and drink and the chatter go on. Then I feel Angela's hands tightening on mine for a lingering squeeze. This time when I look into her face, there is no shyness there, and her eyes are dazzling with mischief.

From the moment I met her standing there on the brow of the Spur Tree Hill, I haven't been able to get my head around her. She has awakened passions in me with a force I have not felt since my teenage years. Yet when she gave me herself, placed herself at my mercy, gave me an opportunity to experience the passions I dreamed of, I hesitated . . . did not have a handle on myself.

I did not know it would be so hard to tell her goodbye.

I look deep into her eyes and there is fire and promise burning there. Everything in that stare is telling me that if I wish, the next moments could be the greatest of my life. And that is the thing. With her I see the present, I feel the power of the next moment, but I cannot see the future. There is an uncertainty about her, a vagueness of things beyond the day. With Audrey, I know. I can tell exactly how tomorrow will be and what we will be in ten years. There is a certainty there and whatever decision I make about us is based on the ability to predict and understand the future and where and how we will be together.

But with this woman I cannot tell. I do not know what she wants from me. I know what I want for my life and my future. But I do not know that she will fit. And I do not want to hurt her. I know that now: I do not want to hurt this woman.

You goin' hate me now, don't it? You goin' scorn me now, don't it?

I do not want to hurt her. I do not want to . . .

Her eyes have all the wisdom of a woman forty years her senior. And the sharp passion of a moment ago has flattened to a warm knowing look. Somewhere on the edge of it, on the softer part of that gaze, is a hint of pain . . . water brims near the edges, and her eyes begin to shine like freshly washed jewels.

While I worry about what my actions may cause, my

hesitation may have already torn something inside her . . . I can see as I struggle to pull my gaze away that *goodbye* has already been received and accepted in her eyes.

TWENTY-SEVEN

There is a presence in my room, a blend of complicated oils that stirs me from a light nap before we leave. It is Angela. She is like a shadow on the open space of the doorway to the bathroom that joins the other guest room to mine.

I have been with models, I have been with gorgeous women, but I have never seen a beauty such as hers. I cannot describe it, for it is not a physical thing, though the space of the doorway in which she pauses frames and outlines every sexy curve she has.

But her beauty is a complex thing. It is in the fullness in that frame, the dimensions of it, enhanced by the dusty light coming through my half-open window that sheens the oils that coat her. It is in the glow around her, an aura of sexual energy that charges the space as she moves. Then there is her sureness, her confidence, her force and magic.

I sense the softness in her face, but I do not see her eyes clearly, I do not know what they are telling me. Her hands are the softest silk against my skin as she urges me onto my stomach. I do not question, I merely obey.

She is in command and there is no doubt about it. Every movement is deliberate yet not harsh. She is an expert caregiver and I am a baby in her hands. Oil, warm liquid, runs down the center of my back and settles in my spinal groove. Slippery hands begin to massage it into me, starting at my shoulders then slowly moving in a circular motion down my back. Her touch is not as deep as a massage, but firm and probing, just enough for me to feel it below my skin. She does not seem interested in muscles but in nerve endings and the quickening of my senses. Her hands are sure, not aggressive yet not overtly gentle, and as she strokes and oils me from my shoulders to my feet, I am in a stupor, a place of comfort, bliss.

She massages my feet for a while. Then there is a pause and the coolness of the room bristles the hairs on my body and stands them on end.

Her hard nipples are on my heels and begin moving slowly up my legs. I imagine her lowering her body onto mine, but it does not come. I do not feel her weight on me, but I feel her breasts caressing, sliding on the oil, making their way along the back of my legs upward. As they get to my ass, I feel them rotate lightly, teasing, creating an unbearable level of anticipation. And as her breasts make their way up my body, I feel the gentle coarseness of her pubic hair begin to follow. Now that is all that touches me. No hands, no stomach, just breasts and pubic hair for the most tantalizing of moments, filling me with a desperate expectation, and a desire for a touch of the rest of her, for her to turn around so I may dive into her.

I find that I am wriggling on the bed. Suddenly, I have begun to gyrate. Just as I cannot take any more, even as I make to desperately spin her, I feel her weight settle on me. Her breasts crush against my back and her pubic hair rests in the rise of my buttocks.

She is now as still as a shadow on a memory. And I am panting as if I have just run a mile.

Slowly she stills me with her lips against my ear and her body merging with the oil on my body and her hands on top of mine, outstretched on the pillow ahead of me.

Now she rises slowly and gently wraps her fingers along my hand, pulling them in tightly against me and I feel her breasts beginning to descend down my body, retracing the path they have just taken. But this time her hands, though gentle, are cupped slightly and her nails are raking my body as she moves down.

By the time her fingers touch my shoulders I am panting again, and as her nails graze my skin I find that I am wriggling like a horse beneath the force of a ride that threatens to break its will. For even as I writhe, she has positioned herself to limit my movements and keep my body in line as if she knows I am about to buck.

She pauses and gives me time to catch my breath, playing her fingers up and down the slippery slopes of my spinal groove, building the weight of the touch with each movement till I can feel her nails again and my body is quickening in ways I cannot control.

Then she rakes her nails along my back, along my sides, dancing in the oil there. She gets to my buttocks, pauses, her fingers pirouetting there, grating my ass, and each movement, each pull of her hand, lifts me from the bed with a high-pitched groan. Now she covers me with her body from the side so I may not move freely and walks her nails slowly on the insides of my legs till I am practically screaming and every muscle in my scrotum is as tight as a drum and I am so convulsed, it is as if the cells of my body are all on fire. And all the time, while her hands play in one part, her breasts trail along at another venue. Like a game of good cop/bad cop, slow soft hard nipples take orders from the contours of my form while further down her urgent expert hands demand and extract passion I never knew I had.

Suddenly I have been turned over and I am lying panting, opened, and without shame to her.

I do not know where she is, for I am in a stupor. Her hands, though, I feel for they are working oil into my body from a reservoir created on my stomach. And the glow of it spreads warmly to my groin and the tissues of my upper thigh. As she works the oil into my body, I crave a fuller touch. I crave the weight of her on me as I did just seconds ago while on my stomach. But again it does not come. All I have are these warm rotating slippery palms sliding over my body, lifting the temperature of my skin, heightening the sensations in my skin till the smallest of touch brings a kind of shock like static electricity.

And here comes the nails again, this time not over my body but on my penis, dragging along the veins, making furrows into the mass of pubic hair, traveling with spiked surefootedness to the softest, most delicate parts of me.

I am screaming without shame. I am hoisting myself without control. And though her palm presses my stomach to hold me down, I am kicking and fighting like a bull out of control.

I feel her now trying to mount me, to hold me down. But I do not care anymore. I want her. I want her so badly I feel pain shooting through my temples. I swing my arm. I find her. I drag her down. I fight to turn her over. But she still has the better of me.

Now she is on top of me and she is cooing into my ear and I am slowly settling back. But not for long, for she spreads upon me and her pubic hair is on my rock-hard penis, as she begins to slowly gyrate back and forth up and down against me.

I am two raging bulls.

I twist and I turn and I hump for the penetration, but I cannot find it. I bite for her neck but it slips away. I want to kiss her, suck her whole mouth into mine, but her lips are on my nose and playing circles on my forehead. I squeeze her to me. I am a crazy man. I am a crying, panting, wild being. I have no control and I do not care anymore. Every nerve in my body is alive. Every place she touches is like fire burning there, every gyration of her crotch upon me has the sensation of a thousand needle pricks. I am over the edge; in my back, in my spine, in my groin there is a gathering storm. Now I am a bursting river, flooding, hoisting from the bed, kicking and screaming and gushing.

And she stays there on top of me, holding me even as I pant and thrash about—working me down from frenzy. Quieting my screams, my spasms, keeping me gently in place, massaging me to a calm, rubbing oil into me, kneading me into me, filling me with a levitated sense of peace.

Now there is no life in me. My mouth is dry. My eyes are tearing. I snuggle into her, pushing my face against her naked breasts to smother the groans, to dry the tears, to quiet the sobs.

TWENTY-EIGHT

We are in Montego Bay and it cannot be too soon. We have been driving for nearly two hours through the hills and I am tired. Father wants us to go straight to the hotel where he expects to meet his Hope tomorrow. But that is another hour and a half around the western end of the island and the journey does not appeal to me now. So I offer to treat him to a night in an all-inclusive hotel. He does not need much convincing.

We find a sprawling property a mile east of the airport called Sea Shell. It takes the price of the air ticket to the US Open to give us access for the night. But who cares; that trip was doomed the moment I ran from my office to find my father.

Another fifteen minutes of signing papers and we are given rooms on the tenth floor with a panoramic view of the sea and the northwestern coastline. The view across the water is so clear and unhindered I swear I can see Cuba glittering in the distance.

After freshening up, we finally find ourselves in a cozy little restaurant at the northern end of the main building. Though enclosed, one side is made of dark one-way glass that gives a view of the property's beach and some of the park-like grounds. It is good to be sitting in a comfortable chair with a drink in my hand.

My father orders a filet mignon. I figure, what the hell, and ask the waiter to bring us two.

Light jazz floats from hidden speakers and gradually conversation eases into the space between us and we are laughing at jokes of the past week. After a while I lean across to him and smile. "You know, old man, there are a few holes in your story."

"Holes in my story? How you mean?"

"Here, for instance." I point to the dim interior of the restaurant with its low lights, its pictures of a subdued Bob Marley on the wall. "Here, why are we here and not in St. Elizabeth? You plan for thirty years to meet a person in a certain place. She does not come and the next week it is another place."

"What's wrong with that?"

"You don't see anything wrong with that?"

"No."

"And then why this secrecy? Why she never talk to you directly, why this secrecy through Tara? It just does not jibe."

"Jibe? What is that? I know what it means!" He waves me silent. "Jibe—everything must make sense to you? Everything must be perfect?"

"Not really, but everything should have a logical sequence. This is a time of cell phones and faxes and e-mails. Why so cloak-and-dagger?"

"Jibe, eeh? Okay, how is this for an explanation? Tara got the wrong date and the wrong flight. Or who said Tara was in Montego Bay to pick her up in the first place?"

"You are making fun of me."

"No more than you are trying to make fun of me. I

tell you about faith already. All you have to do is believe the old man and all things will be revealed, okay?"

"And I must just travel the island with you in faith?"

"Okay, she lives in Germany."

"Germany?"

"Yes."

"I thought it was the States."

"Ah, the first problem with you, always assuming."

"So she lives in Germany."

"Yes. We made the plans about six months ago. And Tara was to get her and bring her to St. Elizabeth for us to meet because she is only coming for two days."

"She's leaving from Germany to see you and only coming for two days?"

"No, she is in Miami with relatives and she is stealing away."

"I see. So Tara missed the date. And why you never pick her up? Why Tara?"

"That is how we planned it, all right? So we planned it."

"So you changed the venue because she missed the date."

"No, Tara misunderstood the message."

"So it was a simple mistake?"

"Yes."

"It's certainly round and round like some le Carré spy story. Why are we here again and not in St. Elizabeth?"

"Tara's memory goes and comes, she has terrible handwriting that she herself cannot read sometimes. It jibe now?"

It does not, but who cares? I have already committed myself, and as he told me, why worry about things that are out of my control? He has his journey that he must take, and I will go with him and hope that if and when reality jolts him, I will be there.

"Okay, Everton, now I have a something to ask you."

"You do?"

"Yes."

"Go ahead."

"Your story is full of holes."

"My story?"

"Yes. For instance, here, what are you doing here and not in St. Elizabeth?"

"Here?"

"Yes, here with me tonight."

So he wants to play a game. "I am spending time with my father. I am staying with him like a good son, so he may meet his lost lover of thirty-five years."

"When you have a sexy woman, the most beautiful woman in St. Elizabeth, at home waiting for you and ready for you as the summer does for the rain?" But he is not laughing. He has that serious look of the instructor about him.

I pause with the food halfway to my mouth. "What do you mean by that? You know why I am here with you. You asked me. Don't do this, Daddy. You know why I am here."

"Yes? I know? But I don't have to meet Hope until tomorrow. The same way you found time to stop here and eat steak, you could have stopped with her."

"But you were forcing me, hurrying. You said the party took too long."

"I wanted to go straight to the hotel too, but you forced me here, promised me all-inclusive." He waves around us. "You never even asked me to stay in St. Elizabeth. The same way you forced me to come here, you could have forced me to stay. We could have left early in the morning.

"I watch you all day, sit down at some stupid breakfast send-off till it turned to lunch send-off and this woman sitting at your side, knowing you goin' leave, reaching out to you. Everybody saw it, every man there would have given anything to just have her look at them the way she was looking at you, and kill each other to climb that mountain. You never even slip away to tell her the right goodbye. It does not make sense, it does not jibe."

My father is a mean and vindictive man and I tell him so.

He only smiles. "Mean and vindictive? That is it? You are not able to venture an explanation?"

"Yes, I can. She is not my type."

"Okay, the sins of the father have fallen onto the shoulders of the son, is that it?" He makes way for the steak.

"It is not like that." There is no conviction; it just fell from my lips because it was there to say.

He has pegged me, truly pegged me. He knows that she has touched me in ways that no woman ever has and that there is something in me that wants her. He sees memories of her in my eyes and notes her absence from our conversation as we came here. It seems my feelings are plain as day before him: in the awkwardness of my goodbye and the way I trembled clumsily when she tried to display a rare outward show of her affection. Having waited for me and seeing that I wasn't going to make a move, she had tried to give me a final hug, near the van, in public, as I left, and I had not given her space or time to do so.

And now I wonder privately how she feels, having opened herself to me and now not being sure how I took it. *You goin' scorn me now, don't it?* Sometimes I wish I had left her there, her head buried inside her shell like a turtle, instead of having drawn her out to offer to me that which I cannot take to hold. But what does she feel now and how does she understand my responses to her?

"She is not my type." I know I sound as if I am trying to convince myself. "I did not want to hurt her."

He smiles to soften the mood. Having made his point, he now moves to console. "You know, son, life shorter than you think, and longer than you can ever believe. It has more time for reflection than it has for action. Why you think all these white people walking up and down about the place and come to drink rum punch and look stupid trying to dance reggae music? What you think them doing? They are creating memories. The time will come when all they can do is sit down and remember all of this. That is all I telling you. I know you have your reasons, the old man just teasing you, that's all. But is a joke God plays. Him give more time to reflect on your memories than Him give you time to create them. That is how it is, son, and in the end, life is nothing else but memories."

The food is good. So we are through it quickly and take our drinks to the lounge outside where the cabaret is in progress. A young group is going through the paces of popular reggae songs. They are pretty good, but they soon give way to the main event: an old crooner, with locks down his back, named Freddie Rocks. Most people would have heard about him. He has been around the dancehall scene for as long as I can remember and now seems to have settled for the steady north coast gig. He opens up with a popular Johnny Cash song, and creates a buzz through the tourists scattered around the lounge. After a few songs, he invites us to come to the floor and dance.

We are sitting beside a group of four Americans, and Father has already begun to engage them about the Grand Ole Opry. I don't know if that is a country group or grand Italian theater, but the Americans seem quite enchanted by him and the discussion is intense. He introduces me as his favorite son and they smile and tell me how good it is for me to be here with my father. People are people, I guess, wherever they may be, and compliments that lack originality are as common as ordinary people.

There is a pause in the conversation and we sit for a while and listen as Freddy takes us from Kenny Rogers to Nat King Cole, Ray Charles, and Luther Vandross. He is in the middle of Elvis Presley's "Make Believe" when Father rises slowly and walks along the edge of the dance floor. As soon as Freddy finishes, Father whispers in his ear and then makes his way back toward us. Suddenly the band strikes up the prelude to my father's favorite song.

As old Freddy leans into the first lines of "Help Me Make It through the Night," Father approaches us and stretches his hands to me and says something I don't quite grasp with all the sounds and conversation around us.

"What?" I shout.

"Dance with the old man."

"Me! Are you crazy? Don't do that, Father. I am not dancing with you."

He has the support of the four Americans and Freddy is looking up and beckoning. But there is no way I am going down there to dance a slow tune with my father.

"Dance with the old man," Jim the cowboy with the bad teeth says. The look on his wife's face is even more beseeching. They begin to chant, "Everton, Everton, Everton!"

This is the height of my humiliation; the more I resist, the more the applause increases and the more attention is drawn to me. If Luther Vandross has a song about it, it must have been done by someone before, so I shut my eyes and rise to follow my father to the dance floor.

Freddy is three-quarters of the way through the song and just to spite me, he starts at the beginning again.

And then Father holds me, rests a palm on my shoulder, and takes my left hand is in his right. And we move to the slow beat of Freddy singing, "*Help me make it through the night . . .*" His eyes are on me, and I try to raise mine to meet his, but it is hard. Even his hands in mine are awkward, not because he is a man, but because he is my father and I have never had to stare at him so squarely. I am not sure what that is in his eyes, and I do not know how to face it. I find my head bowing, for all my emotions are in my eyes, and he will know now whether or not I love him even though I do not know myself. He will see past everything and find the truth that scares me.

"*I don't care what's right or wrong. I don't try to understand . . .*"

He lets go of my shoulders, does a spin thing like a big, big dancer, the crowd roars, and I can't help but smile. And as he holds me again, I feel him pleading in his gaze for me to acknowledge what he is saying to me, what he has been trying to say to me all these few days we have been together.

"Help me make it through the night . . ."

I find his eyes, and there is that glitter in them, that flash of light that usually disappears after an instant. But tonight it fills his eyes and it tells me I am there, wherever it is I wanted to be, whatever it is I have yearned for from him, I am there and he is ready to give it. And it tells me too that I am ready to receive, so I am able now to seek and not be afraid of what I will find, to question and not be afraid of the answers, for whatever I find there will be true and strong as this light that glitters in his eyes.

Let the devil take tomorrow. Lord, tonight I need a friend.
Yesterday is dead and gone and tomorrow's out of sight.
And it's sad to be alone. Help me make it through the night
. . .

Suddenly, I hope she will be there tomorrow, I hope she will not be a fantasy, I hope that when we get to that hill, she will scale the garden like a wind and find his arms, so he can look in her eyes and she can see for herself as I am seeing now that he knows he has been wrong and that he is sorry.

So now, after the dance, after the cheering crowds, I stand with him on the section that overlooks the glimmering grounds of this all-inclusive heaven and I call to him, though he is right here beside me.

"You know that story, that Appleton story, about the rum missing from the casks?"

He smiles and nods. "The angels' share."

"Yes. I am going with you tomorrow, but I want you to know this: what you're looking for may not be there—and nothing is wrong with it not being there. For time and God take what they want from your chances in life, and give you what you must get. You don't have to search for what is missing, the angels have that."

His eyes are glistening in the darkness. "Life is more than a barrel of rum, my son."

"I know. But look at you: sixty-seven, fitter than me. You have a good twenty years left. Remember that after seventy is not even your time. It's God's time—three score and ten—and if by reason of grace, Daddy, you might get a little extra. So what you lose you goin' get back."

He is nodding in the darkness, so I put my hand on his shoulders without fear.

"And that goes for everybody too, you know." I stare at him deeply and squarely. "Sons who use to think their father never loved them and fathers who use to think they never did enough."

"Every man," my father says into the darkness, "should have a son like you."

TWENTY-NINE

Father stands loosely on the deserted meadow, places his foot on a low wall of some discarded structure, and looks sheepishly at me.

I know we are lost.

I had asked him if he was sure of the turn we made as we rounded the North West Point, and he had merely looked across the seat at me as if to say, *Never second guess your old man, boy.* So I had turned without comment.

The shrubbery and trees seemed to have extended too much onto the thoroughfare for a regularly used road, so I asked when was the last time he had visited the place. He said he and Una had been about five years ago. But now we are here, in this place, a mile and a half up a hill as steep as the slope of my windshield, and he is about to grudgingly admit that we are lost.

"Maybe it is farther up the road," I suggest.

"Maybe." He scratches his head. "But the turn from the hill, just as it about to flatten, is how I remember. I can't believe that a hill could flatten and turn into a large open space the same exact way for two different places."

"Well, maybe it's up the road. Come."

It has begun to drizzle but that does not stop him from moving away from me. "And the view . . ." He smiles and peers over the hill toward the north coast and beyond. "The view is almost exactly the same as I remember."

If I had money and could afford to build a hideout or a nice hotel and call it Grand View, I would do it in a place like this. For this must be where all tourist postcards are made.

And the space is large enough—several acres spreading to all sides, broken every now and then by a few gentle slopes. From where we are the land angles down to a small orchard that fronts the dense bush and trees covering the rest of the mountainside.

As I walk the property, I see that there are indeed signs that buildings once stood here and that a large structure has been flattened or bulldozed. Way beyond a cluster of trees, there are heaps of rubble and I can see tractor wheel marks overgrown by grass and weed.

A week ago I would have been angry at having driven all the way up a mountainside for this, but now I just pat my father's shoulder and tell him to come. "Maybe it's up the road," I say again.

"Let us ask that man. He should know where it is."

I beckon to an old man coming from the bush off to the right, a man about my father's age, on the back of a donkey with a cutlass across his lap. For a ways he appears to be a moving part of the hill, but gradually he separates from the background and the foliage and emerges as a solid farmer, squinting from beneath an old felt hat.

He seems unperturbed by the strengthening drizzle, and so is Father, for he goes to meet the man halfway across the meadow.

"How are you doing, my good sir?" Father greets him.

"Howdy," says the old man with a smile. "Onoo lost, man?"

"It seems so," my father answers, "though all the signs pointed to this place till we got here."

"We looking for Grand View Hotel," I call across, as I move to join them.

"Grand View, you say?"

"Yes, a hotel on the hill around the area, can't be far from here," Father replies. "Somewhere we must have taken a wrong turn."

"And you know, sir . . ." The old man leans forward on his donkey like a cowboy. "You know you never make a bad turn at all."

"How you mean?" my father asks.

"They use to have a hotel on this property by that very same name."

"Here?" Father looks to the ground.

"Yes, right here so. Hurricane, 'bout four years now. Christopher, you remember Hurricane Christopher, the one they say turn back from Cuba? They called it the Cuban missile. Well, sir, after it passed, they find the hotel roof way down the hill at Point. Mash up everything."

"Here?" Father is getting wet and something is rising in him.

"Yes." The man disembarks and wipes the rain from his brow. He then ushers the donkey toward the bush and slaps the felt hat on his pants to rid it of the droplets of water. Satisfied, he points around.

"Some Chinese people did buy out the whole place, say them was goin' build bigger place and casino. But I hear the father dead so the work stop. Two years now that work stop. One of the tractors still park and broke down over that ridge down that side."

"Here?" Father blurts again, as the rain intensifies.

"But there were reservations. Calls were made. Reservations were made."

"Come," I tell him. "We have to get out of the rain."

"You right about that." The man trots to join his donkey under a massive poinciana tree. It is closer than the van, so we join him.

Under here the drizzle is unable to pierce the overlap of green leaves and multicolored flowers that spread like a roof on all sides of the massive trunk.

"What you saying to me?" the old man asks as we stop. "You was planning to stay here?"

"Well, yes," I answer, "if this is the place."

"And you know, you not the first person. People come from all about looking for it. People use to love this place, all kinda people come. But the owner them get another place near the coast, you know. Place have the same name. Maybe is there you called."

"They could have transferred the phone number. It is done all the time when people move," I say quietly.

But Father is not listening to me, nor is he paying attention to the old man; he is walking around the tree in a daze, looking at every corner of the property, like a man faced with news that is too much for his mind.

"You okay?"

"I know I wasn't wrong, but look how the place just disappeared."

"What do you want to do?"

"I don't know."

"Do you want to wait a bit? Maybe she will come. You want to go down and check that other place? Whatever you want to do, old man." I have to work with him so he comes to his own truth gradually. I am worried about how he looks, how his hair has come undone in the rain; he is beginning to get a wild, unruly appearance. I do not want him to unravel . . . not here . . . not now.

"Okay." I lead him away and nod to the stranger. "Thanks, this tree won't hold off the rain for long. We will be going back to the van."

"You quite right, sir," he smiles. "But it will hold if it don't get too heavy. Town people can't take too much rain." He says it with such open honesty that I laugh without taking offense.

"Thank you, sir."

Father also waves his thanks before we trot across the yard to the van. Almost on cue, as soon as we enter the vehicle, the rain becomes heavier.

There is more silence than words now. So I put on an instrumental CD, and though I am not following the music, it gives some sort of flavor to the space.

"What a thing . . ." he finally chuckles. "What a thing. Suppose she comes all the way from Germany and find this place and nobody to tell her what happen. It wouldn't be good. We have to wait."

"Yes." I start the engine and flip the A/C on very low to keep the windows from fogging and the air fresh. The rain is persistent, not hard, just half a step up from a drizzle. The old man under the tree has had enough of it, though, and leads his donkey off down the slope a little ahead of us.

After about half an hour, Father straightens in his seat. "You hear that?"

"What?"

"You don't hear it?" His eyes are wide with excitement. I turn the music down and open my window a bit more. Sure enough, there is the sound of an engine laboring up the hill. His face lights up like a bulb. But I am not sure what the reaction in mine is, for though I have taken him here, deep down, I really did not believe she would come. I try for a broad grin. But he sees my discomfort.

"What did I tell you? You don't have any faith!"

It comes curving from the hill onto the flatland, ghostly through the rain, a gray Mercedes SUV almost merging into the background of gray, cloudy skies and falling rain. I watch it all the way till it stops behind my Pathfinder and I feel my stomach turn and my joints weaken at the sight of the woman stepping from it even before the wheels are still.

Una! Holly! Una and Holly. Holly have a Benz!

Una races through the rain, with Holly chasing after her. Before I can open my mouth, she is hammering her fists against the window. Father throws the door open and jumps outside to confront her with an anger I have never seen in him.

It isn't something that you want to see often, two old people who you love and fear for going frenziedly after each other in the mud and rain, especially when you have never seen them quarrel before, especially when the anger is fueled by jealousy. For an instant, I am disgusted by my father. What madness this is! He has taken so much from her, that dignified woman I love so much, that now she has to debase herself to try to get some back. And what she wants, ridiculously, is him.

"I gave my whole life to you!" she is screaming. "I gave my whole life to you and this is how you treat me. I am not letting you go!"

"I not going anywhere, damn stupid woman, I am not going anywhere! But you would not have understood that I must do this. So I had to come alone."

Holly and I are pulling them apart. And I cannot meet Una's eyes; I feel cheap, I feel used. I feel sad. For just in the action of pulling them apart, it seems that Holly and I are taking sides.

Then they turn on us, demanding, screaming that we let them go. Father shoves me off and Holly is forced to release Una. Holly and I come quickly to an understanding on a glance across the space. *Let them go. Maybe the relationship needs this. If it gets beyond the edge we will pull them back.*

So this is what it boils down to, this life thing, this love thing, this marriage thing: two old people fighting, making fools of themselves in the rain, shouting at each other, chasing each other around. One shouting, "Stop and talk to me, I am your wife!"

The other: "Leave me alone, you too damn miserable, what the hell you doing down here?"

Then: "I am your wife, and I am not letting you just run off like this with no damn woman!"

"You don't own me, woman!"

"I am your wife! I have given my life to you for over thirty years."

"So who say I don't love you for over thirty years?"

"Stop and talk to me! Is how people show love?"

So this is what it boils down to, people fighting, searching for answers, reaching back through the years to find the point where the road forked, hoping to correct something that has been formed and tempered by years, by time.

She hammers him with her fists. He holds her arms

and shakes her. She hammers him again. He lets her go and storms away.

A desperation, a panic, a fear that time is running out—a fear of the future which looms ahead like a dark space with a precipice. A fear of being alone. A search for memories—collecting them like a child would collect peenie wallies in a bottle to help guide her through a dark country night.

And what of me? What memories will I have of this fork, this place in my life? Am I making the right decisions? Have I made the wrong decisions? What decisions will I be reaching back to try to fix in thirty years or so? What mistakes will haunt me like a ghost?

There is a yelp. I look over to see my father slipping and sliding, then falling to roll toward the slope where the old man disappeared with his donkey. Una screams as he disappears over the edge. Holly shouts loudly, jumps, and makes a dead run toward the slope. But I find myself reacting less quickly. It seems that I have chased after my father enough these past two weeks, that there are limits to chasing the fantasies of someone else, even if it is your father. It is time now for him to accept full responsibility, or at least for Holly and Una to take over. I have learned by all of this that there are things I must do, that there is someone I must see, memories I must make, decisions that will ensure that I do not chase fantasies thirty-five years down the road. But I am still concerned for him, so I trot over to see how far down the hill he has rolled and how Una and Holly are handling things.

He is a mess of mud from head to toe, but Holly has him and Holly is a big man with huge muscles from working out constantly in the gym. Father's right leg is bent at an awkward angle, but a muddy Una is supporting him from the other side. He still has his wits about him, though, yelling for Holly to take his time. I stand and watch them come slowly up.

"How is he?" I ask as they get to the embankment.

"He has broken his leg," Holly says.

"It doesn't feel broke."

"Holly is a doctor, Daddy."

"Eye doctor!"

"I did do general medicine before I specialized—plus, any blind man can see that it is at an angle."

"Listen," I tell Holly as we near the vehicles. I cannot believe how easily the words are coming from me. "Listen, Holly, you will have to take it from here. There is something I have to do."

"What?"

"I can't tell you now, but get him to hospital and take care of things."

"We have to get back to town this evening."

"I know, but I have to be somewhere else right now."

"Like where?"

I don't respond and instead steer the three of them toward the brilliantly new gray Mercedes. Then I reach inside my car for his bags. As I lift them, I feel the weight and reach inside the biggest one to remove the last bottle of his pimento wine. He will not need this now.

Father has already made an eternal mess of the upholstery of the Mercedes. It is too somber a mood to smile, so I silently place the bags on the floor next to him. Una is on the other side, fixing Father's head in her lap.

"I have to go, Holly," I tell my brother.

"You are just leaving like this?"

"I have to go."

"Okay, whatever. If you have to go, I guess you must."

As I make to move away, he calls me back to say that Father wishes to speak to me.

So I am forced to go over to Una's side and look into the eyes of someone I feel I have betrayed. But she seems so happy to have him in her lap and so embarrassed for her own behavior that she is having trouble meeting my eyes.

"Yes, old man?"

"You goin' back?"

"There are things I must do."

"Mountains to climb?"

"It is not the way you think it is."

"It never is. Both big and small mountains?"

I ignore the comment. I know he means for me to check on that hotel with the same name down the road. I feel the need to kiss him on his forehead and I do.

"Take care of that leg. Stop give your wife trouble. Your adventures done now."

I walk from the Benz to my van without looking back. There is a woman in Ballards Valley I must find. I have things to tell her about decisions I have made about life, about the future, about memories.

THIRTY

And she is there as if waiting for me, leaning against the gate, looking out, in a pair of shorts so skimpy they would probably disappear if I said a harsh hello. Her blouse is just as skimpy, with sleeves of string. It hangs upon her bare, firm breasts, but lies back down against her flat stomach as only the finest weighted silk can.

She does not move while I park the Pathfinder, but watches me come with a look of infinite patience.

I do not know what I will tell her, or rather, how I will express the feelings beating in my chest, but I am here. I disembark and walk slowly across the space.

"You lost," she greets me with a soft look.

"Maybe I am found." I stop with my hand on the gate. She still does not move, but receives me into her space, into her eyes—into a moment of charged silence.

"Where your father?" she finally asks. As if to say: *Let's get the easy conversation out of the way.*

"Daddy is where Daddy should be. But this is not about my father."

"You sure?"

"I . . . I want to talk to you. There are things I want to say to you."

"Things you couldn't say yesterday."

"I really would like to talk to you."

"Things you can't say right here so, ehh? Okay." I think she will go to change, but all she does is push her head through the window to shout, "Mamma, me soon come!"

I must have felt the familiar privacy of the Pathfinder's cabin would make me more at home. But her sitting there like that brings a whole new dimension to it. And she knows, God knows she knows, and is enjoying what she is doing to me.

"You well want to have sex with me, don't it?"

"Wha . . . What?" I am stammering now.

"Talk the truth. You well want to have sex with me, don't it?"

"Listen, can I speak first? May I say what I have to say?" I know I sound foolish. "Can I say what I have to say before we come to that?"

"No, answer my question first. You go round too much corner. Answer the question first. Just talk the truth."

"Anybody would want to have sex with you," I blurt. "Anybody."

"I ask 'bout you."

"Yes, yes, all right, yes, but not so, not just so."

"How many ways somebody can want to have sex with somebody? How many ways?"

"I want more. I want more. Life is more than sex, relationship is more than sex. I can't just want that." I try to find my range, my voice, my control.

"You don't want me." She gives a sad half-chuckle. "You don't want me, I know that. You know that."

"Why you say that? I know what I want, I know now that you can be more to me. We can be more."

"No, Eva, you don't want me, you just don't want to make the same mistakes your father make."

And that is the heart of the matter, isn't it? That is the heart of the matter, the fact that it could be so, that it may be so, but that I now know it is *not* so, for I have thought about it all the way driving here like a madman. It is not because of him but because of me. Not his memories, but mine. "I know me, I know myself. I know what I want," I say.

"Maybe you know what you want now. But what about tomorrow, when you want something else?"

"You think I could just want someone else tomorrow? You think I am like that?"

"*Thing!* Some*thing* else! You think me stupid? Something else. That is what man want. Things, not people. And time change things. And when things change, sometimes people don't fit anymore. I never see anybody go out with a client and it work."

"Yes, but I am not a client. I did not meet you in a massage parlor."

"But you know, and with you that is enough."

"I know myself," is all I can say.

"Yes, but what happen when you go to a party and somebody point me out because they sleep with me or I massage them? What you goin' do? You know what you would do? After a while you goin' start 'fraid to go out with me because you won't be sure who and who I sleep with."

"It would not matter."

She laughs kindly. "So you say now. But it would. I tell you, I know you. I really know you. You have men who can deal with it. But you not like that. You don't make like that. That is why you come here today, 'cause you worry 'bout things—things bother you. You not like your father."

"I'm not comparing. I am trying to—"

"That is why you not goin' make the mistake them that your father make. Because him just do things. You have to think 'bout them first. Him just feel guilty now 'cause him make a mistake. But everybody make mistakes. Is just that him feel guilty now."

"How you so sure about everything?"

"And you know that you know."

I don't know what I know anymore.

Now we are both staring through the windscreen. It's evening, and evenings in Ballards Valley are a little different from those farther south where we were. The sun sets across the land here and not across the sea. And you get a chance to see how the land and the vegetation and the rooftops respond to the rays as they spread to gold. There is a soft reality to it too, for people are moving about and the space is more human.

She turns to me. "I want to, you know, but you put too much meaning to everything."

"What? What you want?"

She laughs again and shakes her head. "How you so fool sometimes? I want to have sex with you from the first time you hold me at Appleton, from the first time."

"It is just that . . . I . . ."

"Talk the truth, man, Eva. You don' have to explain everything." She reaches for the door handle. "Well, since you don't want to do it . . ."

But I beat her to it and hold her hands softly. "Where you going?"

"What?" Her smile reveals that she had just been joking.

"I have somewhere to show you."

"Come then." She reaches across and sticks her tongue into my ear. It is the morning of the massage all over again. She laughs loudly as I jump, leans back into her seat, and places her feet upon the dashboard. "Make we go up by Dorril," she says. "I hear it have the best sunsets."

She is reading my mind.

We are but a few minutes away and the energy in my loins is heating. Suddenly, out of nowhere, a vehicle slots in behind me with its lights flashing. I pull close to the edge of the road to give him way but he stays on my bumper.

"Is Willy," Angela tells me. "Is Willy, him trying to stop you."

Every time I go to Dorril, Willy is there. I stop in a clearing where a young man sits beside a pile of melons. Through the rearview mirror, I see him rise to approach. But Willy is already out and explains to him that the stop is not about buying melons.

"I see you have good company." He gives a wolfish smile through the window.

"Hi," she greets him with a familiarity I do not like.

"Everton, man, you know how long I looking for you? Where is your father?" He seems filled with both urgency and relief.

"Father's gone home. Why you looking for him?"

"This old woman, man—this old woman my mother give me, man. I have this old woman—whole day she waiting for your father. Say they supposed to meet up at the land. We tell her onoo gone but she don't believe. So I have her. I left the boys up on the land looking, to call me when you and your father come. All day them wait and don't see onoo, man. Now she want me to take her up there to look around."

"Which old woman?" My stomach is about to turn.

"The German woman, man, my mother's cousin. She want to see your father about some business. Maybe some land business."

"She exists?"

"How you mean?"

"But we were in Montego Bay, where she . . . never mind. She is real? She exists?"

"Come!" He literally pulls me from the van and I am in a daze as I head toward his vehicle, to find this woman, this fantasy of my father.

She sits there with silver flowing hair, face plump, dimpled—eyes like ackee seed. *Hope.* "Hope?"

"So you are Everton."

There is a quietness to her, a dignity too, and sophistication that comes with age no matter where we start. Also, there is a richness of life in her voice and a force common to those of some means who have still managed to maintain an earthiness.

"You are so tall, just like your father. But say something."

I am overcome with unfamiliar emotions. I feel like there are tears welling up in me and if I speak they may overflow.

"In living color." Willy is standing beside me.

But she is sensing that there is more to my standing

there—understanding, it seems, my emotions, knowing just by a look that I cannot simply blurt things out, not now.

"And Nigel?" She searches my eyes. "He could not make it?"

"We went to Montego Bay. We were at Grand View."

"Ah. He was always like that, giving mixed messages and getting instructions wrong—stubborn."

"That's my father."

"Grand View!"

"He said it was the *first* place."

"Ah." Her eyes cloud momentarily. "Ah, *that* first place!"

I remain silent.

"And he could not make it . . . here?"

"And *now* he cannot."

Her eyes are so black and intense upon me—reading, knowing. "But you are here."

"Yes, I am."

"By faith and coincidence." She smiles. She has seen Angela and has put the pieces together. "How is he, how is your father?"

"My father . . ." I hold her stare. "He won't be coming." There is a feeling that she understands. And there is more she will need to understand. Yet the things we must say cannot be shared with the others. So we speak carefully—staring at each other like old allies in a spy movie.

But then Willy solves the situation: "Why don't you go with Everton, Aunt Hope? Is Everton own everything now, you know." This he says to everyone.

"Yes, Everton," Angela says beside me, "yes." She

pulls my eyes away. She knows there are things to talk about with this woman. "Let Willy take me home."

In a minute Willy has helped Hope from the van and is making space for Angela to enter the vacated seat. He has seen an opening and is making his move. I remember how the first time I saw him I felt I would never introduce him to my woman. Now faith is handing her to him wearing almost nothing, taking her from me mere minutes from memories of a lifetime.

We have swapped women.

Willy pauses by me, smiles, and hugs me. "Just call when you coming. It was good to see you."

"Sure, Willy."

"And don't worry 'bout nothing, man. I will take her home safe." He punches my fist. "Everything is everything and everything is all right."

Sure, I am thinking, as he walks around the front of the van. "Sure."

As the van starts up and Hope and I step aside to allow it to pass, the door opens and Angela runs to me and throws herself into my arms.

"You not telling me you gone." She wraps herself tightly into me.

"I thought you found a new boyfriend."

She presses her lips against my ear. "Him? Is long time me know him. Long time him trying."

"Make him try harder."

She laughs against my cheek. "Make haste and come back."

"Yes? This might take time."

She squeezes onto me. "It not goin' run 'way. Anytime you ready, even if you go home and come back—

just come. When you ready, just call . . . we'll go down to Memories and spend a weekend. Whatever you want."

"Whatever I want? I may want things you cannot give."

"Whatever. If is even one time."

"One time?"

"I could fall in love with you, you know. But we talk 'bout that already. We know how that would go. But make haste and come."

"I will."

"Just don't take thirty-five years."

"I won't."

And so she slips away. I know I will remember this moment forever: how it looks, how it feels, how it touches me. And now I understand a bit how a woman can fill a man so much that a lifetime is not enough to empty himself of her. And if not in a lifetime, then how could he do it in thirty-five years?

So I turn toward this fine portly woman, take her hand, and give her the full force of my smile. "Come," I tell her. "Come! Come and tell me about my father."

THIRTY-ONE

The time for closure has come and I must admit it brings both relief and regret. For whether I wish to admit it or not, I have enjoyed the last several days with my father. But now I am here halfway to Hampshire to put the final curtain on our adventures.

It has been two days since I took the hand of the woman called Hope, for whom my father had left his wife, to reunite after thirty-five years. An evening with Hope did little to alter my image of my father, or the new image I've had since we started on our adventures, but it has indeed filled in a few blanks. She is a wise and clever woman, almost like a female version of my father in how she answered questions and asked them. But I had few secrets shared with me except for what she felt I should know. She revealed a love for my father that seemed to have continued to this day. She too wanted to look into his eyes one more time. She too wanted to ask him *why*, in the same way he had wanted to tell her he was sorry.

After my father, she met a German marine officer who married her and took her with him to Germany. By that time, she hadn't seen my father for a while. He had stayed away and allowed their relationship to die. When the German had proposed to her, she wrote my father about it, hoping he would tell her not to accept.

But he sent her a note to wish her good luck and a long and wonderful life. She said those were not the days I know with telephones, faxes, and zero-wait technology. You were blessed if you by chance found a man who owned a car, and when you did not see him for a while, you waited till he came. She waited for my father, and he did not come. So she moved on with her life, married the German, and moved to Germany. She had resigned herself to not seeing him again, till her cousin wrote and opened the old wounds and reminded her that her relationship with my father still needed closure. So she had come. She wanted to look into his eyes one more time and have him tell her why he left her.

"I wish we had not made it so mysterious," she said. "For once we outsmarted ourselves . . . but it was all so romantic, sending those clues and little messages."

"I understand," I told her. Maybe there is nothing wrong with nostalgia—nothing wrong with trying to recapture old moments that mean so much.

I left her at Tara's. She will be heading back to Germany in another day or two.

Now all that's left is this letter she has given me with her picture in it, and secret words for me to take to my father.

So here I am, threading my way through the dying evening on my way to my father's house in Hampshire.

It has been two days since I saw Hope. Yesterday I slept in; I figured if he could wait for thirty-five years, he could wait another day for his letter. In any event, I was weary from traveling. But I had scarcely had lunch today when Una called to summon me.

"Everton, are you back in town?"

"Yes."

"Your father said you would be."

"He said that?"

"Can you make it here this afternoon? It's important."

I had planned to relax another day and see him tomorrow, Saturday, but Una's call changed that plan.

So I am here with a picture and a letter in my pocket—a message that I hope will bring final closure to the old man's adventures.

I love coming out here to see him; I love the drive through the old estates that give the villages their names, especially in the evenings, like now. And every time I come I wonder why I do not come more often. The colors of the vegetation are magnificent, extending for great distances ahead and around me. All shades of green mixing and blending and dazzling till they touch the heavens. At my speed the hues of blue and green give the evening a mix that you only feel on this stretch of road to Hampshire. The grass is a yellowish green and the rows and rows of orange trees are darker, almost black, and then the vast fields of sugar cane with a lighter dustier shade—and the road stretches ahead toward the dark blue hills rimmed by a lighter blue sky.

Father moved here twelve years ago. He was fifty-five and decided he needed a country estate to retire to. He had worked all his life in the civil service and had been too easy-going to get beyond deputy director, too outspoken to be invited higher, and much too proud to accept promotion as a favor.

But he had fallen in love with a piece of Hampshire that is nestled inside the heart of St. Catherine, half a mile outside Riversdale. Two and a half acres of lush St.

Catherine land; land so rich and pure that "if you see stone on it, is somebody threw it there," as he once said. The only time in his life he used his job to his advantage. The owner had died and Father held it through his office till he secured a loan on his home in Willowdene. When he finished building the house here, he transferred to the agricultural office in Linstead and Una transferred to be vice principal of Linstead High School.

Now at sixty-seven, he is retired, five years after his wife, and they live in their piece of heaven in Hampshire.

"He's been looking out for you all afternoon," Una tells me as she opens the gate for me. She has a classic beauty made richer by stern, responsible eyes and a gentle manner of pure class. Her bearing would be just as suited for the halls of government, walking among dignitaries, as it is here, probably even more so. Her beauty is that of the sharp lines of jagged rocks, and the gray in her hair is like the white of breaking waves crashing against them.

She hugs me.

"The air is so fresh and clean," I exclaim.

"You say that every time you come up here." She pulls away to meet my eyes, but I am still afraid to meet hers.

"But it's true," I smile back.

"How are you, Everton?"

"Fine," I tell her. "Where is he?"

She shrugs. "Around the back."

He is on the back veranda looking out. He sits on a long sofa, one foot in a cast laid flat on the seat while the other rests lightly on the floor. There is a table beside him with fruits, snacks, and a bottle of pimento wine caked with dirt like a newly excavated artifact.

"Old man broke his foot," I tease.

"Old man broke up." He grins and sits up.

"Old man must keep quiet." Una sits beside him on the sofa.

He places a hand on her lap and she grasps it with her own. There is a difference between them. Usually Una would have left us to talk on our own for a while, but this evening she sits and holds his hand.

I feel the letter against my breast; I must wait for the right opportunity to give it to him.

"So you were deep into St. Elizabeth?" He smiles conspiratorially.

I'm not sure what he means by that. "I went back," I say cagily.

"Climbing mountains?"

"Who is to tell?"

"Big mountains, small mountains, what did you find down there?"

He is a handsome man, my father, and his beauty is in his eyes. His features are ordinary. His nose flattish, his mouth full. He has large dimples and the shape of his face is of a young mango—round, full, and a bit long. His hair is gray and he has all of it, but it is thinner and silkier, so it falls around the edges. With the right hairdo he could look like Caesar. But his beauty is in his eyes. Like guides down a mysterious terrain, they tell you how to see his face. You can get caught in them and they dictate to you.

"No mountains, no new roads?" he asks again.

I hesitate. The way Una is holding him and the way

they are soft and easy against each other makes me feel a tinge of guilt. They have somehow found each other again.

"Some roads, some places are just for angels," I finally tell him

He settles into himself and sighs. "Angels' share, no?"

"The angels' share," I nod

"You don't have to talk codes around me," Una says with a smile.

"Codes! No codes, Una. It is just a way of telling my father he should be grateful for what he has."

"I know what angels' share means." She looks at me without blinking.

I glance at my father. "I am impressed."

He winks at me. "You think you are the only one who can give a speech?"

"We talked, Everton." Una pushes a chair to me. "We talked."

I look at her, this beautiful, quiet, dignified woman, and I can't believe it is the same person who traveled a hundred miles to fight for her man. I won't even try to guess how she found out where we were.

"So are adventures over now, old man?"

"For now, maybe."

"Will you stop drinking now too, obey your wife, leave the pimento wine?"

"Well, that would be a new trick, and I am an old dog."

She slaps his cast.

How can I give him this letter now?

"Give him the Heineken bag," he says to Una.

"What bag?" I ask.

Una rises with a mischievous smile and goes to the small closet at the corner of the veranda. She returns with a green Heineken promotional bag and hands it to me.

"What's in here?"

"What does Heineken sponsor?" he counters.

"What do they sponsor?" I ask even as I dig.

He sighs.

"They sponsor the US Open." Una is glowing.

"You think I don't have a few friends?" Father smiles smugly.

In the bag I find airline tickets, hotel reservations, some US cash, and, most astonishingly of all, a tournament-long pass to the US Open tennis tournament in New York.

"Jesus. How did you do this? How did you manage it in two days? No . . . one day!"

"You think you are the only one with friends?"

"No, but in one day?"

"Holly helped, he brought the bag today. That is when I called you," Una beams. "Only a few days of the preliminaries are gone. The real thing starts next week. You should go, Everton." She touches my arm. "You deserve it."

I rise to her with tears in my eyes. "Come here," I say.

"You come," Father says.

"Not you," I tell him. "I am not speaking to you." I pull Una up and hug her tightly. She is surprised, but holds me as I press my tearing face against her neck. "Thanks."

"You see who gets the thanks?" Father complains.

"Thanks for loving my father," I tell her. "Thanks for loving me."

She too is teary and he is silent and everything is all choked up.

"A drink is in order," Father breaks the awkward moment as he reaches for the pimento wine on the table.

I glance at the wine and then at Una.

"It is okay," she says. "The doctor says one glass a day won't kill him."

The bottle of pimento wine is still covered with dust and there is still some mud caked to the bottom. But we want it like that. It would be sacrilege to wash that bottle. I take it from him, do the honors of the opening, and pour everyone a drink. I sip. It bites into me and the shock of the aroma awakens my senses. In my excitement, the sip was too big.

"You always rush your first sip."

I ignore him and savor a smaller sip.

"This is one of the first bottles I buried in the cellar. Ten years old or so. You know that?"

"It's the best yet." I shake my head as if there are wasps behind my eyes.

We are on the verge of night. The light leaves the hills reluctantly and in the distance the peaks are still clear. Though the clouds are bright, shadows have darkened inside them. From the veranda where we sit, the air has already changed and the peenie wallies have begun to flit in and out of the bougainvillea.

I am as happy as I have ever been in the company of my father.

Half an hour later and I am ready to leave. Father has managed to surprise me again. I have come to give him closure, bearing gifts; he had a gift for me as well and a special closure of his own. I must now get home. I have no-pay leave to apply for, I have packing to do. In just a few days I will leave for New York and the US Open to watch Venus Williams play.

"I am going, old man."

"With whatever you found in the country."

"I have packing to do." A thought occurs to me. "And Una . . ."

"Yes?"

I pull her close again, and she is shocked. I slip my hand behind her head and release the clasp that buns her hair, admire the beautiful curls that fall to her shoulders, and cannot help but gasp at her profound beauty and the force of her womanhood. "Take the ribbon from your hair."

I hear a soft sigh with the half-smile he raises at me and I can hardly meet his eyes, but I do. He is ready to enjoy the rest of his life. I see him grasp her hands as I turn, and I can swear I hear him softly whisper, "Shake it loose and let it fall."

But I am out of there. The envelope with the picture, note, and message is still in my pocket. It is mine now, to do with whatever I wish. I pat it lightly as the evening closes on Hampshire.

For every inch of the way from Hampshire to Spanish Town, nothing fills my mind but the image of Venus Williams dancing across the court with the assured elegance of a gazelle. As my mother would say, *Tonight, heaven has come down and glory fills my soul.*

Spanish Town has never looked so good, nor has the left turn that leads to my house seemed so softly paved with silver, inviting me to slip home and prepare for the fulfilling of my dreams.

Yet deep inside I hesitate. And as I pause, the face I see is no longer Venus Williams and the place I want to be is not a certainty anymore. Twenty minutes to my house, my soft bed, my cozy music, my packing for the US Open—and I hesitate. Left turn takes me home, right turn brings to mind a crazy notion. One that rushes at me with a force that takes my breath away. Suddenly, I see her face against the night, I hear her voice like a whisper on the wind, I taste her fragrance like wild musk, I feel the grate, rake, and scrape of her pubic hair.

Right turn and I would be on the highway and if I try hard I could be cutting through the dry grass and red dirt of St. Elizabeth before ten.

I could fall in love with you, you know . . . . make haste and come.

Left turn takes me home, right turn would take me away from everything, away from my flight to New York, away from the US Open, away from Venus Williams. Why do I hesitate?

Any time you ready . . . just come . . . we'll go down to Memories . . . whatever you want . . . make haste and come."

What hesitation? There is none, there are no second thoughts. I swing the wheel right—away from my house and the silver passage. I won't even take the chance to go there and change my clothes. I swing away, and the car speeds up as I point it west toward the highway and St. Elizabeth. Damn if I am going to wait thirty-five years, damn if I am going to wait another week, damn if I am going to wait another night. If I hurry, I will make it by ten. If I press, by nine thirty we will be making our own moments, at a little place called Memories By the Sea.